SWEETS

FORGOTTEN

Connie Shelton

Books by Connie Shelton

THE CHARLIE PARKER SERIES
Deadly Gamble
Vacations Can Be Murder
Partnerships Can Be Murder
Small Towns Can Be Murder
Memories Can Be Murder
Honeymoons Can Be Murder
Reunions Can Be Murder
Competition Can Be Murder
Balloons Can Be Murder
Obsessions Can Be Murder
Gossip Can Be Murder
Stardom Can Be Murder
Phantoms Can Be Murder
Buried Secrets Can Be Murder
Legends Can Be Murder

Holidays Can Be Murder - a Christmas novella

THE SAMANTHA SWEET SERIES
Sweet Masterpiece
Sweet's Sweets
Sweet Holidays
Sweet Hearts
Bitter Sweet
Sweets Galore
Sweets Begorra
Sweet Payback
Sweet Somethings
Sweets Forgotten

The Woodcarver's Secret

SWEETS

FORGOTTEN

The Tenth Samantha Sweet Mystery

Connie Shelton

Secret Staircase Books

Sweets Forgotten
Published by Secret Staircase Books, an imprint of
Columbine Publishing Group
PO Box 416, Angel Fire, NM 87710

Printed and bound in the United States of America
ISBN 1516816439
ISBN-13 978-1516816439

Book layout and design by Secret Staircase Books
Cover illustration © Dreamstime.com
Cover cupcake design © Makeitdoubleplz

First trade paperback edition: August, 2015
First e-book edition: August, 2015

As always, my undying gratitude goes to those who have helped make my books and both of my series a reality: Dan Shelton, my partner in all adventures who is always there for me, working to keep the place running efficiently while I am locked away at my keyboard. My fantastic editors—Susan Slater and Shirley Shaw—thank you so much! And a special thanks goes out to Patty Shepard for planting the idea in my head about Kelly and Julio!

And especially to you, my readers—I cherish our connection through these stories.
Thank you, everyone!

Chapter 1

Samantha Sweet pushed her way through winter coats and touched the keypad on their closet safe. The numerals came naturally to her now and the door swung outward with a tiny electronic beep. Moving Beau's spare service pistol aside, she made room for the large brown envelope she had brought home from town. A year of marriage and they'd finally gotten around to rewriting their wills.

"I hope I don't have to look at you again for a good long time," she muttered to the envelope as she shoved it to the bottom of a stack that included their marriage license and birth certificates, a home inventory list and both passports. Writing a will seemed morbid, even though she knew it was a necessity.

Her hand grazed the curved surface of a wooden box she'd placed there for safekeeping months ago. She felt a little rush of emotion, as if the box's history with her was akin to that of a person. It *had* saved her life, actually, on a couple of occasions. It had imparted the energy she needed to start her dream enterprise, her pastry shop, Sweet's Sweets. For all she knew, perhaps a nice side benefit might have been the near-instant attraction with Beau—they had met shortly after Sam received the box.

On the other hand, there were times when the odd artifact scared the heck out of her, most recently during a showdown over it between two rival organizations. Sam still wasn't sure what or whom to believe about the meaning of the box's powers, and that was a big reason it now stayed in the safe—out of reach to herself or anyone else. She closed the safe, pressed the buttons to lock it and backed out of the closet.

A pair of strong arms closed around her and she shrieked.

"Gotcha!" Beau pulled her to his chest and nuzzled her neck. "Which would you rather have—homemade waffles for breakfast or thirty minutes upstairs?"

"Umm…. Could I choose both?"

He backed toward the leather sofa in the living room, reaching for the buttons on her baker's jacket. "I suppose if we were to skip the part about climbing the stairs …"

A musical tone chimed and his glance slid toward the end table beside them. The readout on his phone showed the department dispatcher's extension.

"Rats!" He reached for the phone. "Dixie, this better be important."

Sam could hear the familiar voice apologizing for the early call. "Sheriff, I'm sorry. You didn't respond to the radio."

"Because I'm supposed to have a half-day off today."

"I know. It's just that all of a sudden we're real shorthanded. Remember how Rico felt like he was coming down with the flu yesterday? Well, five more have it today. Three deputies and a couple others from admin. We need you to reassign duties, and if you could maybe fill in some of the gaps yourself ...?"

Beau sighed. "Okay, then. I'm on my way."

Sam started to pull her jacket over her bare shoulder but his mouth was suddenly in the way. He planted a moist kiss on her collarbone.

"Save that for later. If I can rearrange things at the office maybe we can meet up to continue this line of thought around lunch time."

She indulged him with a long kiss and a smile. They both knew the odds of breaking away for a midday tryst were next to nil. Their lives didn't work that way. He sighed and climbed the stairs, unsnapping his plaid western shirt.

"Don't worry," she called out. "I'll feed the dogs and put something in the crockpot for dinner before I head out."

He returned in under five minutes, strapping on his leather belt crammed with radio, holster, cuffs and other gear, and she could tell that his mind had switched to law enforcement mode just that quickly. She watched his cruiser head down their long driveway before she turned her attention to her own day. The simple chores occupied her hands, and her mind began to focus on business.

With the crisp September days had come seasonal changes to the offerings at Sweet's Sweets—apples, cinnamon and cranberries fit her customers' desires now. Sam had spent several days developing new recipes, especially looking for ways to include the season's abundant

Hatch green chile into her savory breads and muffins. As she checked the lock on the French doors to the back deck, she thought of another twist she might add to the chile-cheese pull-apart loaves she'd been working on yesterday.

Ranger and Nellie, their black Labrador and border collie, watched complacently as she filled their water bowl on the porch and then climbed into her bakery van with its colorful all-over design of pastries. The road to town was crowded this time of day; Sam had nearly forgotten that even little Taos had a rush hour, since she was normally way ahead of the crowd at four-thirty each morning.

She had to admit that adding hired help at the shop was nice. Julio could practically get the store open with his eyes closed, stocking the cases with their signature items in a flurry of pre-dawn baking. Jen would be there by now, arranging the displays and brewing coffee and tea. Becky, Sam's decorator, always arrived shortly after she'd taken her kids to school. Sam thought back to the days when she did every bit of baking from her home kitchen, back when business consisted of specialty cakes and cookies and she also delivered everything herself.

She took Camino de la Placita as a less-congested back way and passed a block west of the famed Plaza, cruising past the front of her shop. The charming storefront in its Depression-era adobe building, with her own purple awnings and pastry-filled display windows, made life a lot more fun even when it wasn't especially easier. She stifled a picture of the upcoming crazy holiday season as she steered into the alley behind the row of shops, vowing to simply enjoy the beautiful autumn weather right now. The scent of roasting green chile from a nearby vendor greeted her as she got out of the van. She took a deep breath and went inside.

"Sam! Oh, thank goodness you're here." Becky Harper stood at the stainless steel worktable with a bag of hot-pink frosting in one hand and a customer's sketch in the other. A two-tiered cake stood on the table, base-coated in white. It was nothing like the drawing.

"How is this," Becky said with a nod toward the cake, "supposed to become *this?*" She waved the drawing toward Sam.

"Good morning to you, too," Sam said, hiking the strap of her bag over her shoulder and taking the sketch and order form.

Sure enough, the cake was described as two round tiers—which it was—but the design clearly showed a hot pink fashion purse, a modified hatbox shape with quilted fondant covering it and black ropey handles.

"I made the buttercream and loaded the bag before I pulled the layers from the fridge," Becky said.

"Maybe the cake was mislabeled. Did you check that?"

Becky nodded. "The same name—Perdida Sanchez—is on both."

"Let's check with Jen," Sam said with a sigh. "She took the order. She'll probably remember the circumstances."

Jennifer Baca, her front counter assistant, had recently shown a few little lapses of attention in her work but this was the biggest error so far. She was probably going to have to sit Jen down for a talk. All she really wanted to do was start on the batch of molded chocolate magnifying glasses she'd envisioned for the Chocoholics Unanimous book group's meeting this evening. They were on a Sherlock Holmes kick this month.

She hung her bag on a hook at the back of the kitchen, tugged her jacket straight, and headed toward the sales room. Female voices came from the other side of the curtain separating the two rooms.

Jen stood behind the counter while the only customer stood at the display windows, which faced the street, admiring the elaborate autumn-themed wedding cake Sam had put on display yesterday.

"Jen, I'll take over here. Becky needs interpretation of an order she's working on." Sam moved into the room. Jen pointed toward the customer's back, trying to convey some message, then shrugged and headed for the kitchen.

"Yes ma'am—how may I help you?" Sam asked.

The woman turned and Sam got her first close look at the customer. She stifled a gasp. The woman's blouse was torn at the shoulder and a bloody scrape blazed across one cheek. Her dark, layered hair had an obviously good cut but was dirty and stood out in tangles. Her skirt and blouse were disheveled and she fiddled with a ripped nail on her right hand.

"What happened to you?" Sam blurted it out without thinking.

"I—I don't …" The stranger turned aside.

"I'm sorry. That was rude of me," Sam said. "Can I get you some coffee? Or would you like to use our bathroom?"

The woman shook her head, as if she were clearing away bad thoughts. Sam began to notice more details. Her clothing was of decent quality although she didn't have a purse, and a glance out the window revealed no car in the parking lot, suggesting the visitor had arrived on foot. However, the lady's complexion and bearing defied the idea that she might be a street person.

"Let me at least get you a cup of tea and a scone or something," Sam said. "Take a seat and just relax for a little while."

The woman pulled out a chair at one of the small bistro tables, a seat facing the door, Sam noticed. She brewed a cup of tea and set it down for the lady.

"Blueberry, almond or cranberry?" Sam asked. "Or maybe a muffin or brownie?"

The woman shook her head again, flinching in pain.

"Look, it's obvious something happened to you," Sam said, taking the chair across from her visitor. "Were you in an accident? Did someone attack you? My husband is the sheriff. He can investigate and find the person."

The woman's vivid blue eyes grew wider at the mention of the sheriff and she set her tea mug down. Sam leaned forward.

"Okay, we don't have to report it until you are ready. Can we just start with your name?"

The shapely dark brows furrowed for a moment.

"Your name, sweetie. What's your name?"

Her mouth opened, then it closed again. Her eyes widened again and a flicker of fear crossed her face. Sam reached out to take her hand but the woman drew back.

"You don't have to tell me," said Sam gently. "Are you sure about the muffin—?"

"I don't know."

"Then a slice of our banana nut bread."

"I don't know my name." Her eyes darted back and forth, taking stock of her clothing, her hands, her surroundings. "I don't even know where I am."

Chapter 2

Jen, can you come back out here?" Sam asked, keeping one eye on the new mystery sitting at her bistro table. "Keep her company. I'm calling Beau."

She slipped into the kitchen as Jen walked toward the case full of pastries. Without asking, Jen picked up a plate and fork and served up a slice of cheesecake. Sam let the curtain fall and walked to the back door. On the small stoop outside, she pulled her cell phone from her pocket and tapped Beau's number.

"Hey you," he said. "Look, I'm afraid a lunch break doesn't look possible—"

"I'm not worried about that, honey, and I'm sorry to bother you but I wasn't sure what else to do."

"Something wrong?" His casual voice had given over to his all-business one.

"There's a woman in my shop and I think she's been hurt. She's extremely nervous and seems to have amnesia and I have no idea who to call."

"You did the right thing. I'm on my way."

He must have been on patrol nearby because he walked in the back door less than three minutes later.

"Jen's serving her cheesecake and tea in the front," Sam told him as she pulled chocolate and sugar from the shelf for her next project. "Other than that, I know nothing about her."

"Go in there and introduce me so she won't freak out at the sight of a lawman," he suggested.

Sam led the way. Her visitor had taken only a few bites of the cheesecake, despite its being their most popular flavor.

"This is my husband, Beau," she said gently. "He's the sheriff and he can help you figure out what to do next."

The woman swallowed hard and pushed her dessert plate away, watching Beau with a wary eye. He sat across the table and took a small notebook from his pocket. A few standard questions and it became apparent the lady couldn't tell him anything.

"Think back," he repeated patiently. "Right before you walked into the bakery, where were you?"

"I ... I seem to have forgotten ..." The woman cupped her mug in her palms and took a breath. "I ... saw your shop from across the street."

She stared toward the front windows. "I guess I crossed by that stop sign and just started walking. The cakes in the window are so pretty."

Of all the shops in the small strip, cakes had been more appealing than the books at Mysterious Happenings or the doggie logo at Puppy Chic, the grooming shop on the other side. That fact might tell them something about the woman and her past. Or, it might have simply meant she was hungry at the moment.

"You have some injuries," Beau said. "Any idea when or where you got them?"

Jane Doe, as Sam had begun to think of her, raised one hand to her face and gingerly touched the abrasion on her cheek. She noticed the broken nail on her right hand and stared at it. Her hands had other scrapes, as if she'd fallen and caught herself as she hit the ground.

"Oh, heavens. I should have washed up before eating." Jane started to get up.

"That can wait for a minute," Beau said. He indicated her torn blouse. "I need to ask this. Do you think you might have been molested? Sexually."

Jane's eyes went wide and she crossed her arms protectively over her chest. "No—I mean, I don't think so!" She looked at Sam, perhaps hoping for verification.

"We should get you in for an exam," Beau said. "I'll call a social worker who can take you to the hospital for that part of it. If your injuries aren't serious we can get you into the women's shelter until we figure out what to do next."

"A shelter?" Clearly, Jane felt some distaste for this idea.

"Can you remember anything about where you live or where you work? The names of any friends or relatives?"

At each suggestion, Jane seemed more bewildered. She shook her head sadly and Sam felt pangs of pity for the poor woman and her situation.

"I don't want to go to the hospital," Jane insisted. "I'm not hurt that badly." She held up the scraped palms as evidence.

Beau sighed. "I can't force you. But seeing as you have no purse, ID or money, I really do think the shelter is the best idea until we can find out where you belong."

"I like the cake shop better. Can I just stay here?"

Oh boy. Sam could see this stretching out all day, and then what was she supposed to do with Jane when it came closing time? She sent Beau a frantic look.

"How about this?" he said. "I'll get out in the neighborhood and ask some questions. Maybe someone on the plaza saw an incident or knows you. If Sam doesn't mind your staying here for an hour or so, we may have this whole thing solved pretty quickly. If I can't find out where you belong, I'll send Melissa Masters over. She's a lady who works for the county and she can find you a place for the night."

"That's a good idea," Sam said. "I know Melissa. She's very nice. And I'm sure Beau will get this figured out soon." *Really soon. Please.*

Poor Beau, she thought, as he brought in a camera and snapped a few pictures of Jane. He had no time to go door to door looking for someone who knew this woman, especially on a day when half his deputies were out sick.

Jen came to the table with a refill for Jane's tea.

"Stay here until you hear from me," Beau said.

Jane seemed preoccupied with her own hands, picking dirt from her cuticles as Beau left.

"Would you like to wash up?" Jen asked.

As long as Jane had no intention of going to the hospital for an exam, she might as well make herself a little more comfortable, Sam thought. She offered to show the way to the restroom at the back.

In the kitchen, Jane stared at the large worktable. A

smile came over her face. "How pretty!"

Becky had obviously gotten the designer purse cake figured out, and the quilted pink fondant with gold trim was coming together nicely. She sent a smile toward the visitor.

Sam got Jane equipped with a clean washcloth and soap, and found a box of adhesive bandages in the medicine cabinet. "Help yourself to whatever you need," she offered. "I'll be right out here in the kitchen."

* * *

Beau sat in his cruiser behind the bakery. "Dixie, sorry to put you on detective work but being so shorthanded ..."

"No problem, boss. What can I do?"

He gave Jane's description: White female, aged late-thirties to early-forties, a hundred twenty pounds, shoulder length brown hair, blue eyes. Wearing a straight black skirt and blue silky blouse.

"See if there are any missing person reports for the county, then go statewide if you need to. Call me if anything close comes in and email me a photo if you come up with one."

"Got it."

He started his cruiser and drove the half block to the plaza. Canvassing was the least exciting part of a cop's job but then sometimes it yielded exactly the right information to put the whole puzzle together. He stared at the crosswalk where Jane indicated she had come over to Sam's shop. It was a small intersection, but a bustling one, with traffic constantly on the move and a number of pedestrians. Everyone was on his or her way somewhere. No vendor carts or school crossing guards. No real reason for someone to hang around here. He turned and entered the first plaza shop he came to, a gallery.

"Sorry, I just got here ten minutes ago," said an effeminate man who bustled about with an air of busyness. Clearly, the sheriff had not come in the door to buy anything and was, therefore, an unwanted distraction.

Beau went on, getting the same result at a fine jeweler, a pottery shop and an upscale clothing store. The art crowd didn't get out early and no one had been around an hour ago. At the drugstore, which actually still had an old-fashioned soda fountain, the clerk was the bored sort who rang up trinkets such as keychains and shot glasses that proclaimed to be from Taos although they were manufactured in China. Beau's inquiry met with, "You gotta be kidding me, man. A thousand people a day come through here."

"I'm asking about the last hour or so. At least look at the photo. She has scratches and dirt on her face—you would have noticed that." He held up the digital screen.

The eye-roll told Beau this guy probably never even looked at faces. The man shook his head.

Out on the sidewalk, he took stock. On the opposite side of the plaza the hotel might provide a lead. He should have thought of it first. He edged between parked cars and crossed the street. In the shady square he circled wrought iron benches and scanned the ground. How much simpler this morning would become if he spotted a scuff on the pathway and a purse with "Jane's" ID lying on the ground. He checked the area carefully but had no such luck.

On the south side of the plaza he crossed the street and entered the hotel's lobby. Four people stood in line to check out, with one busy young clerk trying to handle it all. As he was deciding whether to push ahead and piss them all off, his radio squawked. He stepped outside; maybe Dixie had news.

"Sheriff, we have a next-of-kin notification. APD needs you to get right on it."

Notifying a family of a death was higher priority than a woman who, although she had problems, was happily eating her way through the pastries at Sam's shop.

"Who do I need to see?" he asked.

"We don't have a name. You'll need to speak with the detective in charge."

"I'm nearby so I'll come in. Anything on the missing person I had you checking?"

"Not yet but it's been a little crazy here. I'm still looking."

"Thanks, Dixie." He quick-walked to his cruiser and edged out of the congested plaza. Less than five minutes later he was pulling into his assigned spot at the department.

* * *

Jane Doe emerged from the restroom looking much better. Aside from a bright red scrape on one cheek, her face was clean. She'd put Band-Aids over the abrasions on her palms and the shoulder seam of her blouse was no longer gaping open.

"I found a safety pin in your medicine cabinet," she explained. "I hope it was okay to borrow it."

"Sure, no problem," Sam said, turning away from the pan of half-melted chocolate on the stove. A few more minutes to reach the magical one hundred eighteen degrees and she could take it off the heat and seed it for tempering. She responded to the *bing* of a timer and pulled a tray of fragrant mint-chocolate chip cookies from the oven then carried them to the cooling stand.

Julio, whose concentration was focused on measuring flour into the big Hobart mixer across the room, sent her a look of gratitude. Sam scanned the kitchen out of habit, making sure no one needed an immediate hand with something.

Together, Becky and Jen had sorted out the mix-up on the cake orders. The tiers covered in white fondant now waited at one end of the table, ready to be turned into a fiftieth anniversary cake, while the drawing of the bright pink purse with gold beading and black fondant handles was meant to be a triple chocolate Kahlua cake, all along. Once Becky knew that there were two customers named Perdida Sanchez—who would have guessed?—and found the other cake in the walk-in fridge, she got everything under control.

"I haven't heard anything from Beau—uh, the sheriff," Sam told Jane, although she noticed that Jane hadn't asked. "I know he's hoping to find out where you belong so you can go home."

Jane nodded, a wistful expression crossing her face. She turned to the worktable where Becky had the fashion purse cake nearly finished.

"That's so clever," Jane said.

Her eyes seemed to take in all the decorating tools and the black gum-paste flowers Becky was tucking beside the purse. She smiled fondly at the scene, although many people would have found the table and the several works-in-progress pretty chaotic.

"Do you know anything about decorating cakes?" Becky asked.

"Oh, I don't think so. I don't recall," Jane said. She looked a little lost again.

Not surprising, since you can't remember anything. Sam stopped herself. That line of thinking was petty and unkind. It wasn't as if Jane was in the way or disrupting the work. After all, didn't most of Sam's life consist of one distraction coming along to override another?

She thought of her brief contact with the mysterious wooden box in the wall safe at home this morning. If only she had handled it longer, more thoroughly. The box had led to visions in the past—seeing auras around people, spotting fingerprints that were otherwise invisible. It might have assisted her in observing some unseen fact about Jane this morning, something that would help identify the woman.

"Sam!" Jane's voice held a new, sharp edge. "I think your chocolate is about to burn!"

The stranger was sniffing the air, facing toward the stove with the now-bubbling pot. Sam sprinted across the room and lifted the pan off the double boiler. The chocolate looked fine but there was a tiny whiff on the steam rising above it. Another few seconds and the batch would have been too far gone to save.

Sam turned off the burner and rapidly stirred the chocolate to cool it. A few pieces of solid chocolate helped bring the temperature down.

"Wow, good catch," she said, turning to Jane. "How could you tell?"

Jane blinked three or four times and bit at her upper lip. "I really don't know."

Sam retrieved the pan, dipped a clean spoon into the chocolate and tasted it. Thank goodness, the flavor hadn't been compromised. Now if it would just temper properly, she could finish the chocolate magnifying glasses for the Sherlock bunch and get on with the day. Except that the day had gone off track the minute this strange woman had walked in the door.

Chapter 3

Beau walked into the empty squad room. Every deputy not sick at home with the flu was out on patrol and, judging by the radio chatter, the department was stretched pretty thin. In the dispatch office Dixie was speaking into her headset, typing at her keyboard and looking as unflappable as always.

She caught sight of him from the corner of her eye and held up a handwritten message while tapping computer keys with her left hand. Her eyes rolled slightly as she said, "Yes, ma'am, I'm going to put you on hold for just one moment."

"Sorry I haven't had much time to work on your missing person search," Dixie said, handing Beau the pink slip of paper.

"I can see you have your hands full." For all he knew, the woman at Sam's might not be missing at all. She could have had some small mishap where she struck her head and walked away without her ID. Those things happened.

"This," said the dispatcher, pointing at the message, "is the info on the death in Albuquerque. The caller was an APD detective. His name and number are there."

The phone console beeped, reminding her of the woman still on hold.

"I'd better …"

"Yeah, fine. I got this." Beau read the note as he walked toward his office. The detective's name was Kent Taylor. Beau decided to call him before contacting the local family. According to the brief note, the victim had been found in a hotel room. People always asked questions when they received word of a loved one's death, and knowing something of the circumstances would help him know what to tell them. A death that took place in a hotel was fraught with unknowns. People died in hospitals, in cars, in their own bathtubs—they generally didn't go to a hotel to die, and families were always a little freaked out by the news.

Kent Taylor answered his cell phone on the first ring and Beau introduced himself.

"Yeah, I don't know what will be helpful to you up there," Taylor said. "I can copy you all the ID we found in the guy's wallet. I tried directory assistance and came up with only one Robinet in Taos. First name George."

He read off an address and Beau wrote it down.

"Cause of death?" Beau asked. The families always asked.

"Undetermined—yet. You should know we saw evidence of rough sex play in the room. This was at the Kingston Arms—not the kind of place to attract typical lowlifes. Victim has strangulation marks on his neck, but the OMI will have to say for sure if that killed him." He went into a few more details, things Beau definitely would not tell the relatives.

"So, do you think it was accidental or are we looking at a murder?"

"I'm homicide division," Taylor said. "But you know, things aren't always what they seem."

While Beau waited for the scan of the victim's identification to come through, he looked up George Robinet the old-fashioned way, in the phone directory. The address seemed familiar. When he checked it on the map he remembered why. Greenlee Manor was an assisted living retirement complex, one of those places where, depending on the abilities of the resident, they might be fairly independent or under nursing care. He'd better check a little further before showing up at the door.

He opened his email and saw Taylor's message. Attached were scans of a New Mexico driver's license in the name of Zachary J. Robinet and a business card that showed his name as Zack and his position as partner in a company called ChanZack Innovations, Inc. Beau wondered who Chan was, since the rest of the company name was obviously a play on Zack's name. According to the license, Zack was forty-five years old, six foot one, and two hundred twenty pounds. He printed a copy of the scans, then cropped the driver's license photo of Robinet, enlarged it and printed the face.

The residential address on the license didn't sound immediately familiar. Beau looked it up and found it to be on a winding road on the south end of town, the same direction as Greenlee Manor. With luck, he might find a wife at the home address and she could be the one to inform the elderly parents. No matter who he spoke to, these things were never fun. How do you tell either a wife or a guy's parents that he was messed up in something unsavory in an out-of-town hotel? He grabbed a file folder and stuck the printed pages inside, stopped by Dixie's desk to let her know he was leaving, and went outside to his cruiser.

Goldenrod Lane was a short, narrow road that jutted off one of the through streets, about a half mile from Paseo del Pueblo. The neighborhood was like many in Taos, lots of old-time adobes patched together and added onto for generations, mixed with the new upper middle class ones where money had allowed the owners to build big the first time. The Robinet address was one of the latter. A long driveway showcased a portico of thick logs and a heavy front door with a stylized Zia symbol carved into it. Fall asters and chrysanthemums bloomed in neatly groomed patches of red, gold and purple. A three-car garage at the west end of the house was closed up tight and if any cars were present they were inside it.

Beau picked up the photo of Zack, took a deep breath and walked up to the front door. A doorbell sent rich tones chiming through the house, a hollow sound. He had a feeling right away no one was home. If there was a Mrs. Robinet she was probably at work. He gave the bell one more push but the result was the same, so he turned back to his vehicle and headed toward the next address on his list: Greenlee Manor.

* * *

Sam wondered when she would hear from Beau as she smoothed the melted chocolate with her spatula, cooling it to the proper consistency before it could be poured into the special molds she had purchased for the mystery book group next door.

She sent a sideways glance toward Jane who seemed content to sit on a stool and merely watch the normal hustle-bustle in the kitchen.

Okay, she hasn't really taken over the day. It's just weird having a stranger sitting here staring at me.

Becky had stored the fashion purse cake in the large walk-in fridge and was now piping trim onto the anniversary cake. It was a simple, traditional one that would have a golden 50 on top. As cakes went, it was a relatively easy one. The real work would come later in the week with a six-tier extravaganza of a wedding cake. Cascades of autumn flowers must be made—Sam and Becky had estimated nearly two hundred of them. Those would be fashioned out of gum paste and set to firm up until Thursday, when the massive job of creating ruffles and swags would commence.

Why isn't this lady worried? Sam mused. *I'd be frantic to figure out where I lived, who might be missing me. What if she has kids and they don't have a clue that mommy can't get to them?* She edged a glance toward Jane and smiled half-heartedly when that blue-eyed gaze met hers.

A scream erupted from the sales room, a crash, and Jen's voice. "Sam!"

Sam dropped her spatula on the table and rushed through the curtained opening. Jen was at the beverage bar, holding onto the midsection of the coffee maker, the top precariously balanced and spilled coffee grounds scattered in a swath around her.

"Help—grab that carafe," she panted. "I can barely hold this thing."

Sam rushed to her side, feet sliding on coffee grounds. She moved two carafes out of harm's way and helped to right the machine.

"I don't know what happened," Jen said, wiping her brow with the back her hand. "One minute I was opening the lid to make a fresh batch and the next minute it was coming down on me. Maybe when I cleaned the machine yesterday I didn't put things back right—I don't know."

"At least it's under control now. Don't worry about it." Sam checked the base of the machine to be sure it seemed steady.

"I'll get the broom." Jen headed toward the kitchen but a customer walked through the door and sidetracked her.

"Maybe I can put Jane to work sweeping it up," Sam said as Jen attended to the man who'd headed straight for the bear claws and ordered two.

But in the kitchen, Jane was standing over the chocolate Sam had abandoned. She'd scooped up the tempered liquid and was now injecting it into the molds through the tip of a pastry bag.

"Jane? What are you doing?"

"Oh, sorry. It had cooled and I was worried it would set up too quickly. You would have had to reheat and temper it again, and since it nearly became overheated earlier, I was worried about the flavor."

Sam eyed the perfectly filled molds. "Okay, that's the second time you've saved this order. You know something about chocolate, Jane. Quite a lot, I'd say."

Jane went very still. "I guess I do. I have no idea how I would have known to do that."

Becky and Julio had both stopped working and were listening in.

"It could be a clue to your identity. If Beau doesn't immediately come up with your name, maybe we need to start calling candy companies around the state."

"It was as if I didn't even have to think about it. I just knew what to do." She stared toward the middle of the room. "I don't know what—"

The back door opened and all attention went that direction. Sam's daughter, Kelly, stopped in mid-stride.

"Um, sorry. Didn't mean to interrupt." Her brown curls bobbed a little and a flush rose to her cheeks.

Julio cleared his throat and turned back to his task, pouring red velvet cake batter into the pan for a half-sheet cake. Becky greeted Kelly as she placed the cake topper on the finished anniversary cake.

Kelly looked at Jane, standing frozen in place with a pastry bag in hand and chocolate on her fingers, with frank curiosity.

Sam skipped introducing them—explaining everything would have taken way too long. "What's up?"

"Well, I know I said I would get pizza and come out to your place for dinner tonight, Mom. But something else has come up."

"Okay, no sweat. Something special?"

"A date. I have a date." The twinkle in her eye belied her casual tone.

Sam carried the chocolate molds to the cooling rack. "Oh yeah? Anyone I know?"

"Um, I really can't say."

"Ah ... *can't* say or *won't* say? C'mon, who's the mystery guy?"

"Yeah, well, I better get back to work. I'll talk to you

later." She was out the door before Sam could respond.

"Okay, that was weird. Becky, has she said anything to you?" All young people kept secrets from parents but Kelly was usually fairly candid about her friends and her love life.

Becky shrugged. "No idea at all."

Sam turned her attention to the devil's food cupcakes Julio had baked first thing this morning. They were to be the basis for the Sherlock-themed dessert for the book club. Devil's food lava cakes, mocha cream frosting, molded chocolate toppers—these folks never seemed to OD on chocolate. They even called themselves Chocoholics Unanimous.

While Sam iced cupcakes, Becky began kneading food color into sugary gum paste to make the assortment of fall flowers on their biggest project of the week. After an hour she had almost two dozen orange lilies and yellow nasturtiums done. The time-consuming work on the individual petals of chrysanthemums hadn't even begun and she needed to make pansies and asters as well.

"Jane, you were really good with those chocolate molds," Becky said. "Want to pitch in on these flowers?"

Jane looked a little unsure but said she would give it a try. She washed her hands and stood beside Becky as the experienced decorator showed the simple technique for a pansy.

"The secret is to roll the sugar dough really thin. Then you cut each petal shape individually. Once you have five of them, you gently roll the edges with this tool to give them a pretty little shape, then pinch the five petals together at the center to form the flower. We'll add the shading and details with food color later." She handed Jane the tool and a sheet of the thinly rolled dough, moving her own work to a new spot at the table.

Jane handled the gum paste well enough but her finished petals didn't have the right shape.

"Try again. You can reroll the dough another time or two if necessary."

The second effort wasn't a whole lot better.

"I guess I don't have any past experience with this," Jane said a little hopelessly.

"That's okay," Sam said. She had finished the lava cakes and placed the order on a tray to be delivered to the bookshop next door. "I've got a little time before I have to finish the baby shower cake for Carla Simms."

Jane continued to fumble about with the flowers but her long nails got in the way and she couldn't seem to master the small finger movements needed to deftly pinch and shape the dough. It wasn't long before she moved aside and perched herself on a stool out of the way while Sam and Becky moved into double-time with the flower petals.

Once Sam got into the rhythm of forming the tiny scooped chrysanthemum petals, she found her mind zipping to other subjects: Had Beau made any progress at all in learning Jane's identity? And who was this new guy Kelly was seeing?

Before she knew it, Jen was peeking through the curtain divider to ask if anyone wanted her to order them a sandwich for lunch.

Noon already. Sam straightened her shoulders, rotating them to work out the stiffness. It was another reason she desperately missed the magic box. In the past, when she had an overwhelming amount of work, she'd relied on it—okay, maybe a little too much at times—to give her the energy and stamina to complete an amazing amount of work in a short time. Of course, that was fraught with dangers too. It was impossible for the others in the bakery not to notice how much work she accomplished and comment on it. She massaged her right shoulder. No, it was better that she just move at the pace that fit her fifty-four years and be content with that.

"Let's take a break," she announced. "Jen, yes, sandwiches are a great idea. I'm just going to step out back."

She pulled her phone from her pocket, noting that Becky kept forming flower petals as if her hands wouldn't stop the repetitive movements, even though her stomach said she was hungry.

Outside, it was a perfect fall day with a deep blue sky, abundant sunshine and a crisp tang to the air. She tapped Beau's number and waited while it rang three times. Just as she was certain she would have to leave a message, he answered.

"Sorry, darlin', I don't have anything on your Jane Doe yet. I've been tracking down next of kin for that Albuquerque case. I'm at Greenlee Manor right now, waiting while they track down a couple who lives here. I'll have to get back to you."

"Sure. No problem." She felt a little letdown that he hadn't had time to get Jane taken care of. Not that the woman was posing a problem here at the shop but it was just strange having an extra person looking on.

Okay, don't be this way, Sam. Jane did save your ass when the chocolate was about to burn. And it's not as if she's really under foot.

"I can put in a quick call to social services if you want me to," he was saying.

"No, that's okay. She's not causing any trouble here at

the shop. As long as I have somewhere to send her before the end of the day, okay?"

She walked back through the kitchen, to the sales room, to check in with Jen. The sandwiches were coming from the deli a block over and if they didn't want to wait someone should run over to pick them up. She couldn't very well send Jane to do it, a woman lost and with amnesia. She told Jen she would walk over to pick up the lunches herself.

Chapter 4

Beau looked up to see a gray-haired couple in exercise clothing walking toward him. The assisted-living resident apartment manager had already confirmed that the Robinets had a son named Zachary, who was on record as their next of kin. George and Nancy Robinet certainly didn't match the picture of any retirement home residents he'd ever met before. Both wore athletic shoes and Spandex walking shorts and shirts. They moved with confidence and George held out his hand.

"I hear you wanted to speak to us, Sheriff?"

"Yes. Could we go somewhere?"

"Come along to our apartment," Nancy said, wiping her forehead with a tissue. "I need to shed this jacket. Funny how chilly it seems when we start out walking but how quickly we warm up."

The elevator ride to the third floor took longer than Beau liked. He didn't want to inform these people that their son was dead until he was certain of a few minutes privacy.

"I have to admit that you two surprised me," he said. "You seem pretty young and fit to have chosen life in a retirement home."

"Well, that's the operative word," George said. "We *chose* it. Hey, no more yard work for me."

"No cooking for me," Nancy said with a bright smile. "Our kitchen here has never seen more than cups of coffee and occasional sandwiches. The cafeteria provides three meals a day if we want them."

"Frees up our time for travel, too. Don't have to worry about who's watching our house while we're off to Europe or China or somewhere."

Beau nodded and stood aside as the elevator door slid open on the third floor. Clearly, these two had no clue as to the reason for his visit. He felt badly about the news he was about to spring on them.

George unlocked the door to an apartment with an autumn-themed wreath on the door, and Nancy peeled off her workout jacket as she walked past the tiny efficiency kitchen. The place appeared to consist of the little galley, a comfortable living room and a bedroom. A bathroom probably connected beyond it. The Robinets moved briskly about the room, offering coffee but seemingly unconcerned about Beau's presence.

He cleared his throat. "There's actually an official reason I stopped by today. I'm afraid it's about your son, Zack."

"Oh dear." Nancy dropped her jacket across the back of the sofa. "He hasn't gotten another speeding ticket, has he? There was that time the officer got very upset with him and took him to jail. I had to come and provide bail."

"No ma'am. It's not that."

"No, honey. Couldn't be that," George said. "He's on his way to that tradeshow, remember?"

"Maybe we should all sit down," Beau suggested. Keeping track of them was like trying to round up a pair of leggy young calves. They wouldn't hold still. He gestured toward the sofa and armchair.

"I'm very sorry to inform you that Zack has died."

It took a full minute for the information to sink in and, even then, Nancy looked at him as if he'd rattled out something incomprehensible in a foreign language.

"The Albuquerque police called our department with the news and asked that I contact Zack's next of kin. I'm very sorry."

"Oh my god," said Nancy, finally. George sat on the sofa, his shoulders slumped, a good ten extra years suddenly showing on his face.

"What about Josephine?" he said.

"That would be …"

"Zack's wife. Oh, and my gosh—poor little Bentlee. What will the boy do without a father?" At the mention of her grandson, Nancy's face crumpled and George reached out to put his arms around her.

Beau gave them a moment, feeling that he should leave but knowing he had still more questions to ask. Times like this were when he really hated this job.

"Josephine didn't go to Albuquerque with him?"

Nancy shook her head numbly.

"I'll need to notify her as well," he said. "I went by the house on Goldenrod Lane but no one was home."

George's mouth pursed. "Hm, I can't think where else

Josephine would be this time of day. Except maybe Zack's office. She sometimes helps out with the business."

"That would be ChanZack Innovations?"

Nancy nodded. Giving the couple something concrete to think about seemed to help.

"Chandler and Zack. They hit it off really well when they first met and decided to start the business together."

"I'll stop by there. Can you tell me any more about Zack's trip to Albuquerque? Why he went, who he planned to see, that kind of thing?"

"He went to some kind of computer convention," George said. "I thought it was in Las Vegas. He only went to Albuquerque to catch his flight."

"Those busy freeways in the city," Nancy said. "I knew he shouldn't spend so much time driving around there."

"There wasn't a traffic accident," Beau said as gently as he could. "Zack's body was found in a hotel room."

Nancy's expression said she was processing the information as quickly as she could, working to find the logic. Beau could tell they were anxious, wanting more information.

"He must have driven down there early and decided to stay the night before the trip."

"I don't know ma'am. I was told there was an ongoing investigation. I'm afraid I don't know anything more right now."

There was no way he was going to mention Taylor's comments on the rough sex play, especially to the parents, and especially in light of the fact that the victim's wife had not traveled with him. He repeated his condolences and left them sitting on their sofa, arms around each other, their world instantly shattered by his visit.

Back in his cruiser, he took a minute for a deep breath. The idea of early retirement flashed through his mind. This was certainly not the first grieving family he had visited—it wouldn't be the last. He dialed the cell number George Robinet had given for Zack's wife, hoping to find out where she was at the moment, but after a few rings it went to voicemail. He clicked off. There was no message he could leave for this sort of thing. He pulled out the scanned sheet of Zack Robinet's information and got the address for ChanZack Innovations.

The suite of offices was in Taos's version of an upscale location. Since ninety percent of the businesses in town were in small strip shopping centers or stand-alone adobe buildings, the two-story Appleton Center with its modern façade was it. A local bigwig, Rick Appleton, had made a fortune in real estate in the nineties and saw this building as the embodiment of his achievements. He'd filled the twenty suites with his own offices and other real estate related services, billing it as 'Your one-stop property shop' until the market tanked, helped along by onerous building codes and development rules. Appleton had gone off to greener real estate pastures, although presumably he still collected rent from the current-day tenants. With the one-stop theme gone, the spaces were filled by tech firms, graphics design places and a beauty salon attached to a high-end ladies clothing store. ChanZack Innovations was on the second floor, probably chosen for the corner location and view of Taos Mountain.

With any luck, maybe one of the cars in the lot belonged to Josephine Robinet and Beau could complete his mission quickly. Then he could get back to that other case. Sam's voice had betrayed her impatience at having the stranger underfoot in her shop.

"Mrs. Robinet? No, she hasn't come in today. Mr. Robinet is out of town," said the model-gorgeous receptionist behind the sleek mahogany desk.

"What about his partner? Is he in?"

"Mr. Lane. At the moment, yes. He's due to leave for the airport soon. I will need to ask whether he has any time." She tried sending a coy glance in his direction.

Beau touched the badge on his shirt pocket. "It's official. I suggest that he make time."

He stepped aside, studying a range of colorful art on the wall beside the reception desk, while she made a quiet call. The poster-sized photos pictured trendy and successful people holding cell phones and tablets, staring at their screens with delighted smiles on their faces.

"Sheriff?"

The male voice came from behind him and Beau turned.

"Chandler Lane. What can I do for you?" The man was one of those metro-sexual males with a polished complexion, perfect haircut, complete with blond highlights, and upscale casual clothing you rarely saw on Taos locals, where the tri-cultural blend of New Mexico was very evident—Hispanic politicians, Indian artisans and aging Anglo hippies. Lane was in his early thirties, the sort who knew he was at the top of his game and loving every minute.

"Mr. Lane, you are Zack Robinet's business partner?"

"Yes, that's right. May we offer you some organic coffee?"

Beau declined. "Can we speak privately?"

Lane's deep brown eyes darted toward the receptionist and Beau got the sense of sexual tension between them.

He followed Lane's confident stride as the partner passed his thumb over a tiny panel beside the connecting door. A green light, an audible click, and he led the way into the first office on the left of a short hallway. The man's desktop was filled by two large computer monitors and keyboards. A laptop with the lid closed sat on one corner of a credenza behind the desk. More posters of joyful phone users filled two of the walls in here, as well.

"I swear I paid my taxes," Lane joked, holding his hands up in a no-secrets-here gesture. "That's not why you're here. Okay, a donation to the police and sheriff's association? You got it, you know."

"You might want to sit down," Beau suggested.

Chandler Lane only stood stock still.

"I'm afraid I have bad news. Your partner, Zack, is dead."

"What!" Lane's face went pale beneath his perfect tan. "I can't bel—wow."

He paced the length of the room, running his hands through his hair, pausing, pinching his lower lip.

"What happened? I mean, I'm just stunned. We're supposed to be in Vegas tonight. All our trade show stuff was shipped ahead ..." He crossed back and sank slowly into the chair behind his desk.

"Did you know he was staying the night in Albuquerque?"

"Yeah. Actually, I had planned to go too but then we couldn't get on the same flight and I had some other stuff come up here in town. I'm supposed to leave by two, get to the airport, take a seven o'clock flight tonight. My god, what—what'll happen?"

"Tell me a little more about your business. What types

of 'innovations' do you have?"

Chandler took a deep breath, switching gears. "We, uh, we develop apps. Our biggie is a game called Infinite Star Fighter that seems to have every teen kid and half their fathers addicted to it. Made a couple tons of money on that, I have to admit. Following up was tough. I mean we did upgrades—version 2.1, etcetera. Our big announcement at the electronics show this week is a spinoff that we think will capture the girls' market. Star Fighter Hotties, it's called. You know, every girl wants to think she's so hot she'll hook up with one of the heroes from I.S.F. Sorry, you really don't care about the details on all that." He ran his hands down the sides of his face again. "I just can't take it in—Zack gone. What did Jo say?"

"Jo ... oh, Josephine. I haven't been able to reach his wife yet. I had hoped she would be here. Do you know where I can find her?"

Chandler shook his head. "She comes once or twice a week. She coordinates ad campaigns and double-checks the bookkeeper on tax matters. Zack and me, we're into the gaming kid's mind, know how to come up with action and ideas they love. Not so good with money. Jo coordinates all that other stuff."

"I should probably be the one to notify her about Zack," Beau said, placing one of his business cards on the desk. "If you hear from her can you find out where she is and give me a call? Until then, I'd appreciate it if you don't mention this to anyone else. It would be devastating to a widow to find out from someone on the street if the word gets out."

"Agreed. Totally." Chandler made a zipping motion across his lips.

"Do you still plan to attend the trade show?"

Chandler stared at his clasped hands. "I suppose I'd better. We sent out all these advance press releases about our new product. The sales team is going along to write up orders, but if no one's there to introduce it and do the demos, we've invested about a million dollars in development that we'll have a hard time getting back."

Beau stepped toward the door. "I'm sorry I brought sad news."

Chandler Lane merely stared at the floor and shook his head slowly.

Down in the parking lot, Beau got into his department SUV and had barely reached to stick the key in the ignition when his cell phone rang.

"Sheriff? It's Kent Taylor here in Albuquerque."

"Yes, Detective Taylor. I was about to call you. I've located and notified the parents and the business partner of your victim, but haven't found the wife yet."

"Okay. I mean, let me know when you do. Meanwhile, I've rushed the OMI on this and have some startling results on the autopsy. Robinet didn't die from asphyxiation, as we first thought. Looks like a drug overdose. Heroin."

"Whoa. But the marks on his neck?"

"Yeah, he's got those all right, but that wasn't the COD."

"Meaning—sex *and* drugs at the little party?"

"The Medical Investigator questions whether the victim injected the heroin himself. He definitely wasn't a habitual user. He's thinks Robinet could have been unconscious at the time the drug entered his system."

Beau thought of the clean-cut appearance of Zack Robinet from his ID photo. Apparently there was a lot more to this situation.

"We're looking for the woman who was in the room

with him, but there were a lot of prints. Unfortunately, hotel maids don't exactly wipe down every surface when they clean so we can't be sure when the various prints were left. The desk clerk remembers Robinet heading upstairs with a glamorous woman, so we're running all the prints. Too bad it doesn't go as quickly in real life as on TV."

"So this investigation is going to focus both in Albuquerque and in Taos."

"You got it." A tired sigh came over the line.

"I'll get whatever I can in background on the victim," Beau said, telling Taylor the little he knew after talking with Chandler Lane. "These guys have made a lot of money. That's always good as a motive. The partners were headed to a trade show in Vegas to introduce another hot product so maybe a competitor is somehow involved. I think I'll warn Lane to be careful."

"Let's check in frequently," Taylor suggested. "I have a feeling developments will come from both of our jurisdictions."

Beau took a deep breath after disconnecting from the call. A complicated murder case was the last thing he needed with half his department sick. The phone rang again. Sam. He'd forgotten all about the missing persons reports he was supposed to be checking for her.

Chapter 5

Sam slid an anxious glance toward the clock above the stove, wondering what was going on with Beau's inquiries about the identity of her mysterious visitor. Four o'clock. It wasn't as if Jane Doe was causing any problems here at Sweet's Sweets. It was more like having a guest who'd popped in unannounced and Sam felt she needed to be courteous and come up with ways to entertain her. The bakery was busy enough on any given day to keep her entire crew moving at full speed; entertaining visitors during the work day was putting a strain on her normally ready smile.

She picked up the tray of Sherlock-themed cupcakes and walked toward the bookshop next door. If she hadn't heard from Beau by the time she'd delivered them she would call him. True, his other investigation was more important than this one but, seriously, it was getting late in the day and what was she supposed to do with Jane after closing time?

"Ah, *bon soir*, Miss Samantha!" Ivan Petrenko, the quirky Russian who owned the bookstore greeted her with enthusiasm. "You have bringing the chocolate goodies for the week!"

Sam tended to forget the stories of his colorful past—which supposedly included a daring escape from communist Russia, a life in France where he reputedly became a renowned chef, and a career in a top New York restaurant before he landed in Taos—until she conversed with him and tried to work out his odd blend of languages and syntax.

"You mentioned the club was reading Arthur Conan Doyle this week, so we went with a sleuthing theme," she said, setting the cupcakes on a table with a display of nineteenth-century detective articles, along with the featured book.

"She is perfect, these treats," Ivan said, handing Sam a check. "How is going, your day?"

"Pretty well. We're busy but it's not as crazy as it will get when the holidays begin."

He gave her an odd look, reminding her that the word 'crazy' had several interpretations. There was no telling which one Ivan was picturing in his head right now.

"A woman showed up this morning. She apparently has amnesia," Sam said. "You know that word, right?"

"Oh, *da*, is the forgetting of memory."

"Something like that. She doesn't know her own name or where she lives. Beau is trying to find out if anyone has filed a missing person report but I haven't heard back from him yet and she's just hanging around my shop."

He gave a sympathetic nod.

"Hey, maybe I should send her over here. Seeing some of the books might remind her of something."

Ivan gave a noncommittal European shrug. "I am opening until six. Book club come at six-thirty."

"I'll think about it," Sam said on her way out the door.

What would happen if she sent Jane over and the woman wandered away? Beau might come up with some relatives and then they wouldn't be able to find her again. Plus, what if Jane's amnesia was caused by a traumatic event and something in the bookshop reminded her of it so strongly that she freaked out. Sam couldn't envision herself or Ivan being able to handle the situation if the woman truly went berserk.

She paused on the sidewalk and pulled out her phone. Bothersome or not, there was only one way to find out what, if anything, Beau had learned.

"Hey, darlin'," he said. His voice sounded harried. "Sorry, but I haven't had a minute to follow up on your lady."

"Beau, she isn't 'my lady' and I really don't want her to become mine. I really need somewhere to send her before we close up shop for the day."

A quick flash went through her head, the idea of taking Jane home with her for the night. But the earlier vision of the woman suddenly turning into a whole different personality came back at her. No. Jane needed some kind of professional help.

"I know, I know," he said. "I haven't had any luck with our local databases and there's been no time to take the search further. I'll call Melissa Masters and have her come by your place. Her department is equipped to deal with these things."

"Thank you." Sam breathed a sigh, reminding herself there were times when it really wasn't necessary to fix everything personally. She hung up and went back to the cinnamon-sugar ambiance of her own shop.

"Hey, Sam," Jen greeted. "I was just totaling the register. Looks like we've had a decent day."

Sam crossed behind the counter to take a look. It was amazing how certain days turned out well, even when it didn't feel like a lot of traffic had come in.

"Becky and I were playing a little game with Jane awhile ago, tossing out names to see if she recognized her own."

"And?" A rush of hope.

"No luck. No flicker even."

"Ah well." She told Jen about her call just now to Beau. "I'd better inform her."

It wasn't as if Jane had any belongings to gather, so when Melissa Masters pulled up in front of Sweet's Sweets thirty minutes later she was ready to go.

Melissa turned out to be a woman in her fifties, probably near Sam's age but far more matronly with polyester slacks and a pastel color-coordinated blouse. Her hair reached her collar in short gray waves and her smile was genuine, the sort that radiated kindness and understanding toward those who had endured way too much in their lives. Jane seemed to feel instantly at ease with the social worker.

"We'll go to Casa Comfort," Melissa said. "The sheriff knows where we are."

Sam nodded.

"Jane, you'll share a room with another lady tonight. We have nightgowns and toothbrushes and most anything you'll need. Depending on how many are with us at any given time, sometimes you get a room of your own. We put women with children in the larger ones and there are bunk beds for them. But don't worry about it. I'm sure the sheriff will find your identity and get your home address real soon."

Jane seemed a little confused by all the plans, but Sam knew that must be normal. She watched as Melissa showed Jane out to a white Ford sedan and settled her comfortably in the passenger seat. She'd never thought of the logistics necessary to take people in on a moment's notice, some of them indefinitely.

They drove away and Sam wondered if she would ever see Jane again. Quite likely, Beau would come up with her identity, and anxious family members would come pick her up. With luck maybe Jane's memory would come back immediately when she saw familiar faces and surroundings. Otherwise, she might be in for a long haul of medical and psychiatric care.

"Sam?" Jen touched her forearm. "You okay?"

"Absolutely." She surveyed the sales room. "Ready to close?"

"Here's the bank bag. I think everyone else has already left."

Suddenly, the long day closed in on Sam and she felt an overwhelming need to get home. In the kitchen, Julio had washed and neatly put away all the baking utensils. The oven was off and Becky's orders for the next day waited on the worktable. The lights, other than the one above Sam's desk, were off.

After checking the front door behind Jen, she jammed the bank deposit into her backpack purse, switched out the final lamp, got into her van and drove north. Thank goodness for the crockpot chicken waiting at home; at this moment she didn't even have the energy to stop for fast food.

I miss the box, she thought as she edged through the stop-and-go traffic past the pueblo turnoff. *No, you don't. You can't turn to magic every time you get a little tired.*

An ancient VW with a wheezing engine and bumper stickers all over the back, slowed abruptly to make the turn at the health food market, and Sam had to hit her brakes to avoid rear-ending it.

"Get your taillights fixed," she muttered to the oblivious driver, reminding herself to stay alert. It wasn't that much farther.

The turnoff for the ranch welcomed her, the stone portals on each side of the long drive and the carved lintel connecting them gave the place a solid feel. Beau's big log house, where Sam had moved when they married, welcomed her in the late dusk. Lights at the windows and the sight of his cruiser parked out front comforted her. Both dogs rose and approached the edge of the front porch as she parked her van.

"The chicken smelled so good when I got here," came Beau's voice from the kitchen, "that I went ahead and mashed the potatoes and made some gravy."

What a prize he was. She dropped her pack onto one of the hooks at the coatrack and set her phone on the end table before joining him in the kitchen. He handed her a glass of wine and insisted she take a seat at the small kitchen table while he turned off the gas under a pan on the range top.

"Um, you taste like sugar," he said after kissing the top of her head.

"I should shower. I think I have powdered sugar in every pore of my body."

"I could get that for you." He licked the tip of her nose with a little flick.

"Ugh, honey. You really don't want to do that. There's plenty of sweat in the mix too."

He laughed and clicked his beer glass to her wine glass. "Okay, you win. You want that shower before dinner or after?"

Tiredness was settling over her pretty quickly. She stood up and took his hand. "If you can hold dinner ten minutes I'll make it a very quick one."

By the time she came downstairs, refreshed and wearing a loose caftan, he'd lit candles on the dining table and refilled her wine glass.

"Is there an occasion I've forgotten or do you plan to always spoil me rotten?" she teased.

"Um, probably neither. Although our anniversary is coming up soon."

Sam gulped too quickly and sputtered on her wine. How had she not remembered such an important date, especially when she created fantastic desserts for other people's occasions all the time?

Sam's energy began to return as she ate. Beau talked about his investigation.

"I made a second trip out to interview the victim's parents," he said. "Now that the Albuquerque police are treating this as a suspicious death, possibly a homicide, my department is having to look into the man's background here at home."

"And I'll bet the parents swear their son never used drugs a day in his life."

"Most of 'em will tell you that, yes. Especially the ones who've been successful in their lives and watched their children grow up to be successful too. They really don't think that stuff happens in their own families."

A picture of Kelly flashed briefly through Sam's mind. Aside from a lot of beer and maybe some experimentation in her college years, surely her *own* daughter didn't …

"So the Robinets are swearing up one side and down the other that dear Zack was a wonderful man who never made an enemy, who attended church every week and was probably the next Steve Jobs when it came to his business success."

"And you're not buying it?"

"I think *they* genuinely believe it. I mean, most likely they're not covering up anything. But parents often have an incredible blind side about their adult children. Here's a couple who are vital and active for their ages—they travel and get out a lot. How closely did they really stay involved in their married son's life?" He poured a little more wine for Sam. "I went by Zack Robinet's residence—nice place, by the way. Nobody home there. Most likely, the parents or the business partner will talk to the wife before I do."

"Still, you have to get her side of things."

"Yeah, she'll be the one to verify or deny the things the parents said."

"Do you think she will?" Sam set down her fork and pushed her plate aside. "She might be the one with the most to lose by admitting her husband's weaknesses."

"Losing face, you mean?"

"Well, yeah. Especially when it comes to sex and drugs. She could have been turning a blind eye to all kinds of things, you know, in exchange for lots of money and a fantastic lifestyle."

He nodded. "Some do. You're right about that. The same might be said for his business partner, Chandler Lane. I'd planned on going back to question him some more but he's on his way to a trade show and won't be back in Taos for another three or four days."

Sam stood up and stacked the dishes. "I'm afraid I didn't bring anything home for dessert, but there's ice cream in the freezer."

His smile told her he'd rather have the ice cream than a pastry any day. He picked up the leftover chicken and bowl of potatoes and followed her to the kitchen.

"So, on a completely different topic," Sam said as she rummaged in a drawer for the ice cream scoop, "I don't suppose there's any late-breaking news on Jane?"

He paused with the freezer door open.

"Sorry, darlin'. There's only so many hours in the day. I had Dixie send the photo out to surrounding jurisdictions. Just as I was leaving for the day she said there was one response from a town in Colorado. Pagosa Springs, I think."

He pulled out the new carton of vanilla and proceeded to scoop as he talked.

"For now, Jane's safely in the hands of Melissa and her colleagues so you don't need to worry about her. I'll let you know what we find out, and chances are good that she'll be on her way back to her worried family by this time tomorrow."

Back in the living room, Sam took two bites of her ice cream but felt her earlier tiredness return. When Beau finished off both servings and carried the bowls to the kitchen she found herself dozing on the couch.

Beau came back and kissed her gently on her left temple. "Hey there. You ought to go on to bed. I'll check the horses and dogs and lock up everything. See you upstairs."

He didn't have to suggest twice. She thought once again of the carved box in the safe, feeling very tempted to handle it a little to rid herself of this lethargic mood. But past experience had shown that touching the box at night wasn't a good idea if she wanted any sleep at all. She walked past the closet with the safe and headed upstairs.

By the time she had completed her little nightly routine, Beau was in the bedroom peeling off his undershirt. She spent a moment enjoying the view of his rippling muscles.

"You know why you're so tired this week?" he asked. "I think you're not busy enough. You're between seasons at the bakery and your crew handles everything there really well."

She wiggled her eyebrows at him as he crawled in bed beside her. "I can think of one thing that would keep me busy for awhile right now."

His sexy smile still melted her heart. "Well, that too. But what I was going to suggest is that you help me with this murder investigation."

Sam ignored that suggestion and reached for his elastic waistband.

Chapter 6

Sam pulled her bakery van into the alley behind the shop and gathered her pack and the now-empty bank deposit bag. When she looked up, Kelly's car sat nose to nose with hers, directly behind Puppy Chic. Her daughter had a big smile and her eyes sparkled. Sam hoped her own sexual afterglow wasn't quite so evident.

"So … I'm guessing that the big date last night went well?" Sam teased.

"Yeah. Yeah, it did."

"You gonna tell me his name?"

"Not just yet. I don't know if it'll last. We've only had two dates, Mom. And no sex yet. Really, I'm not jumping into a new relationship *that* quickly!"

"Okay, fair enough. When it comes to a serious guy, I

trust you to pick someone who's good for you, someone I'll like, and who'll produce beautiful grandchildren for me." Sam laughed and shifted her pack to the other shoulder. "I'd better be getting to work. I'm sure the crew has been at it quite awhile already."

Kelly's gaze slid over to where Julio's Harley was parked near the bakery's gas meter. She gave that dreamy little smile again and headed for the back door of the dog grooming shop.

Julio? Oh my god, could he be—?

She shook off the thought and stepped into the bakery kitchen. "I just saw Kelly outside. She seems pretty happy today."

"Oh, that's right," Becky said. "Kelly had a big date last night, didn't she?"

"Apparently so," Sam said with a smile as she hung up her pack and slipped on a clean baker's jacket.

Julio gave his usual quiet "Good morning" and started measuring butter and sugar into the Hobart. She turned off her Mom Radar and decided she better relax about this. Kelly's bouncy demeanor was nothing new, and the sweet smile this morning might have been aimed at something entirely other than the bike. It had to be. Kelly and Julio, a couple? Nah, their temperaments were so different. Sam just couldn't see it.

She chided herself as she picked up the stack of order sheets for the day and spread out the orders to prioritize them. Beau was right—the shop certainly wasn't overly busy right now. Between now and the weekend there were only three weddings and six birthdays. Becky had the autumn flower wedding cake well under way, as evidenced by the dozens of sugar flowers which hung upside down by their stems to dry. One of the other weddings was a very traditional cake with lots of piping and string work. Strings got tricky and Becky hated doing them, so Sam would handle that one herself. The third was a simple fondant-covered two tiers, with satin ribbon and fresh flowers. The bride had ordered the flowers, which would be delivered by the florist on Saturday, then Sam would quickly put the cake together and deliver it Saturday for the Sunday afternoon ceremony.

She made certain the cake flavors were noted and that nothing required a special topper or decorative element she didn't have on hand. Everything seemed well under control. Maybe she really could be helping Beau in some way. She was nibbling on the cap of her pen when her phone rang.

"Hey, girl, what's up?" Her best friend, Zoë. They hadn't seen each other in a couple of weeks.

"We need to get together, maybe 'do lunch'," Sam joked. "Just say when."

"Actually, lunch might be tricky but how about if I pop by for a cup of tea after work today?"

Zoë seemed delighted with that idea. "I have a special Assam that's waiting to be opened."

With a plan in place, Sam set her phone down and picked up the nearest order form. Five minutes later she was happily piping brightly colored frosting onto a five-year-old's birthday cake, turning a square cube of layers into the backdrop for the latest popular cartoon characters, some little munchkins who lived in a cave world and came out often enough to fight off criminals in the way only preschoolers can imagine that they would. That one went into the fridge and she'd just begun a fairy princess castle, complete with sugar cone turrets, when she heard animated voices out front.

Jen's voice came through, asking someone to wait, only moments before Jane Doe came walking through to the kitchen. Evidently, Beau's Colorado lead had not worked out.

"Hi, Sam." Jane wore the same clothing as yesterday. She or someone else had taken the time to sew her ripped sleeve seam back together and the blouse had been laundered. "Melissa took me by the sheriff's office but I guess they didn't have any news for me. They wanted me to go back to the shelter but there's nothing to do there. A lot of the women have jobs and leave during the day or else they are out on interviews or appointments with their counselors. I thought maybe I could help out here?"

Sam stuck a smile on but wasn't feeling the love. Just because Jane had saved a batch of chocolate from destruction yesterday didn't mean she had to adopt the woman and keep her around all the time, did it? She brought herself up short. This poor lady was lost and hurt and no doubt feeling completely disoriented. The least Sam could do was to be hospitable.

"Let's get you a cup of coffee and something to eat first," she suggested.

Jen took Jane's elbow and subtly steered her back to the front room.

"Okay, now what can we do to keep her busy?" Sam said quietly to Becky.

"She wasn't much good with the sugar flowers," her assistant whispered. "I had to redo a bunch of them. Her skill seems to be with chocolate."

Sam paged through the order sheets once more. One customer wanted a ganache-covered cream cake and another had requested "something creative" in chocolate to serve with afternoon tea. She could mention those to Jane and see if the woman's interest piqued. If so, maybe she really could be of help. Meanwhile, she would call Beau while Jane was finishing her cheesecake out front.

"That Albuquerque homicide detective is on his way up here," Beau said, "and no, I haven't had any results on your Jane Doe. The one in Pagosa Springs wasn't a match."

"Last night you mentioned having me help with your investigation," Sam said. "I don't know about a homicide— the pictures always make me queasy—but maybe I can do some of the computer work that's involved in finding Jane's real identity."

He leapt on that suggestion. "You'll have to come to the department. Our computers are on a separate secure network and you can't get into them from yours. But that would be great. Dixie said we've had a bunch of email responses to the notice we sent out, but we haven't had anyone with the time to go through them. How soon can you get here?"

Sam heard Jane's voice again, her coffee break almost done. "Let me assign her something to do and I'll come right away. Say, fifteen or twenty minutes?"

"The sooner the better. I'll have to set you up with access and I have a feeling Detective Taylor will be here any minute and I'll be tied up with him the rest of the day."

Jane's smile lit up when Sam presented her with the idea of making something chocolate for a ladies tea. "Do you have any Grand Marnier? I remember a certain type of truffle …"

Sam scanned the supply shelf and came up with a bottle of the rich liqueur. "Go for it. Truffles sound like just the thing."

She sent a little cautionary glance toward Becky. Translation: taste one before they go out to the customer.

"Oh, Sam," Jane said. "I came across something that might be meaningful." She reached into the pocket of her skirt and came out with a small slip of paper, which she handed to Sam.

The scrap appeared to have been torn from a pad of generic white paper. It contained a string of numbers, handwritten in blue ink—3679854. Sam studied Jane's face.

"I think it's my writing, but I have no idea what they mean."

"Seven digits—it could be a phone number, but it's not a local one."

Jane simply shrugged. It could take days to dial it with every area code in the country, and even if she reached someone, Sam had no idea what to ask. Are you missing a slender, dark haired woman? Surely Beau's department had access to quicker ways of checking. She told Jane she would take it to him.

Ten minutes later she had found a parking spot on the side street near the Sheriff's Department office and walked in to find Beau talking with a man in his fifties whose sport jacket looked a little rundown at the elbows. He had receding hair and tired lines around his eyes. Beau introduced him as Kent Taylor, APD Homicide.

Taylor gave her an almost surly hello that Sam chalked up more to an attitude of 'let's get on with it' than rudeness. Beau pointed Taylor in the direction of the office coffee machine and excused himself, leading Sam into his private office.

"I'm going out with the detective to see if Robinet's wife is home now, and then to interview his business partner again. Here's the file with Jane Doe's photo and information. I've set you up with a user ID and password, written down here."

Sam looked at the incomprehensible jumble of letters and numbers. While she would have preferred an easy password such as Iluvchocolate, as long as she had the little note at her side she supposed she could handle this one.

"I've already got you logged in," he said. "If you leave the desk you need to log out and lock the door."

"Really? Even in your own department?"

"It's a rule. Not that the guys would do anything dishonest with the information but people are always closing out someone else's file and losing information that wasn't saved. It's simpler if we all follow the log-out protocol."

"Got it. So, what am I looking for?"

"Go through these emails. A lot of them will be negative—just saying they don't have our Jane Doe in their files. If they ask for a courtesy check on their own missing persons cases, save those for one of my guys to work later. What you're looking for would be some other department who thinks the MP they're looking for could be your Jane. Compare the photos they will have attached and see if it's remotely possible. Print out any promising ones, file the others." He showed her how he had already set up folders to save the other messages.

"Don't delete anything. You never know how or when something might be of use. Just file them for now."

She showed Beau the paper with numbers Jane had found in her pocket this morning and mentioned their theory that it could be a phone number.

"Pretty generic, but if it's a telephone, Dixie can do some things to cross check it." He took the slip and walked toward dispatch before leaving the building.

It took only a half hour of click-and-drag tedium for Sam to decide that piping roses on birthday cakes was thrilling by comparison to law enforcement work. She felt her eyes glazing over and decided to log out for awhile and stretch. At the coffee machine she poured a cup but it turned out horrendously strong and tasted like the janitor might have made it two days ago. She realized she was spoiled to her signature blend at the shop and the fact that Jen kept the pot refreshed throughout the day. She trudged back to the desk and pulled her login information from the slip of paper in her pocket.

Two hours later she had organized the responses into folders as Beau wanted. Although a couple of them showed dark-haired women of about the right age and build, none pictured the Jane Doe sitting in Sam's shop right now. It looked fairly certain that she would have to spend another night in the women's shelter.

* * *

Beau negotiated Goldenrod Lane, remembering the exact turn to the Robinet house only a moment before he reached it. Kent Taylor looked around with the wonderment city folks showed when they encountered high-dollar homes in remote rural places. The Albuquerque cop was a man of few words, Beau was discovering. Beyond the initial greeting when he arrived in Taos this morning, he'd not said much. In fairness, what was there to say? Reports had been emailed and Beau had read them all—the autopsy, the crime scene details, what little information had been obtained from employees at the Kingston Arms. He pulled into the Robinet driveway, seeing no changes in the house or acreage since his last visit.

Taylor got out of the passenger seat and automatically walked to the roadside mailbox, opening it and pulling out a sheaf of envelopes.

"Looks like no one's checked mail in a few days," he said, flipping through the stack as he returned to Beau's cruiser. "Couple bills, bunch of junk. This one looks like some kind of greeting card. Addressed to Josephine Robinet. Maybe it's her birthday and she took a trip somewhere."

"Anything's possible." Beau scanned the front entry where a skim of dust covered the deck, not mussed by a single footprint. He would look through the mail later.

"Here's something from the Holbrook Academy," Taylor said. "Looks like a billing statement. They got a kid?"

"Yeah, Zack's parents mentioned a grandson."

"That's someone else to notify. Poor little guy."

"I get the impression he's a teenager. Hard to tell how they take news like this. I'll check with the grandparents. They've probably already made the call or gone down to visit."

Taylor stared at the large house. "Looks like these folks have the money to afford sending a kid to Holbrook."

Beau thought about the luxurious office furnishings at ChanZack Innovations and the trendy clothing the business partner wore. Appearances didn't always mean a lot but it was entirely credible that they could send their kid someplace like Holbrook Academy.

He walked up to the front door and pressed the doorbell. Again, the hollow-sounding chimes inside. There was a film of grit on the doorknob. Of course, owners would likely come and go through the attached garage. He walked toward it. Kent Taylor had pocketed the mail and followed along.

"All the tire tracks look old," Taylor said.

"Yeah, I noticed that."

They circled the garage and let themselves into a walled patio through an unlocked high wooden gate. Three sliding glass doors opened onto a huge tiled deck, each door at a different angle to ensure privacy. Peering into the middle one showed a great room large enough to entertain an army battalion or half the kids at the local high school, depending on your preference. Oversized leather couches faced a theater-sized TV screen, and a variety of Indian pottery, mostly in the Tewa and San Ildefonso styles, filled nooks and crannies. No one was in sight, although a discarded shirt over the nearest chair, a plugged-in cell phone and some pocket change on the kitchen counter made it look as if someone could have walked out of the room five minutes ago. Beau tried the door but it was securely locked.

"This one's a pretty fancy master bedroom," Taylor said, his hands cupped around his eyes at the door to the west.

Beau walked to the third door and saw that this room was another bedroom done in grand style. He tugged at the door handle but this one didn't budge either.

"Okay. So the wife's off somewhere out of town, the son is at boarding school and hubby went and got himself killed in Albuquerque." Kent Taylor probably didn't mean for his words to come off so cavalierly. Beau saw it as the attitude of a cop who's seen too much and is facing the end of a long career.

"I suppose we should begin canvassing the neighbors,

see if anyone is a friend of Mrs. Robinet and might know how we can reach her."

They had circled again to the front of the house. Beau faced the road, scanning the neighboring properties and realizing that neither the garage nor the front porch were likely to be visible to any other homes on this curving lane. No matter. It was work that had to be done because you never knew where a lead would come from. Although Beau would have appreciated the chance to stretch his legs, Taylor suggested they take the cruiser to the nearest neighboring house, about a quarter mile up the road.

A sleepy-eyed man of about fifty, wearing only a pair of boxers, answered after their second ring at the doorbell. His expression clearly said "I was asleep, what the hell do you want?" Night shift worker, no doubt. They usually disconnected their doorbells and turned off phones, so Beau didn't have a whole lot of sympathy for him.

"Sorry, never had nothin' to do with 'em," said the man, who gave his name as Randy Walker.

"Within the last few days, would you have seen Mrs. Robinet leave the house, maybe with a suitcase?"

"I tell you, we never exchanged more'n a dozen words in the five years since they built that house. Me, I work nights. Don't see much of anyone. My one neighbor, Buddy, we try to catch some Sunday football now and then." He nodded his head toward the west, presumably indicating the next house along the road.

"Well, if you should see Mrs. Robinet return home, would you mind giving my department a call? We really need to get in touch with her." Beau handed the man his card.

For the first time, Walker's eyes fully opened. "One of 'em done something wrong?"

"Thanks for your time," said Kent Taylor.

The two lawmen headed back to the cruiser parked at the road. The next two houses yielded no answers to their knocks, but that wasn't unusual for midday. It was a neighborhood where people held jobs. They doubled back and walked up to the house directly east of Robinet's.

A woman with a baby on her hip answered the door, her blond hair caught up in a clip at the back, strands hanging across her face. A toddler edged into view from behind her red calf-length skirt. The woman looked ready to slam the door had the visitors turned out to be selling magazines, pans or religion. At Beau's question, she gave her name as Lacy Padilla.

"I might have Jo's cell phone number," she said, her eyes aiming skyward as she worked to remember. "She had me accept a package for her once and asked me to call when it arrived."

"That would be very helpful," Beau said.

She untangled the one kid from her leg and shifted the baby to her other side so she could reach into the pocket of her skirt. One-handed, she thumbed across the cell phone's screen until she came up with it. Beau wrote down the number she read out.

"Did you know the Robinets very well?" Taylor asked.

"No, not at all. I mean, you'd think that Jo and I both being home all day we would have the time to socialize. But we never did. She seemed all wrapped up in charity work and her husband's business. I got pregnant the first time shortly after they moved in next door. Talking baby food and diapers and that kind of thing completely did not interest her. And, unfortunately, the Junior League and all that stuff completely does not interest me. You might check with Sharon across the road and down a little ways. She's about the only other person who's home a lot. Other than Randy—you may have met him." She made a face at the mention of the boxer-clad gentleman.

Beau thanked her for the information and, as usual, handed out his card in case she thought of anything else.

Sharon Redmond answered so quickly after the doorbell rang that Beau knew she must have been watching as they drove up. Chances were she had seen their entire progress up and down the road. She seemed that kind of woman, with her tightly bobbed hair and pursed mouth.

"Well, I heard fights sometimes," she said with a juicy little smile.

"Physical?"

"Nah, I think mostly verbal. Summer nights when windows were open was mostly all I ever got wind of. But you never know. That Zack Robinet has a hell of a temper."

"Does he?"

"I used to see him rag that kid of theirs. Drive him to school, reaming him out over grades or sports and such. That was only the first year they lived here, though. After that, I guess the kid went away to school. I only ever see him on holiday weekends. He was here over the summer and I think the dad tried having the son work at his office. They'd go off together in the mornings. But that lasted a couple weeks. The kid is a teenager with attitude now and he dishes it out as much as the dad does. There was another screaming match and the boy went off with friends and didn't come back for nearly a week."

This was degenerating into blatant gossip but the lawmen let her go on until she'd covered the summer and it seemed the son had gone safely back to Holbrook Academy in August.

"Thanks for your time, Mrs. Redmond," Kent Taylor said. He rolled his eyes the moment he and Beau turned away from the door.

"Well, not much to go on for a morning's work," Beau muttered as they walked back across the road to the empty Robinet home.

He pulled out the number Lacy Padilla had given him and checked it against the one given by Zack's parents yesterday. It was different. He dialed this new one but it went to voicemail. Beau left only his name and number. Then he remembered something.

"It can't hurt to try," he said, leading the way to the back of the house once more.

He stood at the sliding door to the greatroom and dialed Josephine Robinet's number again. Sure enough, a faint tone came through and he noticed that the screen on the phone on the kitchen counter lit up.

"What woman goes anywhere these days without her cell phone?" Taylor asked.

Beau told him about the other number. "She must have two of them."

Still, it didn't make much sense. The neighbor's information was undoubtedly older than that of the in-laws, but when someone gets a new phone the old one normally ends up in a drawer somewhere, not out on the counter. And, the service would have been discontinued. Beau got a ring and voice message. Maybe she had some reason for keeping them both active. Only a few possibilities came to mind.

Chapter 7

Sam reviewed the photos of possible Jane Doe matches once more, but none of them were hers. The face with the closest resemblance was a case more than five years old and the woman was last seen near Buffalo, New York. She set that one aside in case Beau wanted to look at it, but Sam held little hope. She turned out the lights in his office and locked the door. Walking back to Sweet's Sweets would be the best way to take the crick out of her back and would return her to work quicker than waiting for Beau. She covered the few blocks in less than fifteen minutes.

In the sales room Jen was seated at one of the bistro tables discussing a new order with a customer. It took less than sixty seconds in the room with them for Sam to feel the tension. Jen had an order form in front of her and a few penciled sketches, but Sam noticed other pages off to the side. Lots of entries had been made and crossed out. Jen's normally cheery demeanor looked as if it was stretched pretty thin and her smile was tight.

"Anything I can do to help?" Sam asked as casually as she could.

"Mrs. Salazar wants an interesting birthday cake." Jen held out the order form.

"Our specialty," Sam said to the customer. "When is the occasion?"

"I leave for Santa Fe in the morning and need to take it with me." The woman's eyes flashed in challenge. "I thought your shop could provide what I wanted but it looks like I'll have to take my business elsewhere."

Sam looked toward a photograph on the table. The cake in the picture was a variation on a Mad Hatter theme with three tiers set at cockeyed angles, intricate fondant bows, and loads of sugar-paste flowers, in addition to a lot of piping and quirky little add-ons that Sam didn't happen to have in her inventory. Sam knew at a glance this cake would take a minimum of three days to construct because the flowers alone had to be made a day ahead and then allowed time to set up. Baking the layers and trimming cake and fondant to fit was a whole separate operation.

"I suggested some modifications to make it feasible," Jen said.

"To make it entirely different," Mrs. Salazar replied.

Sam took a breath. "If you need an exact replica of this cake, I'm afraid we have to decline. I want you to know that we always do our best to accommodate every customer. With four or five days notice, we could have done this one easily. But overnight? No. Overnight, most bakeries are going to be able to provide you a sheet cake with Happy Birthday, Somebody written in script."

Sam turned sideways to the woman and picked up Jen's sketches. The ideas were good and they were innovative. Even so, it would be a push to make anything like this theme cake for the specified number of guests and to have it done by mid-morning tomorrow. Sam thought again of the carved box in her safe at home.

Clearly, this lady was used to getting her own way and pushing sales girls around to do it. But when the owner handed her photograph back and said 'good luck' she caved.

"That one," she said, pointing at the sketch in Sam's hand. "If you can have that one for me before noon tomorrow, I'll take it."

Sam clarified a few details with her and quoted almost double their normal rate. The job would require overtime by everyone, plus there was just the bitch-factor. Sam didn't like when pushy people hassled her employees. "Rushes like this are cash in advance," she said.

The customer's expression told Sam she wasn't used to being treated this way, but hey. Sam accepted the counted currency and gave a receipt with a smile.

"Noon tomorrow," she reiterated as Mrs. Salazar opened the door and headed toward a silver Mercedes.

"Thanks, Sam." Jen's stress level had gone down about twelve notches, while Sam's was just ramping up. Now that she'd taken the money she had to produce this thing.

In the kitchen, Sam caught an air of taut silence but ignored it and went straight to Julio.

"I need two eight-inch layers in red velvet and two twelve-inchers in devil's food."

"Sam, I have plans tonight. I need to leave in an hour. I got everything caught up so I could, remember?"

She didn't remember but couldn't very well blame him for that. She'd had a lot on her mind. "If you can get the batters made and pans into the oven, I'll watch them and take them out."

He nodded and set to work. Sam made a quick call to let Zoë know she couldn't possibly break away for tea now.

"Becky, I'll need—" Sam stopped in mid-sentence. She'd turned around just in time to catch a glare directed toward Jane, who was sitting at one end of the worktable drizzling decorative patterns over a tray of truffles.

"Becky? Something the matter?"

Her assistant shook her head. "No. I'm fine. What were you saying?"

"For this rush order, I'll need a dozen full-blown roses and they have to be tinted this exact shade of purple." The fabric swatch seemed to be a big point with the customer. "I hate to say this, but I need them before quitting time so they can set up in the fridge overnight."

Becky gave a slightly exaggerated sigh but assured Sam she was nearly done with the birthday cake for a boy's soccer-themed party and could start right away on the roses. Sam was used to her assistant's ups and downs but had the feeling something about Jane had triggered this one. If it didn't blow over quickly, she supposed they would need to have a talk.

She complimented Jane on the truffles, wondering how to work up to the question of where she would go for the night. The shelter again, Sam guessed. Meanwhile, she had more urgent things on her mind.

For this cockeyed cake the customer had okayed

elements from two of Jen's sketches. Sam had already told her because of the tight deadline they would substitute a few pre-made items because there was no time to form every single flower and bow from scratch. She began pulling plastic bins of gadgetry from the storage shelf and stacked them on her desk. None of the purple ribbons matched the given fabric sample but a couple of them were decent complementary tones so she set them out on the worktable.

Yellow always made a nice accent color with purple but the customer had been set on traditional pink, so Sam scrounged up some whimsical butterflies and a string of beading that could be tucked around the tiers to add elegance. She began to gain confidence about the design as she set out the items and played with placement to see which accessory looked best beside the other.

At one end of the long stainless steel table, Jane had finished decorating the truffles and placed them on a drying rack. She seemed a little at loose ends but Sam didn't have a spare brain cell to devote to worrying about keeping the uninvited visitor occupied. The other end of the table had Becky deftly piping large roses onto squares of waxed paper on a flower nail, sliding each finished one onto a baking tray in readiness to go into the fridge for the night. Sam felt a current of tension in the air between the two women even though nothing had been said since she came into the kitchen.

Julio hung up his baker's jacket and told Sam he'd set two timers for the different sized cake layers. He was out the door and rumbling away on his noisy machine within moments.

Sam noticed Jane meandering through the kitchen. "I'm sorry I really don't have anything for you to do," she said. "I can call the shelter if you'd like a ride back."

"Oh, that's okay." Jane said without enthusiasm. She was carrying a borrowed purse that must have been someone's Goodwill donation. "I think I'd like to walk back."

Sam wished her luck and resumed sorting the trims in the plastic bins. As soon as the front door bells tinkled, she sensed that Becky had something to say.

"Okay, you can get it off your chest," Sam said, keeping it casual as she worked.

"I'm suspicious of her," Becky said.

"In what way?"

"She just seems too 'with it' if you know what I mean. She works the chocolate like a pro and yet she can't remember her name?"

"They say amnesia can be like that. Skills from the past aren't forgotten. Otherwise, people with amnesia wouldn't remember their language or how to dress themselves."

"It's other stuff, too. I think she's faking."

* * *

Kent Taylor looked a little haggard by late afternoon and Beau suggested they stop for coffee and a review of what they'd learned so far. He thought of Sam's bakery, a mile or so away, but had a feeling he would get caught up in other topics and would have to explain why he hadn't made further progress on that Jane Doe amnesia case. Java Joe's was only a block over so he headed there.

"We've got zilch at the victim's house," Taylor said as he sat down with his high-octane blend called The Waker-Upper. "The one neighbor was interesting though. Gossipy ones are a little hard to take but sometimes you get the best information."

"Yeah, it's always amazing how people really believe their neighbors can't hear a screaming match. Might be a good idea to put the son, Bentlee Robinet, on your interview list for when you get back to Albuquerque."

"Already have. A father-son battle usually doesn't get told just the way it happened, but the emotion always comes through. I'll know if the kid hated his old man enough to do something about it. We'll know if we have both motive and means."

Beau sipped his own regular-strength coffee.

Taylor continued: "Holbrook Academy is notorious for being a haven of designer drug use," Taylor said. "Those rich kids can afford anything and somebody always makes sure they get what they want."

"You didn't mention 'opportunity' but with Bentlee right there in the city where his father died, it does fill out the trilogy of requirements for a valid suspect."

"I'm not giving up on the wife, either," Taylor said. "She conveniently disappears on the day her husband died."

"Maybe a little fling on the side? She heads out the moment he leaves town?"

"It fits with keeping two cell phones. The boyfriend might be the only one with access to one of the numbers."

"If she and the new honey went away somewhere she might not have gotten the news about her husband."

"That's the innocent explanation. Could be that she and the new honey wanted Zack completely gone forever. She would most likely inherit his half of that multi-million-dollar business. I want more on her background." Taylor's nervous index finger tapped the side of his paper cup.

"Meanwhile, this afternoon I'm thinking we could get some interesting info at the offices of ChanZack Innovations."

"When both cats are away the mice will *really* play?"

"Exactly."

They finished their coffee and got back into Beau's cruiser. Ten minutes later they were taking the elevator to ChanZack Innovations' upper suite in the Appleton Center. The gorgeous receptionist, whose name plate identified her as Amber Carter, was no less model-like today, with her long, dark hair, high cheekbones and porcelain complexion. Beau noticed Kent Taylor subtly straightening his tie as she greeted them.

"We have a few more questions," Beau said after introducing Taylor.

Her deep brown eyes widened slightly. "Um, Mr. Lane isn't here today."

"I know. He's at the trade show. We really only need to speak with the rest of the staff today. Can you give me a list of all the company employees?"

"There are only six of us, besides the two owners. Two sales reps—they went to Vegas with Mr. Lane—two programmers, myself and the bookkeeper. Mrs. Robinet handles taxes so she has the official records in her files. But I don't think I can let you see her stuff while she's gone."

Kent Taylor touched the badge at his belt, a subtle reminder that answering their questions was not optional. "Let's start with whoever's here now."

Amber picked up the intercom. "I'll page the programmers to the conference room for you."

"How about just taking us back to their offices? I'd like to get a better feel for the whole business."

She seemed unsure about that. Obviously, Chandler and Zack required fairly strict security for such a small business. Again, Kent Taylor touched his badge.

"We can get warrants and subpoenas," he said. "It won't be hard to do, considering one of the partners was murdered."

Amber's face went a little paler. She got up and led them toward the inner sanctum, using her own thumb image to open the door. Once past that, the rest of the offices had a fairly open-door policy, it seemed. They passed a very standard-looking office with desk, credenza, file cabinets and a couple of potted plants.

"Helen Melrose's office," Amber said. "She's probably down at the copy machine or making herself a cup of tea in the kitchen. She drinks a lot of tea."

Across the hall, a closed door listed Ed Archuleta and Jamie Phillips on little plaques. An oblong window set into the door showed that the lights inside were off. "The sales team," Amber explained. "Mostly what they have in their office is the artwork for the big ad campaigns. Until they packed everything up for Vegas, their room was practically overflowing with that stuff."

The two programmers shared a large office with dim overhead lighting and, not surprisingly, looked about fifteen years old. The room was full of computer monitors showing everything from incredibly realistic depictions of warriors and battle scenes to full screen images of cartoonish avatars. One screen was full of complex lines of letters and numbers that must have been computer code. All of it was completely outside Beau's realm.

Both young men looked up with somewhat glazed eyes, like moles who had poked their heads out of the ground for the first time in months.

"This is Mike and that's J.B.," Amber said before turning to go back to her own desk.

"Michael," said the tall, plump one. "I prefer Michael."

Kent Taylor wrote down the basics: Michael Anderson, senior programmer. John Bryan Bonds, who went by J.B. Michael had worked for the company four years; J.B. came along two years ago.

"We're investigating the death of Mr. Robinet," Beau told them, wondering whether the tendency for their eyes to dart around to various objects in the room had to do with their work, an aversion to the lawmen, or if it was some inherent trait of nerdy types. "Does either of you know if he had any enemies?"

"Whoa. You think someone did that to him? We heard it was a drug overdose." This from Michael.

Beau realized he had started at the wrong place with the questions. "Okay, what about that? Do you know if he used drugs?"

"Zack? I don't think so. He was a pretty straight up kind of guy," Michael said. "Plus, we all have to get random pee tests. Something about qualifying for the insurance plan or something? You could ask Helen, but I'm pretty sure even the owners have to do it."

Kent Taylor was writing all this down. "Back to the sheriff's question. Did either of you hear of Mr. Robinet having an altercation with anyone in the last few weeks?"

J.B. snickered a little, then caught himself.

"Want to share what that's about?" Taylor asked.

J.B. slid a quick glance toward Michael, who responded with a tiny one-shoulder shrug.

"It's just that I'm not sure I should say this about my boss," J.B. said, fidgeting from one foot to the other.

"Whatever it is, you need to say it," Beau said, trying to keep his tone softer than Taylor's. He stepped over and closed the door to the hallway.

"Well, the truth is that there aren't many people Zack *doesn't* clash with. Helen and Amber are the only ones here in the office that he hasn't yelled at since I've worked here."

"Even the two of you? He's yelled at you?"

"Not so much in the last couple weeks," Michael said. "When we were on deadline for the new upgrade? Yeah, it got a little intense then. He was under a lot of pressure 'cause the trade show space was booked and he's got all these suppliers calling, like, fourteen times a day."

"Yeah," J.B. added, "and the sales team. Some of *those* meetings got really—whew!"

Beau took another tack. "Mrs. Robinet works here sometimes, right? How is she to work with?"

"Oh, she's pretty nice." Michael actually blushed a little. Young guy crush?

"Although she really doesn't come back here much at all," J.B. said. "She and the partners would have these meetings. I suppose they talked about money. That's our impression. She does something with investments or something like that."

After asking if they could think of anything else, Beau and Kent moved again toward the front, stopping at Helen Melrose's office. The bookkeeper was in her seventies, with a short perm and polyester pants suit that would not have been the height of fashion twenty years earlier. She sipped from a pink tea mug and waved them inside.

"Hello," she said, amiably enough. "Amber told me you were here, Sheriff."

Beau vaguely recognized the bookkeeper from somewhere—he wasn't quite sure. They took seats in front of her desk and covered the basic questions with her, then asked about any conflicts between Zack Robinet and his employees.

"Oh, nothing that would lead to a murder, I wouldn't think," she told them. "The young guys pretty much live in their world of computers and blow off steam by blasting away at those games they invent. I suspect Amber might have had a fling with either Chandler or Zack, which led to her being hired here. But it's been over for a long time, if it ever happened. I don't sense any strain between them now. Younger people are so casual about sex these days. All this 'friends with benefits' stuff is way beyond me." She made air quotes when she used the phrase.

"So your particular job is fairly stress-free?" Beau asked.

She snorted. "Hardly. Both partners are constantly uptight about money, so I have to keep my posting up to date and be able to print out a P&L on a moment's notice. Awhile back I couldn't seem to get into the computer banking records, but luckily Mrs. Robinet took over."

To Kent Taylor's inquiry about whether she'd had words with Zack, she merely chuckled.

"I don't let men with tempers get to me. And, believe me, I do *not* take my job home with me. Life's too short for that kind of stress."

"Maybe outside the office?" Kent Taylor asked, ignoring her life's-too-short comment. "Anyone other than staff who might have hated your boss?"

Helen chewed at her lower lip for a moment. "A week or so ago … there was one instance. Zack had gone to the dealership to have his car worked on and he wasn't happy with the bill. He stomped in here and told me to lodge a complaint with the credit card company and not to pay the bill when it came because he was 'pissed as hell'—his words—over the quality of the work."

"Which dealership was it?"

She named the place and Taylor wrote it in his notes. The men thanked her for her time and went on to speak with Amber at the reception desk. As the two programmers had said, it appeared Amber had managed somehow to never have a beef with Zack. She was quite effusive in her praise of how well he ran the company and Beau caught the subtle movement as her fingers played with a decent-sized diamond pendant at her throat. Another of those 'benefits'?

Back in the cruiser, Kent Taylor mentioned the necklace then brought up the subject of the fight between Zack and the car dealer.

"Sounds like it got pretty heated," he said.

"Could have, true. But for six-hundred dollars in car repairs, how likely is it that a guy from Taos would drive all the way to Albuquerque and go to elaborate means to set up a drug-overdose scene in a hotel room? Wouldn't it be more likely that he'd send a couple of his strongmen to catch Zack Robinet in an alley somewhere here in town?"

Chapter 8

Sam kneaded purple food color paste into a huge ball of fondant, enjoying the quiet of the kitchen after hours. Everyone else had left and Beau had called to say that if they had no other plans he really ought to take the detective out for a meal before Kent Taylor got back on the road for the drive to Albuquerque. She told him to go right ahead.

Dividing the sugary dough, Sam left the bigger portion medium lavender and began working more of the color paste to create a violet for the smaller tier. Two small portions of fondant would later become hot pink for the accent pieces and an extremely deep purple for the swags and leaves.

The trick with these lopsided cake designs was to create sturdy bracing beneath the bottom tier so that two heavy layers of cake and fondant could appear to be sitting effortlessly at angles. She had already placed a plastic wedge on the cake board to begin the process. Correct placement of a couple of dowels would assure that the upper tier would seem to be balanced precariously in place. The whole thing would be sturdy but deceptively tippy looking.

A light staccato tap sounded at the back door and Zoë's wavy salt-and-pepper hair framed her smiling face.

"You're working—I know—and I don't want to interrupt. Just brought you this." She held up a large insulated mug with a lid. "The Assam. I brewed a pot and it was so good. Since I had another quick errand I decided to pop by."

Zoë stepped inside and set the mug on Sam's desk, eyeing the lopsided cake.

"It's okay—it's supposed to look this way," Sam said, setting the ball of fondant aside.

She picked up the tea mug and ventured a sip of the steaming brew. "Oh, that's good. Thanks!"

Another sound. "Hey, Mom," Kelly said, breezing in through the open back door and spotting the worktable. She carried a small makeup bag and a garment on a hanger covered in plastic. "Ooh—cute!"

She greeted Zoë with a peck on the cheek.

Sam set her mug down and turned back to the worktable, flattening the large lavender ball of fondant with her hands then placing it into the rolling machine.

"Mind if I change clothes here?" Kelly asked. "By the end of the day at Puppy Chic my shirt smells like soapy dog." She headed for the bathroom.

"Sure."

Zoë watched as Sam caught the sheet of rolled fondant, adjusted the machine to a thinner setting and ran it through again. Roll, repeat. Finally the sheet was just right to cover the twelve-inch cake layers. She wound the entire thing around a long rolling pin and maneuvered it into place, draping it over the cake and the little booster wedge at once.

"I don't know how you do that," Kelly said, catching the last few seconds of the operation. She winked at Zoë.

"Just practice," Sam said, eyeing the positioning of the dough for any possible gaps before she began smoothing the wrinkles and trimming excess, marginally aware that Kelly had ducked back into the bathroom.

"I'm on my way," Zoë said, her hand on the edge of the door. "Enjoy the tea. And let me know when we can work out time for a real lunch or something."

Hands occupied, Sam blew her friend an air kiss.

By the time her daughter emerged ten minutes later, Sam had trimmed the bottom tier's fondant to fit and was running the other ball of fondant through the machine for the second tier. A flash of red caught her attention. Kelly was wearing a low-cut dress with super-short flared skirt that shimmered in the overhead lights.

"Whoa, you're looking more than slightly fabulous," Sam said.

"Thanks. We're going to Romano's. Thought I'd spiff up a little."

This was more than a little. Kelly's normal attire was a pair of skinny jeans and fitted T-shirt. Dressing up consisted of trading the T-shirt for something with glitter or putting on a fuzzy vest over it all.

"I'm guessing that 'we' isn't you and the girls. This guy must be special." Hint, hint.

"Same guy."

"Two nights in a row ... and you're still not going to tell

me who it is, are you?"

"Gotta go!" She pecked a kiss on Sam's cheek and headed toward the door.

"Don't you have a coat? You're going to freeze in that dress." *Oh my god, I sound just like my mother.*

Kelly flashed a smile and walked out. Why on earth was she being so secretive about this guy? Oh well. Sam flipped the fondant sheet back into the roller. The fondant on the second tier didn't fit right and Sam ended up tearing a hole in it with her finger. Then it stuck to the first tier before she was ready, botching the first one as well. More than slightly irritated with the last-minute cake order, and herself, she resisted throwing the whole piece across the room and took a deep breath.

Focus on this cake and try to get home at a reasonable hour.

She sipped Zoë's tea and stared at the ruined fondant coating. Figure it out, she reminded herself. Carefully peeling it from the smaller tier, she kneaded it once more and put it back through the roller. Meanwhile, the small ripped place on the lower tier could be patched with a little water and a careful touch. A big rose could cover the spot anyway. As any decorator knew, there were a hundred ways to fix life's little boo-boos.

The clock showed well past ten by the time Sam switched off the lights to head home. With cake layers baked, filled and stacked, the fondant coating placed over them and the structure of dowels and wedges holding the entire foot-and-a-half confection in place, she was well on her way to completing the rush order. Tomorrow morning she would come in early to add bows and bedazzles and place the roses Becky had made. They would make the noon deadline, even though she felt as if she'd been through the roller machine herself right now.

She drove through the quiet streets, thinking only of a hot shower and snuggling in beside Beau for the five or six hours of sleep she would be lucky to get.

"Hey darlin'," he greeted when she came through the front door. "Can I get you something to eat?"

Sam realized she hadn't eaten anything in many hours, but although the sentiment was wonderful she only wanted sleep. She shook her head and he followed her up the stairs, switching off lights along the way.

"Dixie said to tell you she had no luck with that number you gave us. It's not a telephone number anywhere in the US."

Somehow, Sam wasn't surprised. She was too tired to care right now anyway. By the time she emerged from the shower he'd turned back the covers and was settled on his side of the bed with a book on how dogs' brains work. How did he come up with topics like that?

Sam's eyes closed immediately and she was even able to ignore the ringing telephone, up until Beau answered it and she overheard: "Jane? You mean the Jane Doe who came to Sam's shop yesterday?"

Sam edged one eye open and looked through her lashes at him. He was listening to the phone but watching her, obviously trying to decide whether she'd fallen asleep yet. She mumbled so he would know she'd heard.

"Okay," he said to the phone. "Hold on a moment." He held the phone to his shoulder and turned to Sam. "It's Melissa Masters. She says Jane didn't show up at the shelter this evening. Did she say anything to you about changing her plans?"

Sam was fully awake now and sitting up. "No. Actually, she left the bakery around five and specifically said she was walking back there to stay the night."

Beau relayed the information to Melissa. "I know. It worries me too. Okay. Well, let me know if she turns up. I'll put out a BOLO for our night shift deputies."

He hung up from the call and immediately dialed his night dispatcher to repeat the information about where Jane had last been seen and where she was going. When he hung up, he swung his legs off the bed and Sam seriously wondered if he planned to get up and go out.

"Jane's a free woman, isn't she?" Sam asked. "I mean, she wasn't under any obligation to go back to the shelter, was she?"

"No, not legally. It's just that since she told you she was going there and then she never showed, well, it would be as if Jen said she was going home and never got there, right?"

True, when he put it that way. "Beau, what if she recovered her memory and suddenly knew where she lived and just went there? Could that be possible?"

"I suppose anything *could* be possible. But, knowing we were trying to find her family, and since she's hung around your shop the better part of two days, doesn't it seem logical that someone would call to let one of us know the good news?"

She had to concede the point. Then she thought of what Becky had said earlier. "What if she recovered her memory earlier in the day and for some reason didn't want to tell anyone? We don't know if she's on the run from something or someone … maybe even the law in some other state …"

"Not everyone does the responsible thing, unfortunately.

Even if there's a simple explanation for this."

He yawned and settled back under the comforter. Sam snuggled against him, her mind far too active, but a peek at the clock showed she only had about four hours to sleep now, even if she managed to turn off the big question-machine in her head. With the light out, at last she drifted into an uneasy rest.

Four-thirty came way too early, reminding Sam of those early days in the pastry shop before she hired extra help. She should have charged that belligerent Mrs. Salazar triple the regular price for her stupid specialty cake.

By the time she'd driven the pre-dawn route to the shop and made herself a cup of coffee she'd calmed down. In some ways, even though she wasn't naturally an early riser, it was good to get a head start on the day. She took the decorator frosting out of the fridge so it could warm to room temperature while she drank her coffee, then got the half-finished cake out to work on.

Julio showed up a short while later and went quietly to work on the morning pastries, their standard selection of muffins, croissants, scones and coffee cakes. He had the routine down pat and moved smoothly through the kitchen, with no sign whatsoever that he might have been out late. Sam thought of Kelly's stunning red dress, her flirtatious manner last night, and the tattooed biker. *Get a grip*, she told herself. *You have to admit he's a nice guy, a responsible worker and honest.*

She put those thoughts out of her head and filled a pastry bag with hot-pink decorator icing. Getting into her own decorating rhythm was normally the best antidote for all things troubling but she found her mind zipping with thoughts of Jane Doe, now twice missing, plus Kelly, plus the nagging thought that there was some forgotten important thing she was supposed to be doing.

She piped white swags and elegant fleur-de-lis of tiny dots onto the smaller tier and formed pleated fondant draping for the large one. From the fridge she retrieved the large roses Becky had made yesterday and set them around the base.

By the time Becky arrived, Sam had the super-rush order about ninety percent done.

"It's really looking great," Becky said. "I wasn't sure how we would ever finish on time but you, Sam, are a miracle worker."

Sam smiled, proud of the job and not admitting that she'd sneaked a few moments alone with the box this morning. As she'd handled it, the wood surface began to glow and the artifact warmed to her touch. An unknown power, centuries old, flowed through Sam's hands and arms, lending energy to her tasks. She had missed regular contact with the box, which felt like an old friend now. And, hey, you never knew when a dozen interruptions would come along during any average workday.

She stepped back from the cake, eyeing it critically. Considering the tight timeframe and sleep-deprived hours she had spent on it, she had to admit it had turned out well. A few more little touches, some leaves to accentuate the roses …

Jen stepped into the kitchen. All morning the phone had been ringing but the kitchen staff normally ignored it, letting her handle the calls. Sam glanced at the clock and discovered three hours had ticked by.

"Mrs. Salazar just called," Jen said. "She wanted to remind you the cake has to be there in thirty minutes."

Sam stopped in her tracks. "What?"

"I know. I don't remember her saying she wanted it delivered either."

"She didn't. Did you tell her it was her responsibility to come and pick it up?"

Jen rolled her eyes. "I kind of hinted at that but I know how we aren't supposed to piss off the customers …"

"You're right. You can't win an argument with a customer." Sam set down her pastry bag. "I'll take it."

"Here's her address." Jen held out a slip of paper.

Sam picked up the order sheet and reviewed the details to be sure she hadn't left off anything vital. As much as she really didn't want to go out of her way for this disagreeable woman, she might turn it into a positive thing by meeting up somewhere with Beau for lunch afterward. She carried the cake to her delivery van and secured it inside a box with high sides, then dialed Beau.

"Sure—lunch sounds good. How about if we meet at Paco Taco?"

Thirty minutes later she had handed off the purple and pink cake. Today, Mrs. Salazar wore her gracious persona and effusively thanked Sam for her effort on the cake. You just can't figure out some people, Sam decided as she parked at the outdoor taco place and scanned for an empty table on the patio. Beau pulled in beside her van and got out of his cruiser, talking to the microphone at his shoulder.

"Was that about our Jane Doe?" Sam asked, catching a few words as they took seats in the shade.

"Yeah. I had just radioed dispatch to see if anyone

reported any luck with our BOLO. Sorry, no sign of her yet and she hasn't showed back up at the shelter."

"Sorry to hear that. I wonder if we should be worried."

He was studying the menu painted on the side of the hut-sized building. "I doubt it, darlin'. We know she's not in the hospital or involved in an accident. Other than that, nearly anything could have happened. Most likely she ran into someone who knew her and they got to talking and her memory came back and she's safely home by now. Taos isn't that big a town. Somebody has to know this lady."

"You're right. It would have been nice though if she'd called one of us."

"You'll learn that thank-yous are pretty rare in law enforcement. Everybody wants you there on a moment's notice but they rarely show gratitude when you are. I'm getting the beef taco dinner—how about you?"

He walked up to the order window and came back with tall paper cups of soda.

"Meanwhile," he said, "I need to go visit Zack Robinet's parents again, find out when the funeral will be. Kent Taylor is back in Albuquerque to interview the son at Holbrook Academy. I'm hoping to catch time to talk to the kid myself when he comes up here for the services."

"That's got to be pretty hard, a kid learning that his dad was murdered."

"Yeah, rough. There's no easy way to handle those interviews."

She caught the 'but' in his tone and gave him a look.

"In this case we heard there were some pretty hellacious arguments between father and son. Their clashes were one of the reasons young Bentlee got sent away to boarding school."

"Is he a suspect?" Sam asked after the waitress delivered their tacos in plastic baskets and walked away.

"We've considered it. Zack had battles with several people but the son is one of the few with opportunity, being in Albuquerque. The employees were all here in Taos at the time and the partner wasn't due to head for the airport until the next day." He polished off one taco and started on his second, while Sam dipped her crispy taquito into a small plastic cup of salsa. "There was an altercation at the Chevy place a few days earlier, big argument over the cost of a repair bill. I need to check that out too."

"Really? I bought my truck there years ago. I've always found their service people really pleasant to deal with."

He shrugged. "Could turn out to be nothing. Could just be that Zack Robinet isn't the sweet angel his parents painted him to be."

Beau must have been hungry—he'd nearly finished three tacos before he spoke again. "So, what's the rest of your day look like? Want to come with me to talk to the Robinets?"

Sam tried to remember what was ahead of her at the bakery. Aside from the Salazar order, now safely out of her hands, she thought Becky and Julio had things under control.

"I'll call the shop to be sure but yeah, I think I can break away for a little while."

With the all-clear, she left her baker's jacket in her van and got into Beau's cruiser with him. The ride to Greenlee Manor took precisely eight minutes and they found the elder Robinets in their apartment. The door stood open to the hall and a half-dozen other gray-haired people milled about. When they saw the sheriff's uniform the little crowd shuffled to the corners of the small living room.

"If you all don't mind," said Beau. "I need to speak with the family alone. If anyone has something that might assist my investigation, I would like to speak with you later. Give my deputy here your names and addresses."

Sam had almost forgotten that Beau had deputized her at one point during an earlier case. But it took only a moment to fall into the routine of working with him, taking a notebook and pen and standing near the door as the guests left. All of them lived here in the same complex so it was merely a matter of taking names and apartment numbers of the two who felt they had something to contribute.

With their door closed, George and Nancy Robinet now settled on the couch. Nancy's eyes were puffy and red, George stoic with heavy lines dragging his mouth downward. Beau had seen this often when he delivered news of a death in a family. The first reaction could be anything from stunned silence to almost nonchalance because the news never sank in right away. But after a day or two the reality began to hit them. The visiting neighbors, the covered casserole dishes and homemade cakes with foil over the pans … it all became overwhelming. With this family, the wife became the talkative one.

"I still can't believe it, Sheriff. The feeling is unreal."

"I know. I know it's hard. I'll keep my questions quick so you can get back to your friends." He let Nancy take his right hand and he patted her arm with the left. "We haven't been able to locate Josephine. Have either of you heard anything from her?"

George shook his head. Nancy just leaked a few more tears and dabbed at them with a wadded, soggy tissue.

"And their son," Beau said. "He's been contacted. When

is he coming home for the funeral?"

Nancy spoke up. "The service will be Monday afternoon. George was going to drive down to Albuquerque and pick him up tomorrow. Bentlee has a car here at home but he's not allowed to take it to school. It's a rule for freshmen." She looked at her husband. "But I don't really want George driving. He's too upset."

"We can make some arrangement, I'm sure," Beau told them, making a note to call Kent Taylor's office.

The lack of a car would have made it a little more difficult for Bentlee Robinet to get to his father's hotel—if he was, indeed, still on their suspect list. Sam said as much as she and Beau left after speaking with the two neighbors—who seemed more enthralled about talking with the handsome sheriff in hushed tones than actually providing any useful information—and were on their way to where she'd left her van.

"Never underestimate a teenager's ability to mobilize help," he said. "Anyway, I'm guessing his spending more than two hours riding with a detective might prove very enlightening."

Chapter 9

Sam's dashboard clock told her she'd already been away from Sweet's Sweets too long so she headed that direction. The parking lot out front was full of cars, a cheering sight. She pulled to her normal spot in the alley and walked through the back door. There in the kitchen stood Jane.

"You're back." Sam blurted it out before realizing how it sounded. "I mean, we were worried last night when Melissa called to say you never made it to the shelter. Are you okay?"

"Yeah, I'm fine." Jane put on a smile.

"Where did you spend the night? Did you begin to remember anything?"

Jane wore the same borrowed jeans and T-shirt from the day before, but at least they looked clean. She didn't appear to have slept out in the open.

"Sam!" Jen stage-whispered from the doorway. "I need you on a consultation. The shop is packed and this man needs some specialty chocolates."

"I'll be right back," Sam told Jane. "Don't leave until I'm finished up front."

Jen had not understated the situation; four customers waited at the counter for assistance and all three bistro tables had people seated at them. Jen nodded toward the one with a lone man who sat with his hands around a mug of coffee. Fifty-ish, with steel-gray hair and thick wire-rimmed glasses, he smiled confidently when Sam approached.

"Hi, I understand you're the owner. I'm Stan Bookman. Your girl told me you were the expert in chocolate." He let go of his mug long enough to shake hands.

Sam took one of the chairs at the table. "We do make a pretty great line of chocolates."

"I've heard of them."

Much of the state of New Mexico had heard of them by now, after two holiday seasons in which Sweet's Sweets had barely been able to keep up with the demand. A memory flashed through Sam's mind, the oddball Romanian chocolatier who had showed up that first year and left her with the secrets to the fantastic, practically addictive, taste of really good chocolate. If only Sam had Bobul's finesse in molding and forming intricate shapes with it.

"What I'm after," said Mr. Bookman, "is an out-of-this-world surprise for my wife's birthday. I want to give her the most exquisite box of chocolates that has ever been created."

"I'm sure we can come up with a wonderful selection for you," Sam said, understanding why he hadn't just picked up a box from the display.

"Not to criticize, but nothing off the shelf will do for her. I'm sure your standard chocolates are very good. But I'm going to present these to her aboard a chartered jet on our way to lunch in Paris. They have to be extraordinary."

Wow. Sam worked hard to act as if this sort of request came in every day. "Naturally. I will—"

"Margie's two favorite things in the world are cats and chocolate. I want two pounds of chocolate kitty cats. Each must be unique—different poses, different facial expressions—whatever it takes to make this a gift that no one else in the world has ever received."

Sam could pretty well bet that a box of custom made chocolates presented during a flight to Paris would be right up there in the list of exceptional gifts of all time, but if this man needed them to be shaped like cats she would simply have to figure out a way. Her brain worked at figuring out exactly how she could make this happen while her pen filled in the blanks on an order form.

"Understand, now, that the shape is only one aspect of these chocolates. I want there to be variety in flavor, color and texture too."

Sure—go ahead and make the impossible a little *more* impossible. Sam felt her anxiety level rise. Next, he would probably want the gift box ready by tomorrow. She jotted a few notes as ideas came to her.

"Margie's birthday is next Saturday. I'd like to pick up the order by Friday afternoon if that's okay."

A whole week. Bless him. She put Beau's investigation and the funeral of Zack Robinet and the whole unsolved situation with her Jane Doe visitor on the back burner. Creating unusual desserts was her real love and she was about to get the chance to do something really special.

Stan Bookman reached into the front pocket of his slacks and pulled out a money clip. From it came two one-hundred dollar bills. "If that's not enough, just let me know the balance when I come back," he said.

Sam pushed one of the bills back to him. "One will be more than enough. Depending on what I need to spend on packaging, I'm sure you'll get change back."

He thanked her and stood. "I look forward to seeing my wife's lovely gift."

Sam watched him walk out the front door before turning to see if Jen still needed help. Luckily, the crowd had thinned considerably.

"You do know who that was, don't you?" Jen said, walking over to clear and wipe the empty table.

"Stan Bookman?"

"Book It Travel. The company handles worldwide travel arrangements for all the ritzy-rich who jet about in private planes. He'll charter their flights, arrange stays at the most exclusive hotels, have their dogs shampooed and delivered all fluffy and white if that's what they want."

"Wow."

"I'm surprised he was so nice," Jen said. "I guess I assumed because his clients can be such snobs that he would be, too. Believe me, I saw a lot of them in the gallery before I started working here."

Sam filed the knowledge as a caution. Just because the man was cordial today didn't mean he wouldn't know how to throw a supreme tantrum if his order was not up to his standards. This definitely raised the bar.

In the kitchen, Sam caught a glare Becky aimed toward Jane's back. The sooner she could send their visitor back to the care of Melissa Masters, the better.

"I overheard a little of what that man requested in his order. He wants unusual flavors—how about some apple and carrots with ginger? Or maybe a cinnamon-nutmeg in eighty-six percent cacao?" Jane said. "Sam, I'd love to help with it. I thrive when I'm working in chocolate. And you know I'm good at it."

Her eyes were bright with enthusiasm and Sam wavered. Jane could possibly be a big help. But what was going on with Becky?

"Let me think about it," Sam told Jane. "I need to put some ideas together before leaping into this one."

Jane walked over to Sam's desk, picking up a sheet of paper and a pencil. She found a quiet corner of the worktable and began sketching.

"Becky, help me get something from the van?" Sam headed for the back door without looking back.

The shady alley felt chilly as clouds had rolled in. "I sense that you want to tell me something," Sam said.

"I just don't trust her, Sam. You know that." Becky's normally cheerful demeanor had been off for two days now.

"You said you thought she might be faking her amnesia. Is that it?"

"Well, what was last night all about? Did she go home? If she wasn't at the shelter, where did she go?" Becky's arms were folded tightly across her chest now.

"I suppose you asked her. The two of you seemed to be staring daggers when I walked in awhile ago."

"I did. I came right out and asked."

"And she said …?"

"Nothing, really. She doesn't even have a reasonable explanation."

"Maybe she doesn't owe you one." Sam bit her tongue.

"Sorry, what I mean is that maybe she doesn't owe any of us an explanation."

Becky's toe tapped impatiently. "Beau's department and the social services folks have been called to help her. If she already knows who she is, shouldn't she let them know?"

"If that's the case, yes, she should. But we don't know her story. Maybe there's a reason she can't go home or … I don't know. There could be a lot of reasons she doesn't want to go back."

"Or she *did* go back and just—I don't know!"

"Maybe she ran into someone she knew, came up with money for a motel room … We can't know for sure unless she wants to talk about it."

Becky's muttered response conveyed the idea that she wouldn't trust Jane even if she did decide to talk about it.

"Okay. For now, all I can do is take this whole situation at face value. Beau is still checking out some leads." Although, as Sam recalled, he really had none. "Let's get back to work."

"Are you going to let her stay and work on the chocolates with you?"

"It's a big, complicated order. So, yes, I probably will."

Becky didn't seem very happy about that. Finally, her shoulders relaxed. "I trust you, Sam. And I love my job. I won't give Jane any trouble, but I really want to caution you to watch her."

"This can't go on for more than another couple days," Sam said, reaching out to give Becky a hug. "Go back to that beautiful anniversary cake you were doing and send Jane out. I'll talk to her privately."

Sam had her phone in hand when Jane walked down the steps to join her.

"I need to call Melissa Masters. She deserves to know

what happened last night and whether to keep a bed for you tonight."

Jane pushed a strand of hair behind her right ear. "I, uh—"

"If you remember where you live, that's wonderful. You should go home."

"I don't! I don't remember anything!"

Sam wished she had Beau's eye for spotting truth versus lies.

"If you went places in town maybe someone who knows you stopped and greeted you?"

"No, that didn't happen."

"Okay. Good enough. Let me call Melissa and be sure you have a bed at the shelter tonight. During the day you can come to work here. I really would appreciate your assistance with the chocolate."

Jane fidgeted from one foot to the other. "Sam, please don't make me go back there. I hated it. They're nice people who run the place, but I just didn't fit in. The women were so down-and-out, so abused. I don't know why, but I couldn't handle it."

"Where did you stay last night?"

Jane hung her head. "Here."

"At my shop?" She certainly had not been around when Sam left at ten p.m.

"No, I mean, not *right* here. I wandered the plaza until all the shops closed, then I found an unlocked car down the block. There was a blanket in the backseat."

"Jane! You can't do that. It's not safe. Someone could have come along and harmed you."

"I know. It was dumb. If you could loan me some money I'll stay at a motel. I'll work for free to pay you back."

She sounded so truly desperate that Sam couldn't bring herself to insist upon the shelter. "I'll just let Melissa know you're okay. Then we'll figure out something. For now, go back inside and do an inventory of our chocolate. Find out how much cocoa we have on hand. I have a feeling I'll need to order a variety of supplies."

As she passed along the information to Melissa Masters over the phone, Sam's mind raced. Should she invite Jane to stay at their house or simply check her into a motel and hope for the best. She hung up and called Beau.

"I don't have a good feeling about it either way," he said, "but I have a hard and fast rule about not inviting suspicious people into my own home. It has to be a motel. I wouldn't pay for more than one night at a time, though. Who knows when she'll go dashing off again."

Sam agreed, mentioned the big order for custom chocolates and told him she wasn't sure what time she would get home.

"Tell you what," he said. "How about you get Jane settled into a motel room whenever you get to a stopping point at work? We can meet up for dinner and then you can go back to the shop if you need to."

He was right. With everyone else gone for the day, Sam could work more quickly without interruptions. She clicked off the call and went back inside.

On the worktable sat a bag of roasted cocoa beans. Jane had found the grinder and was turning them to powder.

"I think we'll have enough to get two pounds of chocolate," she said. "A bit more if we do part of the assortment in milks and whites."

Sam lifted the bag, guessing at its weight, and concurred. "Now, I wonder about molding them into cat shapes. I have no idea if any of my suppliers will have such a thing."

"Try Bandenberg Wholesale," Jane said. She stopped grinding the beans and stared at Sam. "I wonder where that name came from? It just popped into my head."

Sam caught the look Becky sent her direction from the other end of the worktable. But when she got online, she readily found the wholesaler and discovered that they did, indeed, have a large selection of unusual chocolate molds. One set featured cats and dogs, some lying down, some sitting. It wouldn't provide the variety Stan Bookman wanted but it could be a great start. She placed an order, including cocoa beans to replenish the shop's supply, and sprang for overnight shipping. That done, she made a shopping list of other items—flavorings and herbal essences—and decided that she could pick them up locally when she went out for dinner with Beau.

By four o'clock, Jane had ground nearly the whole bag of beans and Sam had her shopping list pretty well finalized.

"We can temper and start molding the chocolate tomorrow," she told Jane. "Let's head out now and get you settled for the night."

"I'm meeting Beau for an early dinner out, so you can go ahead and lock up at closing time," she said to Becky and Jen.

In the van she suggested to Jane that they make a stop at Walmart for a few toiletries and another change or two of clothing, to come from Jane's first paycheck. Cash pay, Sam mentally amended, since there was no way she could file all the necessary forms to put Jane on the payroll without a name and social security number. Technically, this was illegal as hell but how could she turn down a woman so obviously in need, not to mention someone with this much knowledge of chocolate?

"I had a few other ideas for cat-themed chocolates," Jane said later, as they walked out of the store with three shopping bags, "being that there isn't a great variety of molds available. How about if I form some from modeling chocolate and we use them to sit on top of a platform, a slab or a cushion made of one of the exotic flavors?"

"If you're good at sculpting delicate shapes, I will be forever grateful," Sam said, her mind flashing again to the image of Bobul the Romanian making his exquisite pine cones.

"It's funny, Sam. I have these little scenes go through my head. I can't say where I am at the time but I distinctly see myself handling chocolate, and there are images … Valentine hearts … little kids getting Easter eggs … It's the strangest feeling."

"But nothing that tells you who you are?"

"Once in awhile it feels very close, but then the memory just slips away."

Sam slid a glance toward her guest, wishing again that she could discern whether this was the truth. Out on Paseo, a truck in front of her hit the brakes and Sam had to do the same. Better to concentrate on her driving and worry about quizzing Jane a bit further tomorrow as they worked together. She wheeled into the parking lot of the Wayside Inn and registered Jane into room 104. With her shopping bags for luggage, Jane settled into the room and Sam left to phone Beau.

"Good timing," he said. "I just wrapped up a traffic stop and Dixie says that Rico is back on duty tonight. I'm ready for dinner if you are. I'll pick you up at your shop."

Sam headed that direction, parked in the alley, and he

arrived about a minute later.

"I was thinking about a burger," he said, "but since it's nearly five I wonder if we could make a stop first? I want to talk to the folks at that dealership where Zack Robinet had the blowup over his repair bill, and I'd like to catch them before closing time."

"No problem. I have to admit that I haven't really thought much about food. I got Jane registered at the Wayside, but I tell you, the woman puzzles me. She told me she slept in a parked car last night, rather than going back to the shelter. Something about how the women there really 'got her down.' And yet I talk to her about baking and chocolate and it's as if she hasn't a care in the world."

"I suppose it's possible for those two subjects to be entirely different, in her mind."

"Yeah, but did I mention to you Becky thinks she faking the amnesia?"

"No, I don't think you did. Some specific reason for that conclusion?"

Sam shook her head. "I really don't know what to think, myself."

"It might be a good idea to keep an eye on the situation," he said. He radioed dispatch and Dixie put him through to Rico.

"I know I told you to do traffic patrol this evening but I've got something a little easier for your first day back," he told the deputy. "Park where you can see room 104 at the Wayside Inn. Watch and report anyone coming or going. The guest is a woman who supposedly doesn't even remember her own name. I'd like to hear about it if you observe anything that seems hinky about her story."

Chapter 10

Friststone Auto sported rows of cars which all appeared to be orange, red or bronze in the late sun blazing through the clouds in the west. Overhead halogen beams tried to overcome this but it didn't seem to matter. No customers roamed the lot and the gaggle of salesmen sat around in their shirtsleeves inside the brightly lit showroom. A couple of them shifted noticeably when they spotted Beau's official vehicle.

"Guy in the blue tie—DWI last week. The one with the striped shirt beats his wife but she won't file a complaint, so all we can do is warn him on a regular basis."

Both of the men in question seemed to have urgent tasks elsewhere in the building when Beau and Sam walked in.

"Hey, Ms. Sweet, good to see you here again. About

ready for a new truck?" Larry Friststone was the eldest son of the Friststone family and apparently the one who caught the late Friday night shift in the sales department.

"I'm good for now on vehicles," she told him. "Actually, I'm just here with my husband this time."

Larry held a meaty hand out to Beau. "Sheriff, congratulations on your marriage to a great gal."

Sam smiled at the compliment. Beau, meanwhile, had suggested Friststone take them somewhere they could talk privately so the trio were headed to a glassed-in office.

"Do you know your customer, Zack Robinet?" he asked, once the door closed behind them.

Friststone nodded vigorously. "Sure do. I heard he died. Wow, kind of sudden wasn't it?"

"He was murdered, it turns out. We're conducting some inquiries and we understand Mr. Robinet got into a fairly serious altercation with someone here at the dealership just a few days before his death."

Friststone's eyes widened but he didn't deny the incident.

"It was over a bill in the service department, I believe."

"Yes, yes, I'd heard about it. Wasn't involved, myself. Our service manager, Donny Vargas, handled it."

Sam thought she remembered someone saying the service manager was actually the one Zack had the fight with, but she kept her mouth shut now.

"I'll need to speak with him," Beau said.

"Certainly. I'll have him paged." Friststone picked up a telephone.

Vargas entered the owner's office a few minutes later. He walked with the strut of a small man who is accustomed to standing up for himself against guys who tried to belittle either his job or his short stature. His shaved head had a five o'clock shadow outlining a forehead-clinging hairline, and his uniform smelled of grease and tires. He shot a defiant look at Beau but answered respectfully when his boss told him to answer the sheriff's questions. Friststone excused himself, leaving the other three alone.

"I hear you and Zack Robinet kind of got into it earlier in the week," Beau said, lounging casually with one hip against the office's massive desk.

Donny Vargas's eyes flashed. "He started it, man. We done the work, everything he wanted, and then he shit a brick over the cost. Hey, we bill according to the published rates on our wall. Nothin' extra. I swear it."

"When was the last time you saw him?"

"Next morning, after we worked on his car. He raised a stink over the bill when he picked up the vehicle but he paid it anyway. We can't release a car until the invoice is paid. So he did. Then he comes back the next morning ready to tie into me. Guess he fumed over it all night or somethin'."

"Did he actually touch you?"

"Nah. He's one of those all-mouth guys. He comes at me, all screaming and acting like he'll punch me? But I show him my fist and then he's all backing away. Growls like some old tomcat. Stupid pussy, that's what he is."

"Was. He's dead."

Vargas paused only a fraction. "Doesn't surprise me, man. He had that kind of mouth on him, always spoutin' off."

"So he treated you badly more than once?"

"Me an' everbody else. Look, I got no love for the jerk. But I'm not the only one feels that way. He's got enemies all over this town."

"Names?"

"I don't know, man. Ask anybody who ever dealt with him."

"What happened after the confrontation that morning? When did you see him again?"

"Never! He backs out of my office, shaking his fist and screaming. But he never came back."

"And you didn't conveniently meet up with him later, sometime after work, maybe another day?"

Vargas poo-pooed the idea but Sam noticed he wouldn't meet Beau's eye.

Beau called Larry Friststone back to the office and asked that he have Vargas write and sign a statement. What he really wanted, Sam discovered, was to keep the service manager occupied while she and Beau walked through the building to the service department.

"Let's just see if the mechanics remember the story the same way, without their manager hovering around."

The crew, at this time on a Friday night, consisted of a senior man who might be a young-looking fifty, plus two young guys who'd probably been out of high school just long enough to take the required training for their jobs.

The older man stepped up to the service desk, asked if he could help them and introduced himself as Scott Montaño.

"Just a few questions," Beau said. "If everyone can come over here I can ask all of you at once."

The others set down their tools and walked over to the service desk, one of them lagging behind and sending nervous glances toward Beau.

"We're looking into the argument which took place here

earlier in the week, with a customer named Zack Robinet. What can any of you tell me about it?"

The young guys shook their heads. "I heard voices is all," said the tall, skinny one whose most notable feature was that his orange freckles managed to stand out behind the layer of garage grease which coated his face. "I was back there in bay six, an oil change."

"Rudy? What about you?" Scott asked when it became apparent the shyer boy wasn't going to speak up.

Rudy shook his head again. "The same. I was in the back. Just heard someone yelling."

"Mr. Montaño? Did you catch any of it—what it was about, how it ended?"

Scott glanced toward the door leading into the showroom, making sure Donny Vargas wasn't coming back. "It was about the charges for Mr. Robinet's car. He was furious over something, but I'm not sure what. He wasn't overcharged. A calm explanation of the charges might have settled him down but it had been a long day and Mr. Vargas wasn't in the best mood. He dished it right back. I felt bad. It wasn't professional of him."

"He said Robinet came back the next morning."

"That's true. He caught Mr. Vargas at a bad time then. He's not a man you want to say good morning to until you judge his mood. Things got a little loud then, too, I'm afraid. The customer had marched right into Mr. Vargas's office." He pointed toward a glass-fronted cubicle a few feet away. "That's one thing you don't ever want to do, cross that doorway unless you're invited."

"Sounds like Mr. Vargas has a pretty good temper, huh?" Sam said.

All three men found other things in the room to look at, primarily their shoes or their fingernails.

"That's okay. I think I'm getting the picture," Beau said. "One more thing: Did anyone see Mr. Vargas confront Mr. Robinet any time afterward? Maybe later in the day, maybe someplace away from the dealership?"

"Not me," said the skinny, freckled kid.

"Nope."

"Afraid not," added Scott Montaño.

Sam took a side door out to the parking lot, while Beau made a show of going back to Larry Friststone's office to pick up whatever passed for Donny Vargas's written statement. He would most likely have to bring the man down to the station to formally go through the same procedure. Too bad one of the other mechanics hadn't witnessed something a little more definitive. Beau had the distinct feeling that one or more of them was stonewalling.

He told Sam as much during the drive to The Scoreboard, the sports bar where he'd heard the atmosphere wasn't the greatest but the burgers were. His source—one of the deputies—was right on the first count.

The noise of five big-screens tuned to football hit full force right inside the door. How a person could follow any one of the games was a mystery, since they all seemed to be running at equal volume. Sam would have left immediately, opting for a quiet spot somewhere, but the tantalizing smells of grilled beef, bacon, onions, chile and cheese filled the air along with what could only be termed eau de French fry.

The Scoreboard's reputation had spread; only one small table remained open.

"Happy hour ends in thirty minutes," said the perky girl

in tight shorts who plopped tiny napkins on their table. She practically winked at Beau as she said it. "I'd sneak you an extra half-price beer but Ray's real strict about it."

She tilted her head toward the bar where a thick-chested man with muscles that screamed steroids threatened to rip the stretchy band around the sleeve of his polo shirt.

"That's okay, I'm on duty anyway," Beau said.

He ordered a Coke and Sam requested the same as she looked over the menu which claimed to serve "101 Delicious Burger Combos." She settled on the Ol' Hickory, something with grilled onions and spicy barbeque sauce. Beau's choice went to the traditional, a mountain of lettuce, tomato, onions and pickles atop a thick burger with cheese.

The waitress turned in their order and brought their drinks before joining a noisy group in the corner who seemed focused on some college game. The fans consisted of a half dozen businessmen who had shed their ties and jackets but bore the mark of white shirts and Cole Haans. With them were three young women who looked way too made-up and too young to be wives. Not to mention that each of the women was paying equal attention to more than one man.

"Do we actually have hookers here in Taos?" Sam whispered to Beau.

He laughed. "Darlin' there are hookers everywhere. If you mean that group, yes. Chief has arrested at least two of those ladies. As long as they don't stray outside the town limits to find business, they're under police jurisdiction and at least I don't have to deal with them. These tend to stick to a middle class clientele and I haven't heard of them getting caught up in anything violent, so I leave them alone. The real skanks hang around outside the Pony after ten p.m. and get themselves tangled up with equally skanky men."

None of the three here seemed at all concerned about a uniformed lawman in their midst, although the laughter from the men had dimmed a little since Sam had looked their direction. She turned her attention back to Beau.

"So, what did you think about the interviews at the dealership just now? Would the service manager have followed Zack Robinet and harmed him?"

"Harm, I can see. The kind of murderer who got Zack, not so much. Setting it up so it appeared he'd been involved in rough sex play but injecting him with heroin instead … that takes some fairly sophisticated planning."

Sam's eyes automatically went to the hookers in the corner, but she chided herself for making assumptions about the type of person who would have gone with Zack to his hotel in Albuquerque. Not someone from here, surely.

Their burgers arrived just then, brought over by the weightlifter-bartender since their server seemed busy at another table. He introduced himself as Ray Belatoni, the owner, as he delivered condiments and assured them they could call upon him or Tina if they needed anything. His words were genuine but his manner seemed perfunctory to Sam, as if he said the same tired phrases to everyone who came in and was secretly wishing the night was over and he could count the till. She turned to the enticing hunk of grilled deliciousness in front of her.

"So, who are your best suspects at this point?" she finally asked Beau, dipping an onion ring into the puddle of ketchup on her plate.

"I think Kent Taylor would pin it on the wife. Have to admit, they're known for loud fights, she disappears the same day Zack left town and hasn't been seen since."

"Even if she was traveling wouldn't she have heard about his death on the news or something?"

"We've asked the media not to release his name since she's his closest kin and we haven't been able to reach her. So, no, there's no news story that gives his or her names. On the other hand, not a lot of Taos men die in Albuquerque, so I suppose she could easily put it together if she heard or read the basics of the story."

"Surely there's a trail of her movements, right? I mean, that's what happens on TV—you can track her credit cards, bank accounts and such, can't you?"

He smiled a little indulgently. "We can and we have, but there's been no activity. Taylor thinks she's probably gone off with another man, which would explain it. He's paying for everything."

"But airline tickets? She has to show identification."

"They travel by car ... maybe by train."

The latter seemed a little far-fetched to Sam. Train travel was not at all the common way to go in New Mexico. But a car—that was surely feasible.

Movement near the door caught her attention. "Beau, look," she said.

Donny Vargas walked in and went straight to the bar. Ray Belatoni greeted him like best of friends and set a shot of golden liquid in front of him, along with a salt shaker and small dish of lime wedges. The auto mechanic slugged back the tequila and Belatoni filled it again.

"Interesting."

Unfortunately, the noise level in the bar prevented them from hearing any of the chummy conversation.

Chapter 11

Jane showed up for work promptly at eight. As per Sam's instructions she said she had taken the about-town trolley that ran up and down the main drag and through the Plaza.

"There was an interesting cooking show on television last night," she told Sam as they washed their hands. "A travelogue of sorts featuring unusual flavors of chocolate from around the world."

Sam's interest perked up. "Something we can use to fill Mr. Bookman's order?"

"Well, some of them. A few were truly weird, like marinating tobacco leaves in rum and infusing the chocolate with the resulting liqueur."

"Uh, no."

"Or, pig's blood? Absinthe?"

"We better skip to the usable ideas," Sam said.

"Japan had one with plum liqueur. It sounded fabulous. And there was a really unusual one from Spain—hazelnut praline, sea salt, and Pop Rocks candy coated in cocoa butter. They say the Pop Rocks explode in your mouth like fireworks."

"Hm, I remember those candies from when Kelly was a kid. She loved them. I didn't realize they were still available."

"I guess they are. We could always check the candy counter at the convenience store on the corner."

Sam added the candy and sea salt to her list of things to buy locally, and Jane started mixing the cocoa powder with cocoa butter in a heavy double boiler.

"This large pot is better than the one you used the other day," Jane said, watching the mixture as it began to melt, stirring carefully.

"You're right. How was your room last night?" Sam asked as Jane inserted the candy thermometer into the dark, fragrant mixture.

"Clean enough, I suppose." Jane looked up. "Fine, really—it was fine."

The woman must have been accustomed to fancier digs but since Sam was paying the bill she hadn't felt obligated to come up with a nicer hotel.

"Still no recollection of your past, though?"

"Not a thing beyond what I'm doing right now. I felt a real understanding of the chocolatier's process while I was watching last night's program."

"Maybe we could play Twenty Questions," Becky said from the worktable, where she was forming sugar flowers for a bridal shower cake. "One of us might ask a question that would help you remember."

Sam sent Becky a look, knowing this was her way of testing Jane, but since she was also keen to learn where Jane belonged she smiled encouragement toward the visitor.

Jane seemed hesitant. "Well, I suppose …"

"Kids. Do you think you have any children?"

Jane spun toward Becky. "What kind of a mother would I be if I didn't remember my own children? That's a cruel question."

Sam held out both hands. "Look, we don't have to do this now. I'm sure Becky was only trying to help you remember things. It isn't about your fitness as a mother or wife or anything like that. Becky?"

"Sorry, Jane. I didn't mean anything by it."

Sometimes I feel more like a mother than an employer to this bunch. Sam looked toward Jane again. "If you think going through some questions would be helpful, we're happy to do it. If not, we'll drop the subject."

"Maybe later. I don't want to lose my concentration on the chocolate."

Good answer. There weren't enough roasted cocoa beans to start over. And the order was an important one.

"When it's tempered, go ahead and mold it," Sam told Jane. "I'm going out for the other ingredients."

Getting away from her shop had never been a priority for Sam but this week, with whatever was going on between Becky and Jane, it was a relief to walk out into the frosty September morning and leave it all behind for awhile. She put her van in gear and headed toward the nearest supermarket. Her phone chimed as she was pulling into the lot, Beau's name showing on the screen.

"Hey there," he said. "I got away so early this morning I didn't want to wake you."

A gesture that was always appreciated.

"Just wondering if your friend Jane said anything about her evening. Rico said no one came or went all night."

"She said she watched a show about chocolate. Her comment on the room itself was less than enthusiastic. That's about it."

"The hotel records don't show any phone calls in- or out-bound, and she doesn't have a cell phone that we're aware of."

Sam thought of the missing evening when Jane's whereabouts were unaccounted for. She could have made it to Walmart and picked up a prepaid phone.

With what money?

Good point.

"So," Beau was saying, "I don't see much point in tying up a deputy's time to keep an eye on her. It's not as if she's committed any crime."

"True. I'll keep watching and listening at the shop. I did tell you she's working for me this week? She knows a lot about chocolate, so that's another clue from her past in case you're still going through missing-person reports."

It was a blatant hint, she knew, one she couldn't hold him to, since he was short-handed and had a much more important case to work.

"Meanwhile, I'm at Smith's. If you can imagine what you'd like for dinner tonight, I'll pick it up now."

A little discussion back and forth and they decided to go with leftovers they already had at home. Sam locked the van and grabbed a shopping cart. Thirty minutes later she walked back into Sweet's Sweets to find Jane spooning molten chocolate into some of her standard-shaped molds.

"I figured I could get these started," she said. "An idea came to me. I can pipe little kittens on some of these, and I think I'll start the figures of modeling chocolate while they set."

"Looks good to me." Not since she'd hired Julio had Sam been able to completely turn over a project to a new employee without quite a lot of training. She unpacked the grocery bags, happy she'd found the Pop Rocks candy, and set everything out for Jane to access.

Jane had already set aside the filled molds and was beginning to mix up a batch of buttercream filling, which could be flavored in a dozen different ways. Sam watched for a minute or two and decided her supervision wasn't really necessary.

The six-tier wedding cake to be loaded with autumn flowers still awaited her attention. It called for swags on the uppermost two tiers, ribbons and beading on another and the huge bottom tier covered in solidly packed sugar flowers, the ones Becky had made earlier in the week. One by one, Sam brought the tiers from the walk-in fridge and began assembling them, making sure to brace everything with extra doweling and platforms. These monster cakes always got tricky. Tomorrow, she would have to recruit some help to get it to her van and set up at the wedding venue. *Note to self: call Kelly or Zoë before this day gets much farther along.* Zoë's husband, Darryl, was always good when muscle power was involved.

With two extra-large pastry bags full of ivory buttercream, she began piping the details. It went smoothly as she hit her stride, and she stuck with it until her shoulders ached. Needing a short break from that, she picked up her daily stack of order forms, browsing to see which were most urgent, still having the nagging thought that she'd forgotten something important.

It probably went back to last night's conversation with Beau and the interviews with his suspects. Somehow, a vital fact had gotten past her. That had to be it. She would call him as soon as she thought of it.

By noon, Becky had finished the bridal shower cake and two for birthdays, Sam had the massive cake for three hundred about half done, and Jane's progress on the chocolates was impressive. Julio, surrounded by bustling women, kept his head down and the bake oven cranking out cake layers alongside the cookies and brownies for the afternoon crowd. When Beau phoned to see if Sam wanted to break away for lunch she rubbed her aching shoulder and agreed. They met in the parking lot at Wendy's.

"I've already been through the drive-up," Beau said. "Got you a spicy chicken sandwich. Is that okay?"

"I love it. The perfect romantic lunch date." She squeezed into the passenger seat of his cruiser, edging aside the radio equipment and a computer screen which was a recent addition to the department's journey into the twenty-first century.

"Detective Taylor is driving up from Albuquerque tomorrow afternoon. Zack Robinet's funeral is Monday morning and Taylor wants to be here for it. I told him he could stay in our guest room. Hope that's okay with you. I guess his department is hassling anybody who wants to do out-of-town travel and he'd have to pay for his own room."

Sam squeezed a dab of ketchup onto a pair of fries. "Sure. I've got to go into the shop and deliver a huge wedding cake in the morning. Afterward, I could plan something nice for dinner. What do you think—chicken or steak?"

"I suspect Taylor is a steak guy. Either one would be a treat. I don't know whether he's married or not, maybe he cooks for himself."

"So, the funeral will go ahead even without Zack's wife? That seems odd."

"His parents are insistent on their need for closure. I've talked to them twice now and get the feeling there's no love lost on the daughter-in-law. Zack's father as much as said he was sure she's been cheating. Dammit—" He wiped at a spot of mayo on his chest. "Now I'll have to change ties. Anyway, from the lack of info on her whereabouts, it could be true. Could be she's gone off with her lover and, if she heard about Zack's death, may decide never to come back."

"Wow—cold. They have a son, don't they?"

"Yeah. Sorry I'm being so cynical. It's probably Kent Taylor's calloused attitude rubbing off on me. You're right. Surely, Mrs. Robinet will contact her son as soon as she learns the news."

Sam finished her sandwich in silence, thinking about what he'd said.

"There could be a hundred reasons for a woman to run off and have no contact with her kid," he said. "For all we know, she *has* contacted him and we just don't know it. I get the feeling the kid's story was a little shaky. I'll learn more about Taylor's interviews with the boy when he gets here."

He balled up his paper sandwich wrapper and shoved it into the bag, along with the few fries he hadn't eaten.

"Meanwhile, I'm trying to keep the department together with half my deputies. Rico came back yesterday but he's still looking peaked and another guy came down with the bug. It hits hard in the stomach and digestion and I *really* don't want to catch this thing."

"Don't share food with them and be sure to wash your hands about eight dozen times a day," she advised with a laugh. "I know, I know. I sound like a mom now."

"Trust me, darlin', you don't want to get it either. So, on that note, I better send you back to work and get myself out there to write tickets."

He kissed Sam on the cheek and she took the paper sack of trash with her, dropping it into a receptacle before climbing back into her van. Back at the bakery, she washed up and surveyed the cake-in-progress.

"It's coming along beautifully, Sam," said Becky, coming back from the fridge with her final project of the day.

Jane piped up: "Yes, that's an amazing pastry."

Her own chocolates were sitting in neat little rows; truffles with the hazelnut and Pop Rocks filling now sported cute little kitty faces. The package with the new molds had come while Sam was gone. Jane had already washed them and brought one over to show Sam which of the variety of shapes she thought would best fit the customer's request.

"If I put pointy ears on this one that's supposed to be a puppy, I think we can modify him to become a cat, don't you think?"

It looked a little tricky but Sam told her to go ahead and try one or two as examples and see how the idea worked out.

"I'm surprised he didn't ask for big chocolate cats," Becky said, "like those bunnies we always make at Easter."

"You have molds for hollow rabbits?" Jane asked. A thoughtful look crossed her face. "I could maybe do something with that, another modification, a sort of grand finale to top off the whole thing."

Sam felt herself wavering. The man had requested boxed chocolates. Would he think a big chocolate cat a little too hokey for his elegant surprise? She suggested that Jane start with the small molds first and see how they turned out.

"We have until the end of next week. There's time to play around with ideas."

She noticed Jane perked up with the knowledge she would be working a few more days. More dollars out of pocket to keep the so-so motel room paid for, but judging by Jane's work so far, it was proving to be well worth the expense.

Sam turned her attention back to the massive cake covered with the autumn flowers. As Becky said, it was coming along well, but a lot of work remained. She brought out the sugar paste flowers Becky had made earlier in the week and began placing them, beginning with the lowest tier where she set the blossoms tightly together, balancing tones of burnt orange, yellow, red and vermillion. As she finished each quarter of the surface she stepped back to get the overall picture, squinting to be sure the colors blended perfectly.

"Sam?" Jen stepped in from the sales room. "We're nearly out of everything up front and it's an hour to closing. Shall I add something?"

"No, that's okay. Let's close a little early, give everyone some extra time at home."

Julio was already washing mixing bowls and pans at the deep sink, his last set of cake layers now on the cooling racks.

"Get all the cooled items into the fridge and close out the register."

"There's a birthday cake to be delivered this afternoon," Becky said. "I can take it on my way home."

Jane was intently focused on a pastry bag with a miniature decorating tip, piping tiny green eyes onto one of the molded kitty shapes. "I can stay if you need me," she said.

"No, that's okay. We have five days next week to get the chocolates done. I'm really impressed with all you accomplished today."

Surprisingly, Becky offered to give Jane a ride to her motel since it was on the way to the birthday cake delivery address. Well, well, Sam thought. Maybe those two have worked out their differences after all. One by one, the employees left and Sam stood back from her creation to see how it was coming along. Times alone like this reminded her of the old days when she baked and decorated at home, solitude feeding her creativity. Sometimes she forgot that the trade-off for having help in the business was that the added energy in the room often zapped her own reserves.

She added a few unusual touches, little flourishes here and there, leaves to complement the spectacular flowers, and decided to call it good. Carefully removing the top two tiers at the spacer platforms she stashed them in the fridge, then moved the large tier in on a wheeled cart. With everything safely stowed and her tools put away, she hung up her jacket and locked the back door behind her.

Kelly's day at Puppy Chic had ended a couple of hours ago and Sam decided to give her a call.

"Hey, how's it going? Another big date tonight?"

"Not tonight. I am taking a purely personal evening to do my own mani-pedi, soak in the tub and read a good book."

Mr. Mysterious not available on a Saturday night?

Sam brought herself back to the reason she had called. "I have a huge cake delivery tomorrow and could use some help. I'd ask Beau, and I'm sure he would do it, but with his job he could get a call at any moment and I'd be stuck."

"Sure, Mom. Anytime."

"I can stop by and pick you up around ten. It really shouldn't take more than thirty minutes, but allow an hour. I mean, in case you have other plans."

"Nothing on my schedule but, um, let me just meet you at your shop. I can get groceries and run a few errands while I'm out."

Kelly still sounded very mysterious but at least they had a plan.

Chapter 12

Kelly didn't seem to have a care in the world when she greeted her mother the next morning, and Sam chided herself for becoming such a busybody. It wasn't as if she had no other concerns to fill her days. Together, they wheeled the heavy cake out to Sam's van and placed the tiers carefully in the spotlessly clean cargo area, securing everything with blocks of Styrofoam.

"I swear, these big cakes get heavier all the time," Sam said, puffing a little as she closed the door.

Kelly wasn't even breathing hard. "Well, Mom," she teased. "Maybe it's time to admit you're getting a little older."

"That, I will never concede." *Not as long as I have Beau keeping me young.* She flushed a little at the memory of their early morning lovemaking. *Can't very well quiz Kelly about her love life, can I?*

Little conversation took place during the short trip to the wedding venue, the ballroom of the town's classiest hotel, which was probably the only indoor spot in Taos large enough to handle the crowd that would devour this cake. The kitchen delivery entrance was around back, not nearly far enough from a fenced enclosure full of garbage dumpsters. Sam commandeered a rolling cart and they loaded the two sections of cake as quickly as possible.

Fortunately, by the time they reached the ballroom they were surrounded by flowers and candles, and her prize confection was safe. The cake table stood ready for its centerpiece attraction, for which Sam felt thankful. It always unnerved her a little to deliver a cake and rely on hotel personnel to set it in place. Way too many things could go wrong.

Within twenty minutes, she and Kelly had assembled the tiers, put spare flowers in place to hide the seam where the tiers met, and arranged the other table decorations to highlight their masterpiece. Ready for "here comes the bride."

Back in the van, Sam noticed Kelly's nails. "I like your manicure. All spiffed up for another big date?"

"Thanks, but, Mom, I'm not telling you anything about my new guy. Not yet. I have no idea whether this will last and, well, he's kind of shy."

A picture of the very-quiet Julio came to mind. Could effervescent Kelly be interested in a man who was always on the gruff side? Sam could see long-term compatibility issues.

"Is it someone I know already? Someone who's worried I might not approve?"

"Not telling."

"Someone who is a lot older or a lot younger?"

"Not telling."

"Somebody famous? Everyone in the country would know if they saw you out together?"

"Not telling."

"Kel, is he married?"

"Mom, no! I've got better sense than that!"

They were back at Kelly's car, and she turned with a smile toward her mother. "If things are still going well in a couple weeks, I'll have everyone over for dinner or something."

She gave Sam's hand a quick squeeze and got out of the van, giving a tiny wave before getting into her little red convertible.

It has to be Julio, Sam thought as she drove back out to the ranch. He, too, had been a little secretive around Sam. He was someone she knew, although not exactly what most mothers would imagine for a long-term relationship with an only daughter. He was a nice enough man, although the tattooed, biker packaging left room for the need to adjust one's attitude. Sam supposed she could do that. For now, she had an overnight guest to cook for.

She stopped at her favorite market at the north end of town and selected three nice filets, three potatoes and some salad greens. Nothing pleased men like a meat and potatoes meal, and this one should do it.

She spent the rest of the afternoon tidying the guest room and bath for Kent Taylor's arrival, dusting the furniture and vacuuming. Not that a police detective was likely to judge her on those things, but it was a pretty sure bet an observant one would notice. Besides, when else would she find the time to do any cleaning? The reward at the end of her little frenzy was a long soak in a hot bath.

A little after four o'clock Sam heard the dogs woofing softly from the front porch. A glance outside showed Beau's cruiser coming up the driveway, followed by a plain white sedan that had to be Taylor's city-issued vehicle. The detective wore an open-necked polo shirt and the same rundown sports jacket as the first time she'd met him. The lines around his eyes seemed a little less tired this time and he gave her a smile and a bottle of wine when she stepped out on the porch to greet him.

Beau ushered their visitor to the guest room where he hung his garment bag in the closet and dropped a small ditty bag on the bed.

"Dinner can be ready any time from thirty minutes onward," Sam told the men.

"We can wait a while. I'll bet Kent could go for a little something to wet the whistle first," Beau suggested.

It didn't take more than a couple minutes to get the guys settled on the back deck with glasses of Scotch. Sam opened the wine Taylor had brought, poured herself a glass and joined them, coming in partway through a conversation about the Robinet case.

"I'll email them to you," Kent was saying. He touched some buttons on his phone.

"Kent says they finally identified the DNA of a prostitute from the hotel room where Zack Robinet died."

"She has to be the one who was with him. We got prints from the bathroom faucets and some used glassware in the room. Name's Krystal Cordova. Age twenty-six. She grew up in Taos but moved to Albuquerque three years ago. Still gets back here quite a bit to visit family and old friends. Apparently got her start as an exotic dancer at some little dive here, then moved on. She's got that combination of good looks and flirtatious innocence that pulls guys in. According to APD's records, she's never worked on the streets there. Connected with an experienced girl who helps her get the high-dollar jobs in the city."

"Yeah, I doubt Taos has room for a whole lot of high-dollar girls," Beau said.

Sam remembered that it had surprised her that Taos had prostitutes at all. You think your own small town is a haven of innocence.

Taylor passed his phone over to Beau, who took a look at the photo.

"I've seen her," he said. He held up the picture to Sam. "Just the other night."

"Yeah, at The Scoreboard. The night we went to try the burgers."

"Yep, that group in the corner." He looked at Taylor. "There were three girls, a group of businessmen. Krystal was one of them. Big, fluffy hair and loads of makeup. Do you think she's still here in town?"

"The drive is only around two and a half hours so she probably runs back and forth from Albuquerque fairly often. So far in this investigation my men haven't managed to find her at home or any of her usual city hangouts."

"If she's here in town I'll find her and bring her in for questioning tomorrow, either before or after the funeral."

"About that—do you think Robinet will draw a crowd?"

"No idea. As far as I know, he's not exactly a celebrity but his partner just got back from a trade show where they introduced a new version of the game that made them a fortune. For all I know, there could be millions of nerdy groupies out there who worship the man."

"Maybe it would be smart to have extra men milling

among the crowd," Kent suggested. "I'm still a big fan of the idea that a killer often shows up to witness his handiwork. We might learn something useful. I have to say, I'm hoping for a break real soon. Too many days have gone by already."

Beau sighed and Sam knew he was trying to figure out where these extra men would come from, since half his force was still calling in sick.

Against her better judgment she spoke up. "I could go. What time will it be?"

Beau leaped at the suggestion, while Taylor seemed a little skeptical.

"Sam's been my right hand on more than one case," he told the detective. "She's got uncanny senses about people."

Yeah, uncanny whenever she'd handled the wooden box. There actually had been a couple of instances where she'd seen auras around people who had turned out to be valid suspects. She shook off the thought of using it this time, though. She had vowed to leave it tucked away in the safe, plus, when would there be an opportunity to get it out and handle it with the cop staying right here in their house? She discarded the idea.

"So, how about we cook those steaks now, and then maybe the three of us go out and hit a couple of bars to see if we can run across our little Krystal?" Beau said, getting up to light the grill.

"In that case," Taylor said, downing the last of his Scotch, "I'd better switch to a soft drink with dinner."

Sam microwaved the potatoes and put the finishing touches on the salad while Beau monitored the steaks. Ready for a glass of wine and quiet evening at home, she found herself hoping the men would change their minds about going out.

However, no such luck. Two hours later they had put together their meager notes. Sam begged off, making the case (with a wink) that if Beau hoped to have a conversation with a hooker his wife's presence would only put a damper on it.

* * *

Beau directed Taylor to The Scoreboard, finding the parking lot even more packed than it had been on his previous visit. Once again, the muscular Ray Belatoni was behind the bar, keeping close tabs on his crew—another bartender and four of those waitresses in short shorts and tight tops. The same three young women hovered at the back booth, although he was fairly sure the men were different ones. Under questioning, he would have to admit that he'd noticed a lot more about the girls than the men.

Taylor surveyed the room with a practiced eye. A few conversations waned but as soon as the civilian-dressed lawmen headed for the back corner most of them picked up again. As before, the television screens blared with football commentary.

"Krystal Cordova?" Beau looked her in the eye and there was no denying who she was. He and Taylor showed their badges. "We'd like to ask you a few questions."

At the mention of her name, Krystal squirmed in her seat. If not for the fact that she was wedged between two of the men on the curved banquette seat, she might have bolted.

"There's nothing going on," one of the other women said.

"I didn't say there was." He took his time scanning the

rest of the table, memorizing faces, although all four of the men suddenly needed to check things in their pockets. "Just a few questions at this point. Krystal, you might want to come outside where we can speak in lower voices."

Her eyes darted back and forth but no escape route presented itself. She gave a ragged sigh, as though she were being inconvenienced, and scooted across the lap of a man who suddenly didn't seem to know her anymore. Beau would bet money that the rest of the table's occupants would be gone if he were to walk back inside five minutes from now.

Krystal tottered on her six-inch platforms and tugged at the skirt that barely covered her butt, working hard to appear unconcerned as she preceded the two lawmen toward the front door. Behind the bar, Ray Belatoni gave her a hard stare, a warning of some sort. He was probably taking a cut of everything the girls made and didn't like the disruption in business.

Taylor put a hand on Krystal's elbow, guiding her toward his car, but she shook it off. "We can talk right here, Mr. Cop. I don't get in cars with strange men."

Taylor laughed. "Because going to their hotel rooms is safer? Come on, Krystal. We know your record and we have your prints in a room at the Kingston Arms Hotel where a man ended up dead. I hate to be brutal about it, but usually that's what happens to the prostitute who goes along with strange men."

Krystal quieted down, her eyes showing a little less flash now.

Beau took over. "Look, Krystal, could we just get to the bottom line here? There's all kinds of proof you were there. We'd just like to know what happened."

She glanced nervously toward the door where a male

voice came through loudly as two guys laughed their way to a small pickup truck.

"Someone watching you?" Taylor asked. "Someone you're afraid of? Cause we can go downtown and ask our questions in private."

She fidgeted another full minute. "Yeah, that might be better."

Okay, that's a new one, Beau thought as he opened the back door to Taylor's car and climbed in after her. Taylor put the car in gear.

Krystal started talking the moment they were out of sight of The Scoreboard. "I swear to you, Sheriff, that guy was dead when I came back to the room. I had nothing to do with it."

"Back to the room? You left and came back?"

Kent pulled into a space in the Sunday-night emptiness of the department parking lot. "Let's get inside and start from the beginning."

Their suspect went along willingly enough and Beau made sure the cameras and recording equipment were functional before they spoke to her again.

"Okay," said Taylor, "so you went to the Kingston Arms with Zack Robinet on the night of September fifteenth. You transacted a little business."

She took a deep breath and began as if she were talking to a child. "I don't remember the date but it wasn't the fifteenth. I was back in Taos by then 'cause that's my mom's birthday. It was a couple days before."

That meshed with the story as they knew it. Robinet had been dead in the room for at least a day before an insistent maid got the manager's permission to enter the room where a privacy request had been phoned to the desk. It was part of what made it so difficult to establish an exact time of death.

"Okay, let's say the thirteenth. Did you go directly up to his room or meet somewhere else?"

"I met him in the hotel bar. It's this cushy place that's supposed to look like some old English library or something. I was told to approach him, to dress down, be classy."

"Who told you?"

"Um …"

"We'll contact Hilde Maya and ask her."

The name of her friend rattled Krystal a little. "No, don't do that. She didn't know about Zack."

"So, who set you up with him?"

Krystal stalled, glancing around the room, shifting in her seat. "Okay, the deal was that I could *never* say who hired me."

"That deal's off. Don't you get it? You're about this close to being arrested for murder. You got no deal with anybody now, honey."

Beau wondered if it was APD policy to refer to a suspect as 'honey.' He suspected not, but sometimes you broke a few little rules.

She fidgeted a little more. "Okay, it was the wife."

"Robinet's wife? A wife hired you to take her husband to bed."

"Yeah." She looked at him frankly. "It's not the weirdest request I ever got. She actually told me to get him to fall in love with me if I could."

Kent's eyes met Beau's above Krystal's head, exchanging a what-the-hell look.

"And you got to the hotel and thought this would happen in one encounter."

She shot him a don't-be-stupid expression. "Okay, so I didn't quite tell it all. I'd been seeing Zack for a few weeks. The plan was coming along and I was about to ask him if he would leave her and we go off somewhere really cool together. I was thinking the Virgin Islands or Bermuda or somewhere like that."

"So you didn't meet him in the hotel bar," Beau said.

"Oh, yeah, the first time I did. Zack was pretty cool. He'd spend money on me and I really liked the Kingston Arms. It's a classy place. He was going to Vegas last weekend and promised to take me along, but he would get me my own room. I couldn't let his partner know I was there. He had some big business show to do but said I could hang around the pool or go shopping and put whatever I wanted on the room bill. I really, really thought he was all into me." Her voice cracked a little at this last part, as if it was just now hitting her that Zack was truly gone.

"Let's get back to the night you were at the Kingston Arms. You and he were in a suite together," Beau said, watching her nod along with the statements. "The sex play maybe got a little rough ..."

She tilted her head. "Well, sometimes he liked me to put my hands on his throat. Oh, god, were there fingerprints? Is that why I'm here? Cause I swear I never did it very hard. He didn't stop breathing—I swear to that!"

Taylor switched topics. "Were there drugs involved in your little party?"

"No. I don't do that shit and Zack said he didn't either. Well, okay, there were a few times we smoked a little pot. That's not really a drug, is it? I mean it's legal for a doctor to give it to you, right?"

"All doctors do is give out drugs," Taylor pointed out. "It counts. But we're talking about something else. Was there heroin in that room?"

"I never saw any." Her eyes were wide now, as if the possibility of a drug charge was more dangerous to her than a murder charge.

Taylor slammed his hands down on the table. Krystal nearly jumped out of her chair and Beau even flinched.

"Zack Robinet died from a heroin overdose. You were in the room with him. Did you give it to him or did he shoot it himself?" The mild-mannered, middle aged cop was gone now, replaced by a man who looked like he might burst a vessel in his head.

Krystal started to cry. "No, no, I never saw no drugs in the suite. If Zack did it himself it was while I was gone." Her mascara had run nearly to her chin now and her face quickly became a wet mess.

Beau seized the new lead and made his voice gentle— playing good cop to Taylor's bad one. He handed her a box of tissues. "You left the room and came back? Maybe you better tell us about that."

She snuffled into the tissue for a couple of minutes. Elaborately swabbing her lower eyelids she finally got her voice under control again.

"We'd spent all day in the bedroom—you know. And then about five o'clock we were getting hungry. Zack suggested room service but I was really in the mood for pizza and they didn't have it. So I said I would run out and get one. There's a Dion's near there and that's my favorite. I got dressed and took my car." She breathed deeply, calming herself and getting the events in sequence.

"I picked up a large pepperoni and came up the elevator. When I walked into the room, I told him 'dinner is served' all elegant-like, you know. He—he didn't answer me. I put the pizza on the table in the living room area and went into the bedroom—" Her voice broke again.

"He was in bed, still with no clothes on, but he looked weird. Not like himself. I said his name again and his face was just so … blank. I told him to quit kidding around and I shook him. He was warm but he was dead." A fresh flood of tears.

Beau wondered if this was the first time in days she had acknowledged to herself what had happened.

"What did you do then?" he asked gently.

"I … I got so scared. I thought he had a heart attack or something and I knew paramedics or somebody would be coming and I just couldn't stick around. I mean, if I wasn't going to get Vegas or the Virgin Islands or anything at all … Well, I figured let the wife deal with all of it. She's the one who got me into this whole thing anyways."

"Describe your actions," Taylor said, his tone far softer than five minutes ago.

"I thought of *CSI* and I got real scared they could figure out I was there. I ran around the room and picked up the lacy little teddy I'd worn earlier and grabbed my makeup bag. And then when I went through the living room I knew my fingerprints would be on the pizza box so I took it with me. I guess that's about it. I drove away and threw my room key in the trash. And the pizza. I couldn't even think about eating it after that."

"Did you check all the rooms and closets in the suite? Could someone else have been there?"

"Oh my god!" Her eyes were huge. "I never even

thought of that. Somebody killed him. And they could have saw me."

She began to look a little frantic.

"You're safe here. But if you can think of anyone who had a reason to kill Zack you need to tell us and do it now. We can't protect you from the killer if we don't know who it is."

She swore there was no one she could think of and finally they had to let her go. Back in Kent Taylor's car, they took her to her own vehicle in the parking lot at The Scoreboard, then followed her home to be sure she made it safely.

"Well, now it makes sense why Josephine Robinet decided to disappear," Taylor said on the way back out to Beau's place. "I'd say she's our number one suspect now. Who else knew exactly where Zack would be and could stage it to implicate the girl she, herself, had paid to go there with him?"

Chapter 13

Chandler Lane met Beau and Sam at the door of the funeral home, apparently taking the role of host. He seemed haggard compared to their previous meeting at the offices of ChanZack Innovations the day after Zack's death. The shock, combined with the rigors of a three-day trade show without the advantage of the business partner's help. His loss would continue to show up in a hundred ways, Beau imagined, as the days went on.

"So glad you could make it, Sheriff," he said. "Are there any developments in your investigation?"

"We've got some leads. We're working the case systematically," Beau replied.

He spotted George and Nancy Robinet near a huge floral arrangement with a guestbook nearby. Solemn music drifted through the doors leading to a chapel where people were already taking seats on long pews. Beau steered Sam toward the parents to say hello. They asked the same question and got the same answer.

"It's hard to believe Josephine hasn't come back to town," Nancy said.

George grumbled a little, Sam catching something about 'her type.' Last night Beau and Kent had stayed up fairly late discussing the case and going over details, especially the bombshell news that Jo Robinet had hired Krystal to seduce and possibly steal her husband. None of them could quite piece together any logical reason behind such a plan. Of course, as Kent Taylor pointed out, Krystal's whole story could be pure b.s. too. Surely, the elder Robinets knew nothing of this.

The detective had brought his own car to the funeral, planning to head back to Albuquerque as soon as he'd had the chance to observe the crowd here. He already had men in Albuquerque talking to the staff at the Kingston Arms and reviewing security tapes and keycard usage to see if what the young woman said gelled with the facts. Sam didn't see him around; he must have already taken a seat inside the chapel.

A slightly built teenage boy slouched across the room and came to stand beside the Robinets. They introduced him as Bentlee, Zack's son. He had the look of entitlement that was probably de rigueur at exclusive boarding schools. Expensive suit, rebelliously unkempt light brown hair to go with the down-your-nose attitude with which he regarded Sam and Beau. Nancy reached out to take his hand but he sidestepped her before she actually touched him.

Sam knew Kent Taylor had questioned the teen back in Albuquerque, the day he'd been sent to inform the boy of his father's death. Taylor's impression was that this kid was no stranger to drugs—he'd practically bragged that kids in his school could get anything they wanted whenever they wanted it. But Bentlee had been genuinely surprised to learn that his father had died from a heroin overdose, Taylor was sure of that. So much for the possibility father and son had done drugs together. Provided Krystal's version of the events of that day was substantiated by the hotel's video records, it looked fairly certain Bentlee wasn't a suspect.

"Oh, it's exactly like her to skip out," the teen was saying in response to someone else's question about his mother. "If it was important to my dad, she hated it. She never supported anything he did, and it's no wonder she can't be bothered to come to his funeral."

Sam wanted to wipe the sneer off his pugnacious little face, just on the principle that kids should be respectful toward the adults in their lives. She took a breath. Thankfully, he was not her problem. This could be evidence of one more crack in the Robinet marriage. It was sad how often bickering parents recruited the kids to take sides.

People continued to pour into the lobby and the Robinets became quickly distracted by friends and sympathizers. Beau moved off, probably to touch base with Kent Taylor, and Sam decided to sign the guest book.

"Hey, Sam. I didn't expect to see you here." She turned to see Darryl Chartrain, Zoë's husband.

"Beau. Work."

He nodded understanding.

"I didn't know you knew the Robinet family, either," she said.

"Me? I did a big remodeling job at their offices a couple years ago, became a huge fan of the game Zack and

Chandler invented."

Seriously? Sam always imagined online gaming as the domain of teenage boys and nerdy young men. Darryl, gray-haired contractor with a successful business and partner in the B&B with Zoë, did not at all seem the type. You just never knew.

"Well," he continued, "that plus the fact that George and Nancy used to be neighbors before they moved to their new place. We knew Zack as a teen, before he and Jo married."

"Is Zoë here?"

"She wanted to come but we had a houseful of guests last night and she needed to stay home to see them off. They're heading toward Pike's Peak this afternoon."

Another of Darryl's neighbors grabbed his attention and Sam turned to look for Beau. True to form, he was standing near the entrance to the chapel, smiling and nodding at those he recognized. Behind his pleasant demeanor she could tell he was processing information relentlessly, memorizing faces and making mental notes he and Kent could discuss. It couldn't be easy to treat every occasion as a grab-bag of clues to be sorted and used in his job. Sam said hello to a few of her bakery customers as she edged toward her husband.

"I'll find seats for us," she said under her breath. "Near the back?"

"Thanks." He shook hands with a man who approached just then.

Sam spotted Kent Taylor sitting alone at the end of a pew in the north corner of the big room. Assuming Beau would want to cover the opposite side the room, she found two spaces along the south wall and staked out spots there.

Already, the chapel was nearly full. Popular guy, this Zack Robinet. Many familiar faces in the crowd. Sam marveled at how closely their lives may have touched upon each other and yet even in this small town the two families had never met.

She settled in for the ritual of the service, monotonously sad music setting the mood with the kind of tunes that brought back unhappy memories from other such occasions. She wondered how funeral directors handled it—avoided becoming depressed around so much grief and gloom every day of their lives. Maybe the same way Beau did it, approaching each day as a job to be done.

At some point the doors closed and he took his seat beside her, reaching for her hand with a little smile, squeezing it when a burst of sobs erupted from the front section where Nancy Robinet sat next to her husband. Sam couldn't imagine what it would be like to lose her only child, especially the way these people had. If she allowed those thoughts into her head she would be a puddle of tears in no time. Instead, she let her mind wander back to the discussion of suspects that had kept Beau and Kent going last night. That quickly became a tangle of statements by people Sam didn't know, and she turned her thoughts to things she could control—the order of fine chocolates which Jane was, even now, working on at the bakery.

Sam let herself envision the special ingredient she would add to a batch later, the thing that made her chocolates irresistible to her customers. A smile formed on her face until she realized how inappropriate that would seem to anyone who might look her direction. The final prayer began and she bowed her head, sneaking a peek at Beau who openly observed people in the crowd. She squeezed his hand once more.

Eventually, talk ended and movement began as the mourners began making their way to the front to offer condolences to the family. Sam hung back with Beau. Somehow, Kent Taylor had gotten past them and now hovered near the doorway at the front of the room where those in the receiving line had to exit.

"So, is that it for your part?" she asked Beau.

"I think Kent wants to go along to the cemetery. Some clue might emerge depending on who shows up there." He watched her face. "I get the feeling you're eager to get back to work?"

"Well, yeah. But I can go along with you. There's nothing crucial right now."

"Do whatever you want. I'm sure Kent and I can handle the crowd. Afterward, I'll probably let the department treat him to lunch before he heads back to Albuquerque and I get on with my interrogations."

Movement behind her caught Sam's attention, someone else ducking out of the condolence line and heading for the rear door. The woman disappeared the moment Sam turned her head, the hem of a long plaid coat the only real look she got. Something seemed very familiar about the person, but Sam couldn't think why. Earlier, she had spotted a number of people she knew but the clothing didn't match with any of them. She shook off the feeling. It wasn't as if it mattered anyway.

She realized Beau was looking at her, waiting for an answer about lunch, it seemed.

"It's simpler if I stick with you," she said, "since we rode together."

They met up with Kent Taylor in the parking lot and decided to take a back way to the cemetery without becoming caught up in the long and slow funeral procession.

"You never know," Taylor said. "Watching people come and go from things like this can be fairly enlightening."

It took thirty minutes for the entire crowd to make the ten-minute drive, park and assemble again once Zack's coffin had been carried from the hearse and set in place. Sam's patience was showing severe strain and she really wished she'd asked Beau to detour by her shop and drop her off at work. She shifted from one foot to the other as the non-denominational minister uttered more of the same tired phrases he'd said back at the chapel. About the time she was thinking of a way to conceal a yawn she heard a ripple pass along the edge of the crowd.

There, not more than twenty feet away, was the woman she'd noticed earlier. There could only be one of those plaid coats anywhere in the state.

"It's her!" someone nearby said.

"Yes!" The stage-whisper attracted more attention than if the word had been uttered aloud.

Sam's attention locked onto the bulky coat, the gray hair and lopsided felt hat. Someone plucked at the woman's sleeve and the coat slipped off her shoulder. The stranger's expression became instantly familiar.

"Jane!" The name slipped out before Sam realized she'd said it. "What are you doing—?"

"It's Jo!" Others called out the name. "Jo Robinet!"

She spun, trying to slip out of the coat and run but her clunky shoes caught on tree roots hidden in the grass and she stumbled. The cheap gray wig went lopsided on her head as the hat fell to the ground. Beau was there in an instant, taking her arm and not letting go.

"Josephine Robinet?" he queried.

Sam rushed to his side and stared the woman in the face. Their Jane Doe could no longer hide her identity.

Chapter 14

Well, this day just got a whole lot more interesting, Sam thought as she followed Beau to the interrogation room where they had stashed Jane—now Jo—when they arrived at the station. She had come along without argument after the final minutes of the funeral erupted in near chaos. The scene flashed through Sam's mind: Nancy Robinet swooning against her husband's side, Bentlee Robinet's open-mouthed astonishment, the long-winded preacher silent for the first time all morning. Chandler Lane and his employees seemed shaken.

Once it became clear that Jo was leaving with the sheriff, the cacophony of voices dampened to a hush. Sam felt sorry for the woman she'd worked with for several days now, watching the downcast eyes and trembling mouth. It took a few minutes for it to sink in that Jane had deceived her all that time, obviously knowing.

"May I speak to her first?" Sam asked outside the department's interrogation room.

She'd caught up with Beau as he was about to open the door. Kent Taylor stood behind.

"I know what you want to ask, Sam. Whether she really had amnesia at all. We'll get to that, but I want to concentrate on the stuff Krystal told us yesterday, too."

Sam fidgeted as Taylor seconded Beau. "Why don't you wait in the observation room while we talk to her? You'll get a chance for personal conversation before it's all over."

Beau seemed taken aback at the glare Sam sent his direction but the responding tightness around his mouth told her that this was, first and foremost, a law enforcement matter. She spun around and walked into the mirrored room that allowed visual and audio observation. Plopping herself into a chair she stewed. Beau entered the interrogation room first, alone. Kent Taylor had slipped into the observation room and stood now beside Sam's chair.

"Mrs. Robinet," Beau said. He offered coffee or a soft drink. Jo declined both.

He began with soft questions: When did she first learn of her husband's death? Where was she when she heard it?

"This morning. The bakery employees said Sam had gone to Zack Robinet's funeral." There were tears in her voice. "I had no memory until last night, but the mention of his name brought it all back."

Beau looked skeptical. "Okay, we'll return to that. You have memories from the past, so let's explore how far back those memories go. Do you remember talking to a prostitute named Krystal?"

Jo said she didn't, but she couldn't meet his eyes as she said it.

Taylor sputtered. "That's bull." He left Sam's side and pushed into the interrogation room, none too quietly. Earlier, he'd been in a hurry to get back to Albuquerque; Beau's slow and easy style wasn't going to suit him.

"Krystal Cordova says you hired her to seduce your husband," Taylor said, not bothering to soften his voice. "She says you knew when and where she would be with him. When she left the room you had ample opportunity to go in there and kill him. I'll be blunt here. To us, it looks like that's exactly what you did."

"What!" Jo's timidity vanished and her eyes flashed. "I absolutely did not kill Zack. That's crazy!"

"Is it? You showed up at the bakery with bruises and scrapes. Looks to us like you confronted him over his infidelity, he got rough with you, you killed him. You figured back in your hometown you could pretend you didn't know anything about it and would find sympathy."

Sam sucked in her breath. That accusation didn't at all fit with the facts. If Jo wanted sympathy, she would have showed up among friends or family. Plus, injecting someone with a lethal drug dose took a lot more planning. His version required that Jo first hire a hooker then—illogically—get angry over the fact that her husband had sex with the woman *and* show up at their hotel with a syringe already loaded with heroin.

Beau left Taylor in charge and came into the observation room where Sam was trying to process what she'd heard. He placed a gentle hand on her shoulder.

"Sorry I got a little short with you earlier," he said.

"What's he *doing* in there?" Sam asked, nodding toward the mirrored window.

"Taylor is just trying to rattle Mrs. Robinet, either to get a true confession of the events or to find out how real her amnesia was."

"I spent a lot of time with that woman," Sam said. "I can't believe she would resort to heroin to kill the man. Beaning him over the head with a heavy ashtray—maybe. But hard drugs? I just don't see it."

"At risk of ticking you off again, honey, you didn't spot her as a woman who would hire a hooker either."

"Neither did you."

"True. That's why we can't assume things about a suspect. We have to ask the questions and gather the evidence."

Okay. She got that.

Taylor's voice grew louder, his quiet-cop persona well hidden now. When he slammed a hand down on the tabletop, Beau moved toward the door.

"Time for good cop to show up again. This time, why don't you come? Now that he's scared her a bit maybe we'll make more progress."

Sam followed willingly.

Jo stood when they entered and Taylor left. She came straight to Sam and hugged her.

"Oh, Sam. I didn't want it to come out like this. It's not at all like I planned. When I heard about the funeral I knew my son would be there. I only wanted to get a look at him, to see if he was all right. The disguise was stupid—things I grabbed out of a charity bin. I only wanted to see my little boy—" Jo sobbed, leaning into Sam's arms.

Beau stood by and let Sam make some there-there noises to calm their suspect.

"Let's sit down and maybe you can tell us more about

what you planned," Sam said. She suggested Beau get them some bottled water.

When he was gone she turned to Jo. "I have a hard time not thinking of you as Jane, the chocolate maker. Having amnesia must be a very weird feeling. Did your memory come back all at once or a little at a time?"

"A little at a time." She wiped her eyes with the sleeve of her shirt.

So Becky wasn't entirely wrong about Jane.

"When?"

"Day before yesterday, as I was working with the chocolate I had a vision of making chocolate rabbits for my son's Easter basket. Seeing the chocolate molds at your shop triggered a lot of things for me."

"I want to know more about that—really, *all* about it. Where you learned so much and who trained you ... but right now we need to concentrate on what the police need to know. About what happened to Zack. You don't really want to be locked up and go through the whole legal system, do you?"

Jo shook her head and another tear slid down her left cheek.

"So, anything you can tell us that could be backed up with facts ... that would be helpful."

"I did hire Krystal. That part is true. I don't know how to explain this, especially to anyone who's happily married like you, Sam." She stared at a spot in the middle of the laminated table top. "Zack was so charming and thoughtful in the beginning. He sent flowers after every date along with these beautiful notes saying what a memorable time he'd had. Such a gentleman. And our wedding—he completely understood my dream of a big wedding and a dream honeymoon to Hawaii. He bought me jewelry and clothes and we always stayed in the best hotels. This was even before the business became as successful as it is now. We weren't rich in those early years but I had the feeling he would spend every last dime, if that's what it took, to make me happy and comfortable."

Sam knew her expression must look doubtful; she couldn't figure out how this connected to recent events.

"Then Zack changed. At first, the abuse was verbal— little digs about what I'd chosen to wear that day or how dinner turned out. I didn't even realize my self-esteem was crumbling away until the first time he hit me. We'd been married nearly two years by then and I was seven months pregnant with Bentlee." Jo's voice became steadier as she related the events.

"My gosh, Jo."

"I couldn't believe it happened. He was so happy about the baby and I really—stupidly—believed he'd tripped and accidentally struck me. *I* actually apologized to *him*! It happened the second time when Bentlee was about a month old. Zack and I were both worn out from waking up during the night, and one evening I complained, saying I really needed to go to bed early. Zack struck out and punched me in the stomach. I fell, and I think I slept right there on the couch, numb and shocked."

Her voice had become almost a monotone, reciting facts without emotion. "Increasingly, I felt stuck. By the time five years went by, I knew he would never stand for me taking Bentlee away. The only thing that saved my sanity was when Zack went out of town on business. He and Chandler were all wrapped up in developing Infinite Star Fighter so there was a lot of travel. I savored those nights alone when he wouldn't force himself on me in bed. If I didn't pretend to enjoy the sex he would just get violent and keep me awake half the night screaming obscenities and punching me in the ribs or stomach. And then it would end, suddenly. After the attacks he would be completely sweet and solicitous, as if nothing had happened. The next day I would get a new fur coat or diamond bracelet or something."

She look up at Sam. "It's humiliating to admit this but I felt like a whore, trading sex for all those expensive trinkets. Sometime after I first had that thought I began to consider hiring a stand-in. I mean, if Zack had someone else to take to bed and to buy things for, maybe he would leave me alone." Her voice cracked. "That's the *only* reason I did it—found Krystal and paid her. I actually hoped he would spend even more time with her."

"You only wanted her to sleep with him? You must have imagined how nice it would be if he died. He would never hit you or force himself on you again." Sam knew Beau and Kent were behind the mirror, catching every word of this.

"It's one thing to imagine it, Sam, but that's not something I would ever have actually done."

"So the idea of Zack dying never came up in conversation with Krystal?" Sam wasn't sure what prompted her to ask. It was as if Beau were feeding her the questions telepathically.

Jo went completely still, her eyelids lightly closed.

"It did? You talked to her again, didn't you? Once the 'job' had become an affair?"

"Not in the way you're thinking," Jo said. Her voice was now barely a whisper.

Sam could practically feel the men in the next room holding their breaths in order to hear all this. She wished it were Beau asking the questions. He would know which way to go next. But she knew if that door opened the mood would be broken and Jo might very well end the interview by calling for a lawyer.

She continued, hoping for the best. "Okay, Jo. If not in that way, in what way did you and Krystal talk about Zack dying?"

"Krystal introduced me to a friend of hers, a man who owns a bar here in town."

"Ray Belatoni?"

"Oh, god, you already know about him?"

Sam nodded. "Tell me what he has to do with this."

"Up to that point Krystal had seemed fairly innocent. In a way she was just this sweet girl who looked great all dressed up and who enjoyed pleasing men. Just Zack's type." Jo took a deep breath and let it out. "Once Ray came into the picture our business deal became tough-business. He demanded that Krystal get more money for her services."

"He was her pimp?"

"I don't think so. I got the impression he was more like a boyfriend who didn't mind sharing her around, as long as she brought in lots of money. I'm pretty sure he dealt drugs out of that bar of his. He might have gotten Krystal hooked so he had a strong hold over her."

"Did you give them more money?"

"Yes, at first. Then the tone of the conversations turned bad. They threatened to tell Zack exactly what was up—and they claimed they had proof—that I had paid them to kill him. I didn't! I swear it. But it would certainly look that way and he would be furious. If he didn't beat me to death himself, he would have told the police and done it in such a way that I would go to prison and never see my son again."

"Blackmail."

"Exactly. They weren't above making up any kind of story—I could see that. I was afraid of them but I was more afraid of what Zack would do."

"What did you do?"

"I decided to get out. Bentlee started school last month so I knew he was safely out of the house. Zack was hard on Bentlee but he *never* treated our son the way he treated other people. With Bentlee he was more intent on showing him the good life and spoiling him rotten."

"So you planned to move out? Go somewhere else?"

She nodded and wiped her face again. "I have relatives on the east coast. It's where I grew up and even though my parents are both gone now, an uncle still owns the chocolate shop my father started when I was a kid. I grew up making cream centers and nut centers, tempering chocolate by the gallons. I figured I could go there, where Zack or Krystal and Ray would never find me."

"When was this?"

"Last week. Zack would be in Vegas over the weekend so he wouldn't know for several days I'd left home. I packed a couple of bags and went to gas up my car. That's when Ray caught me. It was very early in the morning—the sun wasn't even up yet—and wouldn't you know it but he was the only other person at that gas station. He pulled right up beside my car and I could see him looking at the suitcases in the back. He put it together right away. When I left, he followed me. My heart was pounding and I was so scared.

"I started for home but there are some stretches of road out there without much traffic and I decided that wasn't smart, so I looped around back to the center of town. He just stayed behind me. I couldn't make a turn without him being right there. About two streets over from your bakery he rammed my car—hard—with his big pickup truck. I whacked my head on the steering wheel and blacked out. It was the last thing I knew."

"Until now," Sam prompted. "You're remembering it now."

"Trying to get my memory back is all I've thought of during those nights in that motel. By the way, thank you for that, Sam. I didn't know it but you probably saved my life by putting me somewhere that neither Krystal or Ray would ever think to look." She gave a tentative smile. "I began to remember little things, mostly about Zack and me and the good times. When Zack didn't come back, I just ... I didn't know how to handle that. His parents have never exactly been nice to me. If I contacted my son there would be a record and someone would know. If I traveled I would need to use my credit cards. When someone is following you, it feels like they could be anywhere, everywhere. I couldn't stay at home. Making chocolates in your shop was the only thing that felt safe to me."

By this time, Jo's eyes were streaming again and Sam felt herself welling up a little at the idea that she had unknowingly provided a safe haven for this poor woman. She sensed movement behind her and realized Beau had softly opened the door.

"I didn't kill my husband, Sheriff," Jo said between sobs. "Please help me prove that."

"Do you think Krystal and Ray did it?" Beau asked.

"I have no idea."

He told Jo she was free to go as long as she stayed in town.

"What about Ray Belatoni?" she asked, pulling tissues from the box two at a time and swabbing her face with them. "He was ready to kill me in my car that morning."

"More likely he just wanted to scare you out of leaving town. He wanted your money, not your life," Sam suggested.

Beau spoke up. "Now that you can use your credit cards again, I'd suggest you check into a different hotel, someplace with security. Keep your eyes open. We'll be questioning Belatoni again."

Sam walked with Jo to the ladies room where she washed her face and got her emotions under control. "I can give you a ride, if you like. Just give me a minute to tell Beau."

When she walked back into the interrogation room, Beau and Kent Taylor were deep in conversation, trying to find the holes in Jo's story.

"I'm wondering what happened to Jo's car that was run off the road?" Beau said. "Our department has no record of it. That was one thing we checked when looking for Mrs. Robinet in the first place, to notify her of Zack's death—vehicle information, credit cards, the whole thing."

"*Supposedly* run off the road," Taylor added. "I'm taking nothing at face value here."

"I believe her," Sam said. "I've worked with her nearly a week. I think she's being genuine about this."

She realized from Taylor's skeptical look exactly how weak that sounded. Yes, she'd worked with Jo a week, and she hadn't even figured out that Jane Doe had recovered part of her memories. She decided not to tell the men she planned to take Jo to get resettled.

Chapter 15

L ife would be simpler if I had some money and identification," Jo said as they climbed into Sam's bakery van outside the sheriff's office. "Can we go by my house before the bakery?"

"Are you sure you want to work today? It's been a very rough morning. Maybe you should just settle in at home, relax and have a few days to yourself."

In the passenger seat, Jo shuddered. "I don't want to stay there. I was ready to walk away. I can still do that. But I need to see Bentlee and talk things out. I can't let his memories of today end with me being taken away by the sheriff. Would you mind sticking around while I shower and put on something that didn't come from the Goodwill?"

She gave a half-chuckle. "God, my life has been such a disaster recently."

"I'll help you get organized. Beau's suggestion of staying at a hotel with security is a good one. I think we'll all feel better once you are settled somewhere safe."

Sam followed Jo's directions and pulled up to an impressive house on Goldenrod Lane. A three-car garage faced the road and the ranch-style adobe house spread across most of the acre on which it sat.

"You don't have keys, do you?" she asked when her van came to a stop.

"There's a hidden key. I hope I remember the alarm code accurately."

Jo led the way around the side of the garage and approached a cottonwood tree with a small birdhouse nailed to the trunk. She moved a panel in its side and pulled out a ring with several keys. Taking a deep breath, she walked toward the front door, impressively carved with a deep-relief Zia symbol.

"You do it, Sam. I don't know why I'm nervous about this. No one is here."

Sam took the key, which slid easily into the well-oiled lock and she opened the door. A small panel to her right began beeping, its red light flashing.

"Better enter the code quickly," she told Jo, who stepped in and pressed numbers. The red light turned to green.

The foyer contained a padded bench upholstered in Indian-blanket fabric, a table with a bowl for keys and mail, and a couple of potted plants that seemed distinctly in need of water. A wide arch opened into a greatroom where a big screen TV was the focal point and Sam could see a state-of-the-art kitchen. Jo stood in the doorway a couple of long beats, her face unreadable.

"I fully intended to never enter this house again," she

said quietly. "My bags held my most practical clothing and I'd drawn out a bunch of cash—enough to get me through until I could have an attorney inform Zack I was leaving him. It's all gone now. I can't believe I never even made it out of town."

She wandered into the big room, her hand trailing across the back of a cushy leather sofa. Something on the granite counter top caught her eye.

"What's this doing here?" she said, striding to pick up something. "My old cell phone. I didn't leave this here. It's been put away in a drawer for months."

"Maybe Zack got it out?"

"Trying to track me down," she said, a bitter edge to her voice. "Just like him. He would have immediately noticed my things missing and read something illicit into it. Probably thought I would have another man's number programmed into this."

She set the phone down, then picked it up again. "I might as well get it activated again, since I have no idea where my purse and my new phone are."

"You said something about getting money and ID?"

"Oh. Yes." She led the way through another arched doorway to a master suite. Behind a painting that Sam would swear was an original RC Gorman, Jo twirled the dial of a wall safe. She pulled out a large brown envelope and a stack of cash bound with a paper bank wrapper.

"That will keep me going awhile," she said about the cash. She dumped the contents of the envelope and separated a passport and MasterCard from the rest of the items. An oversized parchment-colored page looked identical to Sam's own marriage license from the county. Jo stuck hers back inside the envelope without a second glance.

Sam held her hand out. "Beau will want to hang onto the passport until he's sure he has caught Zack's killer. Sorry."

Jo paused before handing it over with a sigh. "I suppose you're right."

"I'm really sorry, Jo, but you do understand don't you?"

Jo didn't respond.

"If what you told him checks out, I'm sure you'll get it back soon." She didn't mention that when the real killer was caught Jo would probably be required to testify about everything she'd told them today. It was unlikely Beau would want her leaving the country for a long time.

"Mind if I look around while you're packing?" Sam asked. "Maybe Zack left something behind that would be an important clue for Beau."

"Knock yourself out."

Sam walked through the foyer to the greatroom and kitchen. Both rooms were spotlessly organized. Either the Robinets were a very neat couple or a maid had come earlier in the week. Down a hall, she found a boy's bedroom and guest room done in Southwestern diagonal prints. A door from the kitchen led to a pantry and another to a garage. She reached for the wall light switch. Two of the three bays held cars—a shiny new black Corvette and a white Lexus crossover. She pulled the door shut.

Wait a minute. If Zack drove a car to Albuquerque and the Corvette belonged to Bentlee, as Beau had mentioned, the Lexus had to be Jo's.

But she'd claimed that it was wrecked.

Sam's heart thudded. She turned and listened for a moment, hearing faint sounds of Jo moving about in the master bedroom. She ducked out to the garage, closing the door softly behind her. Circling the Lexus, she saw no evidence that it had been involved in an accident. The light wasn't great in here, but still, even a scrape down the side would have showed. She walked around the vehicle twice before it occurred to her to look inside.

She prayed it wasn't equipped with some kind of alarm that would go off when she touched the handle. Decided to take the chance. The car wasn't locked and the door opened with that solid, heavy feel of quality. There in the back were two suitcases. Nice designer luggage, Sam noted.

What was going on here?

A scream ripped through the cavernous space.

Sam bumped her head on the door frame, half expecting to face a drawn weapon. She backed away from the car, staring at Jo who stood transfixed in the kitchen doorway.

"My car! What's it—?"

"Doing here? I'd say that's a great question, one that the sheriff will want to know the answer to."

"Sam, I *swear* the last time I saw this car was when I ran away from it. The back was bashed from Ray's pickup truck and the front had hit a concrete fence post. It was *not* drivable."

Sam left the door standing open, wondering what to believe. Jo's story had been so convincing. She pulled out her phone and told Beau about the discovery.

By the time she hung up Jo was crying again.

"How did this get here?" she asked between sobs. "It was wrecked, really wrecked."

Sam didn't know whether to comfort her or slap her into silence.

"It's like someone's trying to drive me insane," Jo blubbered. "It's the kind of thing Zack would have done in his cruel moments but how could that be? He was in Albuquerque."

She sat on the step with the kitchen door open behind her, holding her head in her hands.

"Beau is sending his forensic people to dust the car for prints and check it over. I'm sure they'll find out who drove it here." Including you, if you are lying about this whole thing. "Meanwhile, he suggested we stick with the original plan and get you into a hotel. I'll take you."

"I don't know," Jo said. Her voice had a ragged quality to it. "I can't think. Maybe I *am* going insane. I feel like everything is spinning out of control."

Sam walked over and sat down beside her. "For now, don't try to figure it out. Let's just get you to a safe place for a few days and let you rest and absorb it all. It's been a horrible week for you."

Jo leaned into Sam's shoulder. "It has," she agreed with a resigned sigh.

"Come on. Let's go." Sam led her into the house, locking the kitchen door behind them, pocketing Jo's set of house keys.

In the foyer sat a small wheeled suitcase and a purse.

"Did you come up with everything you need for a few days?"

Jo nodded, looking a little numb at this point.

"I was thinking I'd take you to El Monte. It's quiet and private and visitors have to enter through a lobby. Is that okay?"

Jo allowed Sam to take the handle of the small bag and lock the front door, following along like a puppy that had recently been whipped.

Thirty minutes later, Sam was wheeling the suitcase into a third story room where she checked the windows and informed the desk not to let any calls through without first checking with Ms. Robinet.

"I still want to come to work tomorrow," Jo said, coming out of the bathroom with a clean face and freshly brushed hair.

"Call me in the morning. I can pick you up but I want to be sure you're ready for this. You might change your mind and decide to simply hang out in this luxurious room and rest up for a few days." Sam fully expected Jo would soon want to return home. She faced many adjustments right now.

The sheriff's office was on her way to Sweet's Sweets so Sam stopped in to drop off Jo Robinet's keys.

"The car was parked inside her own garage all this time?" Beau asked.

"I only know it's there now. Jo swears the last time she saw it was after Ray Belatoni ran her off the road. She ran away without even taking her purse, apparently, because that's how she ended up walking into my bakery last Thursday morning." Sam recalled Jo's torn blouse and the scrapes on her face.

"But you said there's no damage to the car, no sign it was in an accident."

"I sure couldn't see anything."

He tapped his pencil against the desktop. "I guess I better bring her in for more questions."

"Beau, I think she's telling the truth. You should have seen how upset she was when she saw the car there. It was genuinely a shock to her."

"Or maybe she freaked out because you found the car. It's the key that makes her whole story fall apart."

Sam felt herself bristle. "Are you saying I don't know when someone's lying to me?"

He gave her a long, steady stare. "I'm only saying you seem to have a blind spot about this woman. Maybe you've gotten close to Jo because of working together and you're not seeing the obvious."

He *was* questioning her judgment. She dropped Jo's keys on his desk and walked out of his office. In the squad room, Lisa the forensics technician was checking supplies in the black boxy kit she carried to all her assignments. Beau came out of his office and handed the key ring and an assignment sheet with the address and details of the tests she was to conduct. Her glance wavered between Sam and Beau before she ducked out the back door with her things.

"If Jo knew the car was there, why didn't she try to keep me from going inside with her? Why didn't she hide her vehicle in a better place?" she said defiantly.

"For that matter, why didn't she just go home and let herself in and drive herself to the funeral in her own car, wearing her own clothes?" he countered.

"Okay, you're right. None of it makes sense. We're on the same team here. I would never take someone else's side against you." She reached out to touch his hand.

"The forensic results will tell us something," he said. "Meanwhile, I thought I'd drop by Zack's former office again. I overheard Chandler Lane saying something about holding a small gathering at the offices for business acquaintances and customers to stop by for a toast to Zack. The sales team will be back from Vegas, and that could get interesting. Want to go along?"

Sam called the bakery where Jen assured her everything

was fine. "Spend the afternoon with Beau if you want. We're rolling along and it's only a couple more hours anyway."

Rolling along, but there was still work to be done, Sam thought. The deadline for the big order of chocolates was only four days away. At least she would have Jo's help again tomorrow—unless Beau decided to arrest her.

The parking lot at the Appleton Center was full so Beau took a spot at the curb. Voices and waves of very un-grief-stricken laughter filled the vestibule and hallways as they made their way to the second floor.

"I'd heard that Zack wasn't well liked. Add booze and maybe his death is a cause for celebration," Beau said under his breath. "I guess we'll keep our eyes open for whoever's celebrating the loudest, huh?"

"Maybe it's just a case of everyone showing up for a free party."

Beau had pulled out the little notebook he carried, reviewing names he'd been given on his previous two visits. He showed her the list. "Remember, we want to know who might have been angry enough with Zack to have killed him. Formal questioning isn't going to happen here, but pay attention to conversations and attitudes. The two sales reps were out of town when I came before, so I want to chat with each of them. I've spoken with the partner and the bookkeeper but you might see if either of them has anything interesting to say."

"Got it." Sam caught Jo's name several times as they approached the offices. The missing wife's sudden appearance today had apparently sparked a lot of talk.

The double doors to ChanZack Innovations stood wide open and a half-dozen people had stepped out into the corridor. Beau recognized the two programmers he had interviewed earlier; three young women appeared to have the nerdy guys completely enthralled with a story about their favorite club in Santa Fe. The men nodded to Beau as he and Sam entered the office's reception area.

"Oh my god, I know, right?" A trilling giggle escaped a teenage girl who apparently had something stronger than soda in her plastic cup.

From across the room Chandler Lane noticed Beau and shot the girl a strong warning look. Zack's business partner strode over and plucked the cup from her grasp, setting it on Amber's desk and signaling to someone else, a woman apparently responsible for the girl's attendance.

"Sorry about that," Lane said to Beau. "Believe me, we do not condone underage drinking. Jamie will see that she gets home safely."

"Jamie Phillips?" Beau asked. One of the two company sales reps who had recently returned from the Las Vegas trade show.

"Yes," said the woman who approached. She had the build of a waif, with spiky black hair and huge blue eyes. Certainly, she did not appear old enough to be the mother of the teen. She took the girl's hand with a grip that cautioned her to stay quiet. "I apologize for my sister's behavior."

"I wouldn't want to see either of you get in trouble for doing anything illegal," Beau said. His expression remained friendly in a no-nonsense way. "Meanwhile, Ms. Phillips, I've been wanting to speak with you. Privately, if possible. It's about the day Zack died."

"Really, Sheriff—" Chandler Lane sputtered a little.

"I realize this is a social occasion," Beau said, eyeing the conference room where a large table was loaded with food and a credenza served as a bar. "But please understand that my department is trying to figure out what happened. To your boss." This last with firm eye contact toward Jamie Phillips.

"We can go into Ed's and my office," she said, smiling at Chandler and steering her young sister into the company of Helen Melrose, the bookkeeper.

Jamie hit the wall switch and bright fluorescents came on overhead.

"What a week," she said, ushering Beau and Sam into the large office she shared with the other sales rep. She shuffled a couple of empty easels aside and found chairs, which she pulled up to a table stacked with poster-board flats. "I just got in from Vegas last night. I apologize that the place is so disorganized."

"Completely understandable," Sam said.

"Chandler told me you were bringing out a new game?"

"Yeah—Star Fighter Hotties. It's a companion product to Infinite Star Fighter. It's testing really well in the girls' ten-to-fourteen market. It's why I've brought Cass here—my little sister. She's given us some decent ideas on how to bring the sixteen-and-up girls into the fold. Basically, we're going for a game that's interactive with the one the boys are so crazy about. You know, girls and boys … get them talking about something other than sex and drugs at that age."

Sam couldn't exactly picture how a game called Hotties was about anything except sex, but who knew?

"Chandler told me Zack had been pretty hard on you and Ed, really pushing to get the ad campaign done?"

"No kidding. He's like a tyrant—I mean yeah, he was … a … very *driven* man, at times."

"To the point of becoming abusive?"

She shook her head and the dark spikes of hair didn't budge. "Zack could get loud. He was willing to work 24/7 to get a thing done and he couldn't see why everyone else wouldn't do the same. The argument 'some of us have a life' absolutely did not matter to him."

"So, somebody around here might have gotten sick of his behavior and thought the company would be better off without him?"

Jamie held both hands up. "I didn't say that at all. ChanZack pays well—*really* well when you consider the bonuses and retirement contributions. With that nice paycheck comes the knowledge that you'll have to put up with some extra shit. That's all."

"Fair enough. But there might have been someone who didn't look at the situation as practically as you do. Maybe Zack crossed the line with somebody else in the office?"

Her mouth did a little twisty move as she considered the question. "Sorry, I really can't think of anyone who would have taken it that far."

Beau knew an almost-rehearsed answer when he heard one. He waited, not letting up with his eye contact.

"Well, J.B. has been stomping around for weeks because Zack rode his case pretty hard."

One friend goes under the bus.

"But, really, I'd look most closely at Amber. There's no such thing as a purely friendly failed romance, is there?"

Chapter 16

Beau dismissed Jamie, asking her not to discuss their chat and to send in Ed Archuleta, the other sales rep. Sam busied herself by flipping through the poster boards on the table, wondering how ads that depicted cartoonish avatars with breasts that bulged from their shiny skin-tight suits could possibly make either boys or girls think of anything other than sex.

"I'm definitely getting old," she said, showing one of the Star Fighter Hotties posters to Beau.

Ed Archuleta looked like the male version of Jamie Phillips—young, trendy clothes, bed-head hair.

Beau posed the same questions and Ed essentially gave the same assurances as Jamie. Yes, Zack was hard on them. He was hard on everyone. You didn't take it personally.

Sam noticed despite his salesman smile and all the right words, a twitching muscle in his jaw revealed a lot of tension beneath it all. She mentioned it to Beau after Ed left.

"Yeah, the guy was definitely selling me on an idea he didn't fully believe in, wasn't he?"

"What about Jamie's statement about Amber?"

"The receptionist. Yeah, but I've seen Amber and Chandler in the same room. He's the one on her list now. My guess is that there was probably a little fling with Zack but being married he was too complicated to stay with. Chandler, on the other hand, could be prime husband material and she'll want to reel him in before he has presence of mind to suggest a pre-nup. She wouldn't need to get rid of Zack to reach her goal."

They left the empty office behind and went to rejoin the party, noticing the crowd was about half the previous size.

Chandler Lane met them near the reception desk. "Sorry about that little thing with Cass earlier. None of us realized she'd spiked her Coke. Jamie's taking her home."

Beau waved it off. "As long as she's not driving, she's the least of my worries right now."

"Yeah, mine too, actually," Chandler said. "Can I offer you guys a drink? Something to eat? We have tons of food in there."

Beau shook his head, scanning the remaining crowd with an eye toward whom he could talk to next. Sam edged to the food table and found herself next to a man who was loading his plate with sliced deli meats, cheeses and pickles. Judging by his girth, he probably should have stuck with the cucumbers and carrot sticks.

"Could have knocked me over with a feather when Jo showed up today," said a woman across the table from him.

"Me too," said the chubby guy. "I really thought she'd finally had the good sense to get out of this town."

"Really?" The woman had come to the cookie platter

and didn't seem inclined to leave it. "You know, I always thought she loved Taos, although she did become a little uppity once they moved into that big house."

"Me, I was surprised to see her go there." The man had eaten half the goodies on his tiny plate and was stacking it high again.

Chandler Lane walked into the conference room, Beau beside him. "Go where?" Chandler asked.

The chubby man suddenly had a mouthful and wagged his head back and forth with an I-can't-talk-right-now movement.

Chandler turned to Beau. "Meet Will Valmora, Zack's golfing buddy."

Valmora swallowed hugely, wiped his hand on his napkin and extended it. "Sheriff. I recognize you from your last election campaign."

"Sheriff Cardwell is working with the Albuquerque police to figure out what happened to Zack," Chandler said.

"Yeah, wow, what a shocker this was," said Valmora.

"You knew Zack pretty well, then?"

"Golf once or twice a week. Now and then we'd bring the wives. Mine loves golf. Not so sure Jo did, though."

"A minute ago you said something about being surprised Jo hadn't left him," Sam said, stepping to Beau's side in an attempt to look more sheriff-wifely than bystander-ish.

Will gave her a second look, realizing his earlier conversation had probably revealed too much, considering he didn't know who he was standing next to.

"Well, yeah …" he said. "I just meant, you know, I felt for her. Zack could be kind of hard on her."

Kind of? From Jo's version of the story, Sam knew it was downright abusive.

"I imagine the game can get pretty tense," Beau said. "I never got very good at golf myself, so I sort of understand the pressure."

"Oh, it does. Picture a whole bag of clubs being pitched into the pond. Hers. Jo stood there red-faced and didn't say a word."

Public humiliation. Did this move Jo back to the top of Beau's suspect list? Sam wondered as she picked up a sugar cookie.

"After that, my wife refused to golf with the pair of them. I considered cutting Zack off and finding another partner but he and I were so evenly matched, it was what made the game fun. When I went on playing with Zack, my wife joined a ladies group."

Maybe Valmora had caught a lot of flack at home, but still, golf surely wasn't a vital enough reason for either Will Valmora or his wife to have tracked Zack down and murdered him. Sam nibbled at the edges of the heavy sugar cookie, privately thinking her own were much better, while she mulled over the possible suspects in what she hoped was the same way Beau would do.

Valmora's eyes kept edging toward the platters of food and he had just spooned up a big scoop of crab dip when Beau's phone rang. Sam saw the name Lisa on the screen. Beau excused himself and walked out to the corridor to take it. Less than a minute later, he made eye contact and gave a nod that he needed to leave. She excused herself and offered condolences all around before joining him.

"Lisa's at the Robinet house, gathering evidence from Jo's car. She wants me to come out there and see something."

A knot of dread crept into Sam's gut. Or maybe it was just the sugar cookie.

Fifteen minutes later they pulled up outside the Robinet home. Lisa's department vehicle was parked at one of the garage doors.

"Sheriff, I wanted you to see this for yourself, not that you wouldn't believe my report," Lisa said when she met them at the open door.

"I trust you." The tech was young but very good at her job. He'd never found fault with her thoroughness.

"But still … It's evidence that will come out in court, so two sets of eyes are better than one."

He nodded. Sam stayed near the rear of the parked Lexus while Beau followed Lisa to the open driver's door and shined her high beam flashlight inside.

"There are no prints. At all." Lisa said "You can see where I've dusted. Steering wheel, clear. Gearshift, clear. Dashboard, clear. I even did the edges of the leather seats, where a lot of people touch as they're getting situated inside a car. There's nothing."

"The whole car's been wiped down."

"Exactly."

Sam piped up. "If Jo had been in accident she wouldn't have had the presence of mind to do all that."

"No," Beau agreed. "She wouldn't."

He walked around the car, pulling out his own flashlight to check it. "But this car shows no sign of being bashed or scraped. Even the most minor contact would show up on a paint job like this one. There are suitcases in the back, just like she said."

"How does this fit with what she told us?" Sam asked.

"Maybe she packed her stuff intending to leave. Went to Albuquerque and got rid of Zack. Maybe something he did that day set her off."

"She could have packed the car," Lisa said, "then changed her mind."

Sam felt her blood pressure rising. "It doesn't fit. She was ready to leave an abusive man. She had him fixed up with another woman as a distraction. She would have gotten as far away from here as she could. She said she intended to go to the east coast where she has relatives. If her story about Ray Belatoni running her off the road isn't true, why didn't she just follow through and get out of New Mexico?"

"Good point. But if it *is* true, why isn't the car damaged and why aren't her prints inside it?"

Lisa had gotten down on the floor, shining her flashlight into the wheel wells of the car. She scooted around from the front of the vehicle to the back, lying down to face the undercarriage as she reached the rear bumper.

"I may have something here, boss."

Beau got down, craning his neck to see where the light pointed. Sam watched his good pants become instantly covered in dust.

"Here," said Lisa, "and there. Those are new parts. There's no wear on the axle and barely a thin layer of dust inside this panel. The one on the other side has some erosion and flecks of mud."

"We had a lot of rain in August and it takes a very thorough undercarriage wash to get rid of all the mud."

"Exactly."

"This car has been repaired, very recently," Beau said.

Sam's pulse quickened. "Here's a possible scenario. Ray Belatoni runs Jo off the road and she takes off running. When he can't catch her he goes back to her car and figures he can cover his tracks somehow."

"By enlisting the help of his buddy, Donny Vargas,"

Beau said. "The dealership could get replacement parts and make the repairs in just a few days' time. Vargas and Belatoni are sharp enough to know that they want to erase any trace of their own involvement with this car, so one of them drives it here, puts it in the garage using Jo's opener, and they wipe down the car completely."

"Don't dealerships have to report extensive damage repairs?" Lisa asked.

"They usually do, for insurance purposes. But Vargas could have possibly worked on this one after hours, or he fudged the records by making up a story about the owner not having insurance or not wanting the wreck on her driving record. He's seen it all, believe me. He could come up with something."

Lisa had her camera out, capturing photos of all the details under the car.

"Beau, what do you think?" Sam asked. "Did those two men simply want to cover up a traffic accident, or could this be part of a plan where one of them killed Zack and they decided to frame Jo for the murder?"

"If Jo's story is true, Ray Belatoni's motive was blackmail." Beau had pulled out a notebook and was tapping his pen against it as he voiced his thoughts. "Vargas, of course, had been angry enough at Zack to do almost anything. His rage might have built until he actually killed Zack. But I can't quite see how Vargas killing Zack connects to Belatoni running Jo off the road. I need to think about this."

Lisa scooted out from under the car and began snapping photos of the interior with the hatch open, getting shots of the suitcases inside.

"Let's have this towed to the department garage," Beau

suggested. "I'll get you some extra help and you can go through it inch by inch."

Lisa sent him a grateful look and began packing her kit. Sam realized she hadn't checked in with the bakery in awhile, so she plucked her phone from her pack. It had been on silent mode during the funeral and wake and she discovered she had messages from both Kelly and Zoë.

Kelly didn't answer her phone. Zoë suggested a glass of wine together if Sam happened to be out and about.

"I'm with Beau on a forensic scene right now," Sam said. She glanced at the time and asked Beau when he thought he would be free.

"Not until late," he told her. "If I can't round up another forensic person to help Lisa I should go along to process this car. I'll drop you at home first."

"How about the bakery instead?" It was closer and she could pick up her van. She gave Zoë an estimate of an hour before she could be there.

"Stay for dinner then," Zoë suggested. "I heard Beau say he would be busy and I've got a pot of my green chile stew on the stove."

No one in her right mind would turn down Zoë's green chile stew. Sam agreed without hesitation.

* * *

The tow truck driver couldn't possibly be any slower, Beau thought as he waited in his cruiser at the department's inadequate impound garage. With no luck at finding someone with more than minimal forensics training to assist Lisa in processing the Lexus, he'd been forced to take that task himself. After dropping Sam at her vehicle he'd come here, expecting the truck and Lisa's department Suburban to already be here. No matter—he could use the time to return Kent Taylor's call, which he'd missed.

"Just got back to Albuquerque," Kent said, "and I've been reviewing the security tapes from the Kingston Arms. Our guys narrowed down the hours of the day for me. Now we're trying to figure out exactly what we're seeing."

"Anyone we know?"

"Well, not Josephine Robinet, if that's what you mean. I'm looking at the footage for the entire afternoon and evening." He murmured something as he apparently forwarded the tape. "Here's Zack and Krystal walking down the hall together and going into a room. Unfortunately, his room was at the far end of the hall away from the camera. There are these little alcoves up and down the hall and each one leads to two rooms. So it's impossible to know if, say, a person stepping out of our sight went into room 933 or room 935."

Beau tried to fix an image in his head that fit Taylor's description.

"The ninth floor has the pricier, deluxe rooms and a couple of small suites, so there wasn't a lot of traffic. I've got a couple of businessmen arriving and never leaving their own rooms. Another one who comes and goes. Krystal is pretty identifiable—the only female with that fluffy hairdo. She leaves and comes back at pretty much the intervals she described to us. Even has the pizza box when she comes back. And it's not but a couple minutes before she bolts from the room and runs to the elevator with a wad of clothing bunched up in her arms."

"That fits with her story, all right."

"Okay, let's see here … I've got an unknown male who took the elevator to the ninth floor then walked toward Zack's room. Again, can't say for sure if he went into 933 or 935 but he didn't stay long and he never returned all night. Not exactly the movements a guest would make."

"Can you tell if he used a keycard or did Zack let him into the room?"

"Can't tell. It's those damn little alcoves."

"I assume you don't recognize him?"

"No, dammit. He's wearing a hat with a fairly wide brim. I think he's aware of the camera because he keeps his head down so there's never a clear look at his face."

"What about stature, gait? Anything familiar there?"

"I'm gonna have our film technician copy and send you this short clip. You know these people better than I do. Maybe you can tell."

The lead seemed skimpy—after all, a guy walking down the hall in a hotel could be anybody in the world—but Beau agreed to take a look.

The tow truck hauling Jo Robinet's Lexus arrived just then, followed by Lisa in her Suburban. By the time the luxury car was offloaded, Beau had received a message from Taylor with thirty seconds of video attached. He watched it while Lisa pulled a stack of evidence envelopes from her kit and began earnestly gathering bits and pieces from the interior of Jo's car. She would use sticky tape to pluck up hairs, fabric fibers, skin cells—anything that could later be used to tie the occupant(s) of the car to the case.

On the video, Beau understood Taylor's frustration at not being able to see what went on within those little alcoves. They were no more than twenty-four inches deep, but a person and his actions disappeared from camera view the instant he stepped toward any of the guestroom doors. The man in the hat was no exception. There was no way to say positively that he even entered the room. He could have been standing in the alcove, although it was unlikely, for the full five minutes he vanished from view. Instead, Beau gave his attention to watching the man walk down the corridor and back, memorizing the way he carried himself. Something about him seemed familiar.

Chapter 17

Sam handed bowls to Zoë who ladled them full of her hearty stew, so fragrant with onions and meat that it nearly made Sam's knees buckle.

"It's just the two of us? Where's Darryl?" she asked, carrying one of the hot bowls to Zoë's large round kitchen table.

"Bowling."

"Seriously? Darryl?" Sam had a hard time picturing the tall, white-bearded contractor in a bowling alley. He was much more mountain-man than beer-and-fries and bowling shirts.

"There's a new guy on his crew for this house they're building now who invited him. Darryl likes him and agreed to this before he really thought it through. He'll have a backache in the morning." Zoë brought spoons and napkins to the table and topped up their wine glasses.

Sam blew the steam that was wafting off the stew and scooped up a spoonful of the combination of pork, tomatoes, chile and potato.

"I suppose you heard about the big surprise at Zack Robinet's funeral today," Sam said, waiting a moment for the stew to cool.

"Um, no ... But I'm guessing there's a story. Funerals and surprises don't generally go together."

"Remember Jane, who's been doing chocolates for me at the shop?"

Zoë turned her palms up, a tad impatient at the switch in topics. Sam laughed and told her about the ugly plaid coat and wig. "I tell you, I was completely shocked when someone called her Jo Robinet."

"No! Wow." Zoë had set her spoon down. "So, this Jane who's been in your shop all week ... Did she really have amnesia at all?"

"She says she did. Says she only began to remember things in detail the night before the funeral."

"Do you believe her? I guess I should ask, does Beau believe her?"

Sam shifted a little in her chair.

"Come on, you guys didn't fight about this, did you?"

"Oh, no. It got a little tense but no fight." Not really.

"So where on earth did Jane, uh, Jo learn so much about chocolate? I gather that Zack Robinet's wife wasn't a candy shop owner here in town or you would have already known about her."

"That goes back to her childhood. Her father was a chocolatier somewhere back east."

"So she's still working for you?"

"Yeah. I mean, she's fantastic with the chocolates and has some really creative ideas for a special order we're doing right now."

"And Beau doesn't see her as a suspect in her husband's death? The papers are full of the story of sex and drugs and all kinds of creepy stuff." Zoë looked a little sideways at Sam, questioning the sanity of her keeping Jo on at the shop.

"He's ruled her out completely." Well, Sam *hoped* by now it was completely.

"If you say so." Zoë passed a basket of tortillas and turned back to eating her stew.

Sam's phone rang and the readout said it was Kelly. Perfect timing for a change of subject. She apologized to Zoë and took the call.

"Hey, sorry I missed you earlier," Sam said. "What's up?"

"Not much. I wanted to let you know that Jen dropped off your bank deposit with me when she left the bakery this evening. I'm going out, so I can either leave it here at my house for you to pick up or bring it to work in the morning."

"That's okay," Sam said. "Just bring it when you come to work. I'll break away sometime in the morning and get the money to the bank."

She clicked off the call and looked up to see Zoë watching from the corners of her eyes.

"What?"

"You said 'that's okay' but it didn't really sound so nonchalant as you wanted it to. Kelly's still being coy about the new guy?"

"She is, and I have a sneaking suspicion … something I don't want to admit even to myself."

Zoë gave a long stare. "What on earth would that be?"

The barrier broke. "I think the new boyfriend is Julio Ortiz, my baker. And I keep having these creepy thoughts about his past trouble with the law and the tattoos and the loud motorcycle. Am I horrible, or what?"

Zoë smiled indulgently. "Okay, for one thing, Kelly hasn't even indicated that she's very serious about this new guy. But with you it's something more—are you talking about prejudice? You think you're prejudiced against Julio? That's the dumbest thing I ever heard. I've known you twenty years, Samantha Sweet, and I've never seen a scrap of prejudice in anything you do. You hired the man, you trust your business to him. Is he the picture you had in your mind for a future son-in-law? Probably not. But as you've told me yourself, he's a nice guy who has been nothing but hardworking and honest. There are clean-cut guys out there who don't have that going for them."

Sam immediately thought of everything Jo Robinet had told her about the horrible secrets within her marriage. Yes, Kelly could do a lot worse than Julio.

* * *

Beau handed Lisa the final envelope, which contained a numbered sample of human hair taken from the headrest of the Lexus. He hated forensics. Well, he loved it when a DNA sample or distinctive carpet thread connected the impossible dots in a case and allowed him to make an arrest that would stand up in court. He hated the part where a team had to spend hours collecting, bagging, and labeling those samples. Revise that: he hated the part where he was on that team. He thanked heaven for people like Lisa who thrived on the details. For himself, he'd rather be out in the field, putting clues together and tracking down bad guys.

Since viewing the video from the Albuquerque hotel it was all he could think about. Although Ray Belatoni might be too stocky, both Belatoni and Donny Vargas fit the general height and build of the man in the hat. And he knew of one place where he could go to observe both of them: The Scoreboard.

He saw Lisa to her vehicle and felt pleased that she was excited to get back to her small lab and start running tests. Of course, most of their evidence would have to be sent to the state crime lab in Santa Fe and would fall into a system that was way overloaded. Contrary to what people wanted to believe from television, lab tests rarely led directly to a quick arrest. They could, however, be invaluable in verifying whether Beau's own footwork in finding and bringing in the right suspect had paid off.

Lisa drove away and Beau got into his cruiser. He was halfway to the sports bar when he remembered he was still wearing the suit he'd worn to Zack Robinet's funeral this morning. Maybe that was a good thing. Being out of uniform would allow him to walk a little more unobtrusively into the bar.

He parked his cruiser at the edge of the crowded parking lot, rolled up the sleeves of his dress shirt and did a quick job of brushing off the dust his pants had acquired during the inspection of the Lexus. Running his fingers through his hair he decided he fit the part of a guy having a beer after work well enough.

Ray Belatoni was behind the bar again. He recognized Beau and remembered his preference for a Dos Equis. Beau took a stool near the end and made sure he could see most of the room in the mirror. Krystal and two other overly made-up girls were again at the corner table, this time with some locals who were most likely friends rather than clients. Donny Vargas was one of them. They had been watching one of the big screens across the room but once Vargas made eye contact with Beau, the laughter at the table grew a little more raucous.

Showing me how unconcerned you are? He sipped his Dos Equis, realizing Sam would tease him about being as cool as the suave guy from the commercials. The idea put a little smile on his face.

Belatoni seemed in constant motion, checking on his patrons or clearing empty glasses. Beau thought of the video again but couldn't place the bar owner as the man in the hat. His way of moving behind the bar was entirely different from a guy walking down the corridor in a hotel and there wasn't an easy way to compare. As for Vargas, he was sipping some type of amber liquid from a heavy glass, a beverage that probably wouldn't send him to the men's room for a long time, so Beau was unlikely to observe the way he walked for awhile yet. He memorized each of the men's facial features as he finished his beer.

It was nearing ten p.m. by the time he paid his tab and walked out to the cruiser. Sam was probably home in bed by now so he didn't follow his first impulse to call her. Most of the televised games would be over soon, so odds were The Scoreboard would empty out and he could be home at a reasonable time. He got in his vehicle and moved it across the street where the shadow of a big cottonwood might help conceal the fact that he was watching the bar.

His luck held. Donny Vargas, Krystal and one of the other girls came out about fifteen minutes later. Beau had used the time to review the hotel video on his phone but it wasn't a lot of help. He could not definitively say that Vargas was the man in the hat.

An hour later, six cars remained in the lot at The Scoreboard and Beau had a feeling Ray Belatoni would not leave until the last customer had spent his money. He decided to pack it in for tonight.

At home, Sam was fast asleep. He brushed his teeth and undressed as quietly as possible and snuggled in beside her. When daylight brightened the north-facing window, he discovered Sam gone and a slip of paper propped against his alarm clock.

You worked late, so I bought you some extra sleep, her note said. Although he normally would have been up before dawn to tend to the ranch chores and get to his office well before the day shift began, he appreciated her thoughtfulness. Obviously, he'd needed the rest.

While he showered, dressed in his uniform and went to the barn to scoop oats for the horses, he thought again about his little surveillance mission last night. Still no answers. He would check with Lisa to be sure she'd obtained all the evidence she needed, then he supposed he could release Jo Robinet's vehicle.

* * *

Sam counted the pieces of chocolate for Stan Bookman's unconventional order. Allowing for a little breakage in handling and those that were not quite perfect, she and Jane had completed about half of what they would need. She sat back against the edge of the worktable, holding her first mug of coffee between her palms and contemplating the candy. What more could they do to make the assortment unique?

Her eyes drifted to the shelf above the stove. In a small tin box were three little cloth pouches, each containing granules of a special powder. Sam had no idea what they were; the chocolatier, Bobul, had given them to her. The magical ingredients gave Sweet's Sweets something no other chocolate shop could duplicate. Whatever they were, they made her candies irresistible. Sam was half afraid to put the enchanted powder into a full box of candy. She supposed a person might overdose on the stuff somehow. But if a few of the pieces contained Bobul's secret ingredients ... there was no way Mr. Bookman's wife wouldn't flip out for them.

She quickly set her mug aside. She would have to work fast to perform the act before anyone else arrived. Julio was due in ten minutes. She pulled a container from the storage shelf, a now-cold block of chocolate Jo had cooked and tempered on Saturday. They'd run out of time before she could pour it into molds, but since chocolate could be re-melted and tempered it was no problem. Sam tipped the block into a pan with a low flame and reached for the tin above.

The mixture had just begun to melt nicely when she heard Julio's motorcycle in the alley. Quickly, she took a pinch from the red cloth pouch. Then the green. Then the blue. The chocolate foamed upward for a millisecond, then settled into gentle bubbles. She replaced the tin on the shelf as the back doorknob turned.

"Good morning, Sam," Julio said, removing his leather jacket and rubbing his hands together.

She thought again of her conversation last night with Zoë and felt a rush of warmth toward him. He smiled, washed his hands and began pulling ingredients from the fridge for the early morning breakfast pastries. Not a trace of secrecy in his demeanor. Sam, herself, felt more guilty for sneaking special ingredients into the chocolate than Julio exhibited right now. She pushed the thought aside and checked her candy thermometer.

By the time Jo arrived, Sam had divided the dark chocolate into a couple of smaller batches and was adding cream to one.

"Oh, I do love milk chocolates," Jo said. "I know the trend these days is toward dark, but if it's done right milk chocolate just takes me right back to childhood."

Sam found herself smiling with similar pleasant memories.

"Now that you're remembering a lot more, I'd love to hear about your past. Where did you learn your chocolate-making techniques?"

"Ah, now that goes back to my grandfather," Jo said, tying an apron over her spotless baker's jacket.

Sam's phone rang, interrupting the story. She signaled for Jo to hold that thought. The call was from Beau.

"Good mornin' darlin'," he said.

She could tell the extra sleep had really helped.

"I have some news for your new employee," he said. "We can release her car today. Would she like me to bring it by? Save her having to take the bus or depend on you."

Sam posed the question to Jo whose face registered mild panic.

"I don't know, Sam. What if Ray Belatoni is still after

me? He knows the Lexus."

"Beau, she needs to think about it awhile. Do you need to deliver the car right now?"

"Soon," he said. "I'll come by when I can break away, let's say midday. We can talk about it then."

Sam passed along the information as soon as she hung up.

"I do want to get to my in-laws' place and talk to my son. I tried calling last night, but they told me he was asleep already. Hard to believe, since this is the boy who never wanted to go to bed before midnight. If I'm going to talk to him I think it needs to be in person."

"So, take your car back. No one can stop you driving around town in it."

Jo had poured the milk chocolate mixture onto the table for tempering. Automatically working it with a flat spatula she chewed at her lower lip.

"Or, what about driving your son's car instead? Would Ray Belatoni know about that one?"

"The Corvette is pretty flashy. Not exactly a car for getting around unnoticed."

Sam almost opened her mouth to offer the use of her pickup truck, which sat unused in the driveway a lot of the time since she'd not taken a caretaking job in awhile. She stopped, reminding herself that she barely knew Jo.

"Well, you think about it." Sam turned to her stack of orders for the day.

With Jo handling the chocolates, she and Becky could start their cakes and pastries. Sam had a birthday cake depicting an artist's easel halfway done when the back door opened. Beau stepped in and greeted everyone.

"Jo, I've brought your car with your suitcases in the back," he said, walking over to the worktable where she was piping dark chocolate whiskers on a white chocolate kitten. "We don't have the space to keep it at the department yard, so I either need to hand it over to you here or take it back to your house."

Jo stared at the candies for a half minute before she set down her pastry bag and turned to him.

"I'll take it," she said. She looked across the table at Sam. "I need to get to the DMV for a duplicate of my license and maybe I should make the drive over to George and Nancy's place now, before I lose my courage. If that's okay with you? The chocolate needs to set up anyway."

"Sure. No problem," Sam told her.

Jo made a quick call and told her mother-in-law she was coming over. She placed the tray of new chocolates on a cooling rack and removed her apron, taking a deep breath as Beau handed her the key. As soon as she was out the door, Beau turned to Sam.

"Now I need a ride back to the impound lot where I left my cruiser. Can you break away?"

Since he could have easily called one of his deputies, Sam assumed he wanted to talk to her alone. She was somewhat at a loss for what to paint on the artist's easel anyway, so the break came at a welcome moment.

"Don't get too attached to her, Sam," he said as soon as she started her van and pulled to the end of the alley. "We've *almost* ruled her out as the person who administered the fatal dose to Zack but she could still be in this up to her neck. Murder for hire is every bit as serious. She's admitted she hired Krystal. Things may have gotten out of her control, as she said, or she could have masterminded it all."

"But—really? You saw her in the interrogation room, Beau. That woman's been abused."

"I'm not saying she wasn't. I'm saying she might have acted on her desperation, to a lot bigger degree than she's letting on."

"Beau, I really don't think—"

He turned in his seat, facing her with a stern look. "The only reason I didn't forbid her working in your shop is because she's right where you can keep an eye on her. If I had the evidence against her I'd be holding her."

"Forbid? *You* just gave her car back!"

"With a tracking device attached. I'm not that stupid, Sam." His tone was sharper than he'd ever used with her before.

Sam bit back a retort. Nothing would be gained by letting this escalate.

Chapter 18

Beau kissed Sam's cheek before getting out of her van, already regretting that they'd had words. Especially over a case. He'd vowed never to allow his job to come between them, and now he had let it happen. He'd better pick up some flowers before he went home tonight.

However, that was hours away. Seated in his cruiser, he turned on the computer and watched the blinking dot that represented Jo Robinet's Lexus. She'd spent a record short time at the DMV and now it appeared she really was on her way to Zack's parents' place. In case she tried to get tricky about this, he'd planted another such device on the other car in the garage, the son's Corvette. Jo had access to it, plus Bentlee Robinet wasn't completely in the clear either. According to Beau's last conversation with Kent Taylor, the kid's alibi was shaky.

Meanwhile, he would touch base with each of the people he'd talked to yesterday at ChanZack and see if he could verify alibis for each of the employees who had locked horns with Zack in recent weeks. The sooner he could assure Kent Taylor that no one from the Taos circle of acquaintances would have driven all the way to Albuquerque to kill Zack Robinet, the better. He got the feeling the detective wasn't looking too hard for suspects on his own turf.

Chandler Lane was standing at the reception desk, ostensibly going over something with Amber on a sheet of paper, conveniently positioned so he could see straight down the front of her blouse. He looked up and took a step back when Beau entered.

"Sheriff. Two visits in as many days. Are you making progress toward finding Zack's killer, I hope?"

"Are Ed and Jamie here?" Beau asked, choosing not to explain.

"Amber?" Chandler said in his best let's-be-cooperative voice.

She checked something on her computer screen, as if the office had so many employees that a person wouldn't know who was in or out at any given moment.

"They both are. Back in their office." She sent a smile toward Beau. He decided it must just be her way. Surely she didn't intend to flirt blatantly with every male.

"I'd like to chat with each of them, separately. And your programmers, in a minute. Can you call Ed to come out here first?"

"I'll get him," Chandler said, turning toward the keypad which led to the inner sanctum.

"I'd prefer that he be paged. Don't tell him why, just ask him to come up front," Beau said to Amber.

Both Chandler and his receptionist seemed a little surprised by the request but neither said anything. Amber picked up the desk phone and pressed a two-digit intercom number. Ed Archuleta definitely seemed startled when he walked through the double doors and realized the sheriff was waiting.

"Let's take a little walk outside," Beau suggested. "We'll just be a few minutes." This last bit directed to the boss.

They strolled the hallway to the elevator, Beau reaching for his little notebook.

"I just need to get a few more details. This is routine stuff, information the police in Albuquerque needed. Can you tell me where you were last Wednesday?"

"That's the night Zack died, right?" Ed started to reach for the elevator button but hesitated. "Sure. I was here. I was in the office every single day and half of each night for the month leading up to the Vegas show."

"Was everyone working that many hours?"

"Most of us. Well, Jamie and me, both the programmers. Zack left a day early, which wasn't completely unusual. I suspected he had a little something going on the side. Female something, I mean. I don't know—I shouldn't really say that, him being my boss and all."

"No, it's fine. I need to know the truth." Beau left the notebook in his pocket and leaned casually against the wall. "Did Zack say something to give you that impression?"

"Nah, not really. It was more of a look. You know, a guy comes to work in a T-shirt every day of the week and then suddenly a trip comes up and he's wearing cologne."

Beau nodded, hoping Ed would go on. He didn't.

"Anyone else in the office acting a little out of character?"

"Well, Chandler is panting around all over Amber. He's

either getting some already or he's hoping to, real soon."

Beau chuckled. "Yeah, I got that impression too. I'm sure those of you in sales become pretty good at reading people, don't you?"

"That's what selling is all about. Figure out what motivates that customer and how to tell 'em they can have it. But no. Jamie and I been busting butt for weeks. Aside from the bosses coming and going from our office, I couldn't tell you who else was around."

"Okay, thanks." He walked back with Ed, keeping him in conversation in the lobby until Jamie showed up. No way he wanted these two comparing notes before he'd talked to each of them separately.

He posed nearly the same questions to Jamie and got essentially the same answers, except that her observations about Chandler and Amber were a little more graphic and came from Amber's point of view. The receptionist had apparently confessed over the coffee maker one morning that the previous night had been "woo!" Other than wondering what day of the week the conversation took place, Beau had no interest in the office sexcapades. He jotted down Jamie's responses, walked her back inside and called for one of the programmers. Michael Anderson was the one who showed up.

He swore—on a make-believe stack of bibles, while crossing his heart—that the programmers had been even more harried than the sales staff.

"You would not believe it, man. We were here, like, twenty-seven hours a day. No shit. And it still wasn't good enough. Every time *we* tested the program it ran fine. Zack or Chandler would come in and try it and *bam!* there's a glitch. We're starting at square one, like, every other day."

"Bet you were happy to see the prototype go out the door for Vegas."

"Uh, yeah, it's called a beta version. But yeah. Office goes from madhouse crazy to so quiet you could hear yourself breathe. Which was kind of nice."

"That was Wednesday night?"

"I guess it would have been … No, that had to be Thursday. Zack had taken off Tuesday or Wednesday, something about going on ahead to Vegas. Chandler said he couldn't get the same flight so he was leaving Thursday, I think. I don't know, man. I can't keep up with those guys. All I know's that we had to have the beta up and running without a single flaw by Thursday morning, so we pulled several all-nighters. You didn't notice we had sleeping bags on the floor in our office?"

"Let me go through it again," Beau said. "Zack was gone Wednesday. Chandler left Thursday, as did Jamie and Ed?"

Michael nodded.

"The bookkeeper never left town?"

"Helen, nah. She's just this quiet older lady who pays bills and prints out reports, I guess. I only ever see her in the breakroom getting herself some tea."

"What about Amber? Was she going to the show in Vegas?"

"No. There was some flack about that between her and Chandler. I remember commenting to J.B. about us having her to ourselves in the office for an extra couple days. But then he didn't leave early. I was thinking of suggesting we three go out for happy hour one night. I'd have made sure I sat next to her."

"I thought you computer guys were so wrapped up in

codes and programs that you never noticed that kind of thing."

"Yeah, well, that'd be J.B. Him and me, we work together real well but I tell you, he's *completely* not interested in having a social life. He's intense, man—goes home, works on computers there. Or plays games, or whatever he does in that man cave in his parents' spare room." Michael edged a glance down the hall toward the ChanZack offices. "I like the guy. Don't get me wrong. Really."

"Oh, no. I see what you're saying." Beau stood straight up again, giving the idea the interview was about over. "So you were at the office all day and most of the night Wednesday … and everyone else was, as well?"

Michael stared toward the ceiling for a moment. "Okay. Amber and Helen both left at their regular times, around five. They never really have to work late. Jamie and Ed were scrambling around and I heard some kind of panicky thing about someone had forgotten to get the brochures from the printer, or something like that. Me and J.B. … No, wait a second—J.B. did leave early that afternoon. Once we'd tested the game for the final time, he said he had something important. I guessed it was a run to that mega comic-book store in Santa Fe because he said he might be late the next morning."

"So, J.B. really didn't have an alibi for Wednesday night?"

"Oh, hey, I'm sure he does. Just ask him. He'll get it straightened out." Michael suddenly seemed eager to go.

While Beau waited for J.B. to answer the page to the front, he flipped back to his notes from the first office visit, the one with Kent Taylor. All the junior programmer had said was that Zack had a temper and had clashed with nearly everyone in the company. Could J.B. be hiding his own guilt? Sometimes it was the quiet ones who fooled you.

* * *

Sam's challenge now was to find suitable packaging for the impressive collection of chocolates for Stan Bookman's order. She'd been through her stash of gift boxes and canisters, most of which were far too winter-holiday themed to work for this one. She stared at her computer screen, scanning the offerings from her normal suppliers, not finding anything quite grand enough. One box she loved was out of stock and wouldn't be available for months.

"What about something that isn't a candy box?" Jen said, looking over Sam's shoulder on her way from the fridge with a customer's bridal shower cake.

Sam looked away from the frustrating array in front of her.

"Millie's Attic has lots of cute things," Jen said. "Boxes covered in fancy paper, vintage tins, that sort of thing."

"Great idea. I'll find the time to get over there sometime today." Sam switched to her email, which she hadn't checked for anything other than bakery orders in days.

From the sales room she heard a riffle of voices. A moment later Jen stepped through the curtain into the kitchen, her arm around Jo's shoulders. Sam looked up to see Jo sobbing noisily. Jen steered her toward Sam.

"I've got a customer out front," she said in a low tone.

Sam stood up and took over. "Jo, Jo … come in and take my chair. What's the matter?"

Becky stepped forward with a box of tissues and even Julio paused while removing a layer cake from its pan. Jo sat, yanking a fistful of Kleenex from the box. A good three minutes went by before she could speak. Sam motioned the others back to their work and went to the front to make a cup of tea.

"Is it something you want to talk about?" she asked, putting the tea mug in Jo's hands.

"My son—" Jo's lower lip quivered and tears threatened to spill again.

"Is he all right?"

Jo's head bobbed somewhere between an affirmative nod and a negative shake. "They've poisoned him against me. All the Robinets. Starting with his s.o.b. father. Bentlee just spent the last hour unleashing this stream of … of … hatred at me."

"What!"

"He said it. He hates me for what I did to his dad. I asked him to tell me what that was—all he could do was to spout back Zack's nasty words, the same things he's said for years to tear down my self esteem."

Sam tried to think of a response but realized Jo only needed to talk it out.

"Apparently Zack went by Bentlee's school when he arrived in Albuquerque last week, on the pretense of taking his son out to lunch. Then he proceeded to unload a bunch of lies. He told our son that I had repeatedly cheated on him! When was that supposed to happen? He watched me like a hawk and questioned my every move. He said I'd never loved my own son, that the business was more important to me than my kid. The business belongs to Zack and Chandler. Aside from occasionally going over the ad campaigns with the sales team or the financials with Helen, I had nothing to do with it."

"Bentlee's grandparents were there, right? Surely they could provide a voice of reason about all this."

"Oh, no." Jo's eyes flashed. "They've bought the whole story too. I mean, George and Nancy were never huge fans of mine. We've all kept a polite wariness around each other. There's no reason—other than Zack's word—for them to believe any of it. But they stood there, right behind Bentlee, going along with everything he said. It was like being ganged up on from three sides. I couldn't believe it."

Wow. Sam felt sorry for Jo and, not for the first time, was thankful Kelly's father had not been in their lives.

"When you think about it, the whole thing *should* be laughable. Here was Zack, talking to his son about me being such a horrible wife when he was on his way to spend the afternoon and night with another woman."

Uh, yeah. A hooker *you* paid to be there. Sam was beginning to tire of the dramatics in the Robinet family. Maybe they all deserved each other.

"Maybe you should go home and try to put all this behind you, Jo. I'm sure Bentlee will come around once he cools down. He'll remember the good times you had together and he'll see the truth."

"I won't even get a chance to talk to him alone. George made it clear that he intends to drive Bentlee back to school this afternoon and that none of them want me around. It was so humiliating." The sobs started again.

Sam felt her attention wandering. She wanted to be supportive but so much of this was unsolvable at this moment. She really needed to get on with other things.

"I don't want to go home, Sam. I'll just sit around and cry all day and feel sorry for myself. Can I stay here and work, finish the chocolates?"

Sam wavered. The downside was she really didn't want to get caught up in Jo's crying spells. On the other hand, the order of chocolates needed to be finished and Jo was much quicker at the work, freeing Sam's time to finish several other orders. Plus, she knew Beau wanted to keep Jo on his radar. At least by having her at the bakery they would know where she was and what she was doing. Unfortunately, that sounded a little too much like the way Jo's husband had treated her. Sam cast aside that train of thought. With a sigh, she agreed to have Jo stay and finish the chocolates.

"I'm going to follow Jen's suggestion and run out to see if I can locate the right box for this order," Sam told the group in the kitchen.

Getting into her van and driving away provided exactly the breath of fresh air Sam needed. Beau could be right about Jo's involvement in Zack's death. How well did she know the woman, anyway? Just because she was a master at chocolate-making didn't mean she wouldn't crack under the strain of an abusive marriage and estrangement from her son. For that matter, the whole breakdown in the interrogation room could have been an act. How many times had Beau told her never to trust what a suspect told you? Anyone, under the right circumstances, will lie to save her own skin. She shouldn't have been so sharp with Beau earlier. As she steered down narrow Martyrs Lane to find parking at Millie's Attic, she decided to make his favorite chicken parmesan dinner tonight.

She'd no sooner put her hand on the doorknob of the quaint, tiny shop than she heard a familiar voice.

"Time for shopping? I thought you were swamped with work this week." Zoë's grin teased her.

"I wish it was casual shopping, but this is work."

She explained about the box for the chocolates and Zoë followed her inside.

"Last time I was here I did see something like that," she said. She greeted the owner, whose name wasn't Millie at all, but Linda. Zoë explained that it was the current owner's grandmother who had started the concept of selling spare things out of her attic when the Great Depression hit the family hard.

Linda steered them toward one corner of the shop, where handmade fabric flowers filled pottery vases and the shelves contained vintage toys from the 1940s and '50s. A stack of cardboard boxes on a low table glowed with colored light from stained glass ornaments hung in the nearby window. The boxes were covered in various papers with a Victorian feel.

"I'm not sure whether the classic look will appeal," Sam said, scanning the choices. "We're designing the candy around the woman's fav—"

She stopped short when she spotted a box covered with colored pencil drawings of felines. It was slightly larger than she'd had in mind. They would have to turn out another dozen or so candies in order to fill it.

"This one is perfect," she said, picking up the feline box and handing it to Linda, who carried it to the register. One way or another, she would manage the extra chocolates.

"Now, if only Jo can continue to work another day or two," she told Zoë. "I have a feeling all the drama going on in her life right now will take over, right when I really need her."

After paying an incredibly small amount for the decorative box and carrying her shopping bag outside, Sam asked Zoë if she wanted to stop somewhere for a coffee.

"As busy as you are?"

"I need it. I get to the bakery and feel like I'm at my wit's end."

A half-block away one of the cafés with outdoor tables appeared to be experiencing a mid-morning lull. They quickly found a table and ordered lattes.

"We could have done this at my place—for free," Sam said

"But then you couldn't talk quite so freely. C'mon, something's bothering you."

"Nothing major. It's just an unsettled feeling, wondering whether Jo is being honest with me. Beau still considers her a suspect, and I don't see that. I can't believe she's a killer. We had a bit of a fight over it this morning."

"A real fight?"

"Oh, no. More like testy words."

Zoë chuckled. "You two are so good together. Do you know how rare it is for a couple to make it a whole year without a fight? I see honeymooners at the B&B who are already fighting and they haven't been married twenty-four hours."

Honeymooners. The B&B. Sam's mind flashed back to their wedding, held at Zoë and Darryl's place, the perfect September weather and beautiful decorations. The forgotten thing which had been nagging at her all week. Their anniversary—tomorrow—and she had wanted to do it up special.

Chapter 19

Beau sat in his cruiser in the shade of a cottonwood in the library parking lot and watched the blinking tracer dot as Jo Robinet parked at Sweet's Sweets. As long as it didn't leave again right away, his suspect would most likely stay put all day. Sam had mentioned a special order she'd assigned to her temporary helper, and she would be there to keep an eye on the woman. He dialed Kent Taylor's number and the detective thanked Beau for the report on the junior programmer's alibi for Wednesday night. J.B. had made a purchase at the comic book store, which could be easily verified. Beau mentally ticked another suspect off their list.

"In other news," Taylor said. "We've verified Ray Belatoni's alibi. He wasn't in Albuquerque at all that day. Krystal is still on our radar. She admits to being in the room both before and after Zack died, and the cameras agree. It's looking like she's our best bet right now."

"So, should I quit monitoring Jo Robinet?"

"Not yet. We know she and Krystal had hatched a plan together. Jo inherits Zack's half of a multi-million dollar business, which could give Krystal a whole lot of reasons for wanting to help the lady out. And with that much cash at her disposal, the recent widow could afford to go nearly anywhere in the world.

Beau had to agree. Money was such an enticing little motive. Or, in this case, a big fat enticing motive. "Too bad for her, I've got her passport."

"That's good," Taylor said. "Got something else for you to check out. Our lab folks performed some kind of photo-enhancing thing on the footage of the man in the hat. Still couldn't quite get the face, but the hat is a particular brand popular with golfers. We found two shops in Albuquerque that sell them and one in Taos. I'm sending you a picture of the hat."

"Zack Robinet played golf."

"And one of those golfing buddies recently had a run-in with him, right?"

"Will Valmora. Seemed like a pretty mellow type when I talked with him, and I pretty much discounted him."

"Still, let's find out where he was that day. Wouldn't hurt to drop by the sporting goods shop that sells the hats and see if they sold one to Valmora."

"I'll do it." Beau smiled as he retrieved the photo on his phone.

This was his kind of police work, tracking clues and looking for facts, rather than endless interviews with suspects who all proclaimed their own innocence. He put the cruiser in gear. He was familiar with the store Taylor had named; cutting through Martyrs Lane was a quick way to get there.

A huge box of pastries caught his eye—the custom artwork on Sam's bakery delivery van. It was parked at the curb in a block of cutesy little shops favored by women tourists. Two doors down, he spotted Sam chatting beside Zoë's vehicle. He thought of his recent statement to Kent Taylor and pulled to a stop beside the van. Zoë got into her Subaru and waved as she started the engine.

"Hey, you," Sam said, walking toward him with a smile.

"I thought you were sticking close to Jo Robinet all day, making sure she didn't skip out." His displeasure must have showed on his face.

"Excuse me?"

"She's a prime suspect, Sam."

"Well, how was I to know that? You let me believe she was pretty much off the list. And I don't recall being assigned to babysit her. Your department can still track her car, can't you?"

He took a deep breath. "It just took me by surprise, seeing you out here shopping and socializing this time of day."

Her eyes narrowed. "You aren't telling me how I'm supposed to spend my day are you, Sheriff?"

"Sam, I—"

But she'd already marched past him and gotten into her van. Oh boy.

Since this seemed like a situation best left to cool awhile and then resolve with a rose bouquet at the end of the day, he continued his route toward Paseo del Pueblo Sur and the sporting goods store Taylor had named.

The young man behind the counter gave Beau a blank stare when he inquired about the hat by its brand name. He held out his phone, showing the picture.

"Oh, yeah, those. We have some, over there in the corner by the golf clubs and shirts."

"I don't need to buy one," Beau said, working to keep his voice patient. "I need to know if you've sold this particular style in recent—"

Again, the blank stare.

"Is the owner or manager here?"

The kid disappeared through a half-door, beyond which Beau could see shelves packed with rental ski boots and racks holding skis. T'would soon be the season. A man followed the clerk back out, a guy who might be anywhere between thirty-five and fifty. Beau showed the photo again.

"I assume your sales are computerized?" he asked. "Could you tell me if you've sold any of these recently?"

The man squinted, then pulled a pair of low-power reading glasses from his shirt pocket.

"This is last year's style. The ribbon band is bandanna print. This year they went with tropical flowers. I don't know why—men don't really want to be wearing flowers on their hats, now do they?"

Beau stood patiently while the manager tapped keys on the computer.

"Looks like we sold three, two of them marked down to clearance price at the end of the season. Had to make space for ski caps and gloves."

"I need to know who purchased them, if that's possible."

The man sucked air through his teeth. "A credit card purchase, maybe. Cash, no way."

"Check them for me. Please." Beau felt almost guilty for asking. It would only prove Valmora owned such a hat, not whether he was the one in the hotel hallway outside Zack Robinet's room. His lawyer would have great fun with this, but it was necessary to establish the full chain of events if they had any hope of eventually proving a case. Meanwhile, he could take another tack.

He left his card with the store manager, asking to be informed of the names of the hat buyers. Glancing through his notes, out in the cruiser, he didn't see where he had actually asked Will Valmora his whereabouts last Wednesday night. It wouldn't hurt to do that and tie up one more loose end. And there was no time like the present. He got Dixie on the radio, obtained the address, which turned out to be surprisingly near his own home out in the ranchland, and debated. He could drive out there now or, more importantly, catch the Robinets and their grandson before they left to drive Bentlee back to his Albuquerque boarding school.

He opted for the latter. He would be more likely to catch Will Valmora home at the end of the day, on his own way home.

Greenlee Manor was buzzing when Beau pulled into the parking lot. He got sidetracked when someone shouted, "There's the sheriff. Tell him!"

A huge Buick, about four sizes too large for the tiny woman driving it, sat butt-to-bumper with a Prius and a small crowd had gathered.

"She backed into me!" said a gray-haired man with a decided hump between his shoulder blades.

"I did not." The woman might be tiny but her eyes held a lot of fire. "Your car is outside its space. You pulled out without looking. Sheriff, give him a ticket."

"Is anyone hurt?" Beau asked, surveying the minor damage. Both drivers were walking around and he guessed the impact must have happened with the cars barely rolling.

Across the lot, he spotted George and Nancy Robinet with Bentlee at their side. The teen was pulling a suitcase. Beau scanned the looky-loos at the accident, choosing two women who seemed the least befuddled among them.

"Ma'am, I'd like for you to go inside and get someone from the staff to come out and make sure no one is hurt. And could you," he said, turning to the other lady, "please wait with them until the town police arrive? I'm actually here on another case and need to get going."

As he strode across the lot toward the Robinets, he keyed his mike and asked Dixie to report the fender bender to the town cops. With such a minor accident on private property they likely wouldn't do anything, but maybe they could give reassurance to the two oldsters and make sure a battle didn't erupt. A few of the onlookers lost interest and trailed after Beau.

Hoping for a more mellow tone than Kent Taylor had used with the boy, Beau approached the group with a smile.

"Hey, Bentlee. Looks like you're heading back to Albuquerque?"

The teen sent out a so-what kind of look. What ever happened to basic politeness?

"He's got school, Sheriff. A place like Holbrook Academy, they fall way behind when they aren't there. It's a top school."

"I imagine they would be lenient in this case, knowing families need time together in times like this, especially his mother."

"My mother doesn't need anybody," Bentlee said with a

snarl. "She's a self-centered bitch."

Neither of the grandparents contradicted him, a fact Beau found astounding.

"Well, I imagine everything is hitting her pretty hard right now," Beau said.

"Sheriff, he's not wrong about Jo," George Robinet said. "The woman was completely—"

Beau held up a hand to cut him off. "This really isn't the time or place," he said. Whew—tough group. Even after his warning, Nancy Robinet continued to mumble criticism of her daughter-in-law.

"Anyway, that's not really why I wanted to catch you before you left. I have a few more questions about the day your dad died. Could we go inside and chat?" He eyed the nosy neighbors who lingered just out of range.

Both grandparents made impatient gestures. What was it today? Beau wondered. Was he giving off some kind of unfriendly vibe? It seemed nearly every conversation became a confrontation.

Since none of the other three made a move toward going to the apartment, Beau took the reins. "All right. Mr. and Mrs. Robinet, you may wait here at your car. I'll talk with Bentlee in mine. We'll just be a few minutes."

He gestured for the teenager to precede him to the nearby cruiser. When Beau opened the passenger door, curiosity won out. Bentlee slid into the seat, eyeing all the special equipment while Beau walked around to the driver's side.

"Okay, let's just cut to the chase and get this done," Beau said. "You talked with Detective Taylor in Albuquerque and told him where you were last Wednesday night. Unfortunately, what you told him proved not to be true.

The police check that kind of thing. They also check out your friends and it turns out your best buddies seem to know a lot about drugs."

Bentlee went a little white around the edges at the mention of his friends. "Okay, look. I did lie about where I was that night. The school has a strict policy about drug use and I couldn't let it get out that I was smoking a little dope and trying these new pills with my friends. Holbrook will kick me out and I'd have to go back home to live. It might be better without my dad there, but things aren't great between my mom and me either. Know what I mean?"

"Your dad died of a heroin overdose, son. You really don't want to start down that path yourself, do you?"

"I'm not—"

"No one *starts* with heroin. I'm just saying, be careful."

"You won't tell my grandparents, will you? I'll quit the drugs, promise."

Beau tilted his head, not really committing. "You might not realize it now, but your mother loves you very much. Both of you are in shock right now over what happened, but when it sinks in there will be some rough emotional times ahead. I think the two of you might like to be able to turn to each other."

"Is that what this is? A lecture on how to be nice to my mom? Seriously?"

"Just saying. It's been hard on her." Mentioning the abuse didn't seem necessary. The boy had been there.

* * *

Sam took a deep breath as the last of her employees left for the day. Between Jo's emotional story and the near-argument with Beau, not to mention the pressure of increasing the output of their chocolate order, she felt drained. And she still hadn't begun the anniversary cake she wanted to do for tomorrow. She and Beau really needed some time to themselves—a special dinner out, the cake. They could not start taking their marriage for granted this early on.

She mulled over all this, including what on earth she might get Beau as a gift, as she drove home. His cruiser wasn't there and she felt secretly a little glad about that. She would have time to shower, phone for tomorrow night's dinner reservation, and regroup before he arrived. Not for the first time all day, she thought of the carved box. She'd missed its presence in her daily routine.

The dogs greeted her with their perpetually happy faces and wagging tails. It might be quite pleasant to come back in her next life as a dog, she thought. Their carefree attitude seemed like the right way to approach each day.

Once inside, she glanced toward the hall closet. The box was in the wall safe, waiting for her. It had been three months since her unexpected encounter with the woman from The Vongraf Foundation, Isobel St. Clair, and the story she'd told of the existence of two other boxes like this one. Especially bizarre was the fact an organization existed whose members were intent upon getting hold of the boxes, supposedly to use them for some nefarious purposes.

At the time, especially after one of these men had nearly killed Isobel in her car, Sam had felt on high alert, worried for her own safety and that of the box in her possession. But months had passed without incident. No one had come snooping around. Not even a casual mention of the box from any stranger. Maybe the whole story was a fabrication or a bunch of silly superstition. Sam punched the buttons for the safe's code and the door swung quietly open.

The lumpy surface of the box felt familiar as she pulled it from its hiding place. She held it close to her body and the wood began to warm. By the time she'd closed the safe and walked upstairs, the normally dark stain had begun to glow to the color of honey. Her mood rose, her steps feeling lighter. She set the box on her bathroom vanity and undressed for the shower, allowing warm water to further soothe her tired muscles.

In her mind, a picture emerged of the cake she would bake for their anniversary. If she got up early in the morning and went straight to the bakery she could create to her heart's content before the bustle of the real workday began. Shower finished, she dried and dressed quickly, locating a piece of paper in her nightstand drawer and quickly sketching the design for the cake before any of the details could escape. If inspiration had come from her handling of the box, she knew the effect would be temporary. Folding the page, she stuck it in the pocket of her work slacks, draped over the bedroom chair, then headed for the kitchen.

She seasoned two chicken breasts, grated parmesan and cut the florets from a head of fresh broccoli. Outside, she heard Beau's cruiser, his happy greeting for the dogs, the front door.

"Sorry I'm a little late," he called through the open doorway. "Had to stop off for one final interview."

She couldn't see him from where she stood and found herself trying to read his tone of voice. Would their earlier testiness resume?

"Dinner in about twenty minutes," she said. "I can hold it a little longer if you want a shower or a drink first."

His head peered around the doorframe. "Let's do a drink out on the deck first. It won't be long before the evenings are too chilly to sit out there."

She set the vegetables aside and dried her hands, heading toward the living room.

"Sounds good to—" She came to an abrupt halt. On the coffee table sat an enormous bouquet of yellow roses—her favorite.

"Beau—"

He came up behind her and wrapped his arms around her waist. "It's a little early for our anniversary, but I don't think it's too early for an apology. I'm sorry for earlier."

She turned to him, her throat suddenly tight. "Me too. I don't know why I—"

But she couldn't talk just then because his mouth was on hers. Dinner somehow got delayed as they stumbled up the stairs and undressed more quickly than she ever remembered. The evening became a pleasant blur of warmth and togetherness, wine and a good meal, back to bed to settle into each other's arms. Sam had reached that most pleasant state of bliss.

Then the phone rang. Beau rolled over and picked it up.

"Robinet?" he said. "I'll be right there."

Chapter 20

Sam shivered in the passenger seat of Beau's cruiser, waiting for the heater to provide some bit of warmth. The midnight phone call had startled both of them awake, their fuzzy mood disappearing like a wisp of smoke in a gale. Dispatch had said only that there had been an incident involving Josephine Robinet at the El Monte Hotel. Sam knew there was no hope of her falling back to sleep once Beau left, so she opted to come with him. He switched off his strobing lights as they pulled under the hotel's portico.

"I swear, Sheriff, no employee here at El Monte gave out private information about Mrs. Robinet. We don't even have her real name on the registration." The night manager fluttered about, covering his bases. He seemed young, inexperienced, and worried for his job if one of the hotel's important guests should complain to upper management.

"Where is she now?" Beau asked.

"Was she harmed?" Sam blurted at the same moment.

"She is shaken but unhurt. We have installed her in another room and sealed off her old one for now."

What on earth happened here? Sam wondered as they followed the manager to the elevator. Beau suggested that they first speak with Jo, then check out the room. The man inserted a key into a slot on the elevator panel and pressed the top button, one with a small symbol on it but no number. The car glided silently and opened to a small foyer decorated in Southwestern chic. A private suite? Who knew Taos had anything quite this exclusive? He gave a series of short knocks, evidently some code devised for Jo. Beau seemed to approve of the extra measures.

A uniformed hotel guard opened the door, surveyed the three, then admitted them.

"Sam!" Jo rushed forward wearing a hotel robe over her long nightgown. Her hair was in tangles and without makeup her face seemed young and scared.

"What happened?" Sam said, meeting Jo's outstretched arms and pulling her in.

Jo's words spilled out, her hands fluttering. "Phone calls, shadows … the window … someone at the door."

"Maybe we should all sit down," Beau said. He turned to the guard and hotel manager. "I think we'll be all right from here. I'll need a key to her previous room, please."

The guard handed it over and the two men left. Sam saw that the suite included a small kitchen, elegant living room and two bedrooms. She offered to make tea or pour Jo a glass of wine from the rack on the granite countertop.

"Nothing right now," Jo said.

Sam filled the electric kettle anyway.

Beau led the way into the living room and let Jo take her choice of seats.

"I know this is upsetting and probably a little disorganized in your mind, but if you could walk me through it and tell me what happened and when?"

Jo took a breath and clenched her hands to keep them still. "The first incident happened last night, shortly after I checked in and settled into the room. The phone rang—I assumed it would be Sam or someone from the hotel staff so I answered it. The caller quickly hung up."

"You didn't say anything about this to me at work today," Sam said.

"I didn't really think anything of it. A wrong number, I assumed."

"It might have been. What time did it happen?" Beau was taking notes now. Sam shut off the kettle and brewed two cups of tea, carrying them to the coffee table and setting them down for Jo and herself.

"Early evening ... maybe six o'clock," Jo said, in answer to Beau's question.

"That's all?"

"Last night, yes. Tonight, there was another phone call. I had specifically asked the front desk not to put any calls through. I let it ring four times but it just wouldn't quit. I thought of my son. Maybe he needed to reach me."

"Had you told him you were staying here?"

"Come to think of it, no, I hadn't." She twisted a little in her seat. "The ringing began to worry me so I picked it up. That time, someone was breathing. Just loudly enough to let me know he was there."

"So it was a male?"

"Well, I said 'he' but I can't really be sure."

"What did you do? Did you speak?"

"I think I asked who it was. But they didn't say anything. It was creepy. I asked one more time then I hung up. I think I paced the length of the room a time or two then took the phone off the hook. Obviously, the desk people were not taking me seriously."

Which would explain the manager's current state of anxiety.

"You said someone came to your door?"

"That was later. I watched some TV and tried to put the phone calls out of my mind. I went to bed and turned out the light. I was almost asleep when I heard a noise at the window. On the third floor I couldn't imagine—"

"What sort of noise?" Beau asked.

"Small, at first, as if someone threw a handful of gravel. That was my first thought but it seemed crazy. I decided it was probably a tree branch, leaves brushing the glass, something like that."

"Did you get up and look?"

"Not right away. I kept telling myself it was only the wind. But then I remembered what a still night it was. And then I pictured the view from my window and realized there were no trees close enough to the building. I stood to the side and peeked around the edge of the curtain but couldn't see anyone. The room looked out over a garden with small pathway lights. It's fairly dark out there."

"We'll check it out." Beau seemed skeptical of actually finding the stalker on the premises by now. "But that wasn't all, was it?"

"Right. The door. I laid awake for about two hours and finally relaxed enough to doze off. But then I heard my door handle rattle. I just froze to the spot, thinking I had dreamed it. But it happened again, and a voice called my name. This creepy half-whisper. I think I cried out. I'm not sure. My heart was pounding so hard and my hands were shaking. I reached for the phone but it was still off the hook so I fumbled around for my cell phone, but then I realized I didn't have the number for the front desk programmed in and—all this time I was shaking so bad. I put the regular phone back and it took a minute for a connection, and then I called the desk and by that time my voice was so shaky I don't think they could understand me. I had to repeat everything a few times."

Sam reached out and took Jo's hand.

"While I was talking, the door opened. I know it did—a beam of light from the hallway came in. I screamed and yelled for the desk clerk to send help right away. The door closed again."

"How long before the hotel guard came up?"

"I don't know …" She was sobbing again. "I … It's the first time in my life I remember feeling genuine panic. I couldn't move, I was so terrified. The guard opened the door with a passkey and called out to me."

"Okay," said Beau, "you don't have to go back over that part. I'll ask him about it. And we can post a deputy in the suite's foyer for the rest of the night."

"Do you feel safe enough to stay here?" Sam asked.

"I won't sleep, if that's what you mean. But, yes, I'll be all right if there's someone guarding the door." She reached for the tea, which was lukewarm by now. "I need to be rid of the Lexus. I'm sure having it outside is how the man knew I was here. I'll take it back to the house and put it in the garage again."

"How about afterward?" Sam asked.

"I'll have to think about that." Jo sipped the tea, while Beau looked over his notes.

"I can't think of anything else right now," he said, "but we'll check back with you in the morning."

Morning, Sam thought as they took the elevator down. It was already after two a.m. According to her original plan, she would be getting up at four-thirty and heading to her shop to bake their anniversary cake. Barely a moment's sleep and already the new day was way off track. She stood to the side as Beau spoke with the hotel manager, warning him nothing better happen to Jo, and they would be answering directly to the sheriff's department if there were any further disturbances of this guest.

"Let's go home," he said, draping an arm across Sam's shoulders as they walked to his cruiser.

She leaned into him, all her earlier energy from handling the box completely gone now.

When Sam's cell phone jangled on the bedside table, she rolled over, wanting badly to ignore it. Catching sight of the readout, however, she saw it was Jo.

"Sam, I hope I didn't wake you."

Ugh. Even though she and Beau had agreed not to set their alarms, it still felt awfully early.

"I wanted to let you know that I've decided what to do. I stayed up all night and still didn't feel safe alone in this hotel. So I called my best friend this morning and I'm going to stay at her house. I'll take the Lexus home and put it out of sight in the garage again. I'll get a rental to drive around town. Surely, this person will be caught soon, don't you think?"

Evidently, Jo had several cups of coffee under her belt

this morning. Sam's fuzzy mind struggled to process this raft of new information.

"Hold on a second." She turned to Beau, who was rubbing his eyes, and told him what Jo had in mind.

He reached out and took the phone. "Jo, I don't think this is a good idea. Think about it. Anyone who knows you and your movements will know your friends. You could be putting both of you in danger."

"Sorry, Sheriff. I've made up my mind. Brenda lives in a very secure neighborhood, gated condo complex, and she's got a great alarm system. She practically begged me to come there when I told her what happened last night."

"Have you told anyone else?" He rubbed the stubble on his chin.

"No. And I won't. You'll catch the man soon and then I can go home. Until then, at least I'm not a prisoner in a hotel."

She hung up and Beau groaned as he handed Sam's phone back. "There's some people you just can't protect from their own stupidity."

He went into the bathroom. Sam's phone rang again almost immediately.

"I meant to tell you," Jo said, "I'll be at the bakery this morning. I don't want you to think you can't count on me."

The bakery. Sam realized she was running more than three hours late for everything she'd hoped to accomplish today. She pulled her clothes on, raced through brushing her teeth, and was out the door ten minutes later. Jo's Lexus sat in the alley near Julio's motorcycle. That was another subject Sam wanted to address soon, to get Kelly to admit that she and Julio were dating.

"Sam—I'm glad you're here." Jo was boxing up chocolates from the assortment they had already completed. On the worktable sat a new bag of cacao beans, ready for processing. "Can we talk for a minute?"

By her bright-eyed appearance, Jo obviously meant right now. Heavens—Sam hadn't even removed her coat yet.

"I need at least one cup of coffee before I have to process a single scrap of information," Sam told her.

She greeted Julio and Becky and went to the front where Jen had—bless her!—freshly brewed their signature blend coffee. A woman in business attire was choosing a dozen pastries and a man with a bulging gut called out his order for three bear claws. Sam bagged those, picked up her own coffee mug and joined Jo back in the kitchen.

"Maybe we should talk privately?" she suggested to Jo.

A quick glance toward the other employees and Jo agreed. She slipped on a fleece jacket against the frosty morning air and they stepped out to the alley.

"Let's walk. It's too cold to stand around in the shade," Sam suggested. "I assume this is about your plan to stay with your friend. You know Beau isn't crazy about that idea."

"I know, but I told him how I felt about it. Would you be willing to follow me over to my house sometime this morning so I can leave the Lexus? The rental car company will deliver a car here to the bakery around noon."

They turned the corner and crossed the street toward the plaza.

"Which brings up the other thing I wanted to talk about. Sam, I'd really love to continue working for you. For free, of course. Now that I have Zack's half of the business I don't have money worries. I just need something to fill the hours and I love working with chocolate."

"Jo, I—" Sam started to say she didn't normally get all that many orders for chocolates.

"I'll continue to help out at ChanZack as needed, but that's far from full time. Helen handles all the daily entries so it's usually only at tax season that I'm involved. With Zack gone I'll be needed to move money around among the investment accounts. He always handled that." She seemed to be clarifying all these details for herself more than for Sam's information.

"So, what do you think?" Jo said, stopping in mid-sidewalk and facing Sam. "About my working for you."

"Well, definitely until we get this big order finished. After that, let me evaluate the situation. I don't know how much I'll be able to keep you busy right now. Maybe more around the holidays."

Sam didn't feel quite fueled up yet, although her coffee was gone. She subtly steered Jo back toward Sweet's Sweets. Her mind not geared toward work yet, she suggested that this would be a good time to take Jo's car to its home garage. She poured more coffee into a paper cup and got into her van to follow Jo home.

As they approached, the middle garage door slid upward and Jo steered the Lexus inside while Sam waited in her idling van in the spacious driveway. Jo trotted out a minute later.

"I thought of some things I want to get from the house," she said through Sam's window. "Want to come in with me?"

"I can wait out here."

"It'll only take a minute." Jo went back in through the garage, the door slid down.

Less than a minute later, Jo came running out the front

door, breathing hard. "Sam! I think we better call Beau. Someone's broken into the house."

Now I'm awake, thought Sam. She dialed Beau and handed the phone to Jo.

"Is the intruder still inside?" he asked.

"No. Well, I don't think so. I'm sure I made a lot of noise, and I walked through several rooms before it hit me that little things are messed up."

"Stay right where you are. I'll be there as soon as I can."

Jo bounced on the balls of her feet, looking toward the house and back at Sam as rhythmically as if she were at a tennis match. All the while, she chewed at a cuticle. It would be a wonder if she didn't manage to scratch off half her lip, Sam thought.

"Do you want to just go on inside?" Jo finally asked after about ten minutes, still nibbling that cuticle.

"Beau said to wait out here." Sam thought of the near-arguments between herself and Beau this week, balanced by the complete and beautiful reconciliation last night. The sound of a siren down the road spared her from having to make a bad choice. His cruiser roared into the driveway thirty seconds later. She got out of the van and stood beside it with Jo.

"I'm surprised," he said as he got out of his vehicle. "I honestly thought you would have gone back in there, no matter what I said." He was facing Sam as he said it.

She merely smiled and gave him an innocent gaze.

"I'm fairly certain there's no one inside," Jo said.

"Still, I want you both to wait here while I check it out." He placed one hand on the grip of his pistol and approached the front door.

Sam found herself almost holding her breath. Watching

Beau walk into a potentially dangerous place was far more scary than doing it herself. Five whole minutes ticked by at the speed of a garden slug. Finally, Beau came out and motioned to the women.

"Jo, I need you to tell me what's out of place."

The three of them went inside. The house had obviously not been ransacked, Sam could tell at a glance, but Jo pointed out little things.

"This should be out in the garage," she said, pointing to a red metal toolbox on the floor by the kitchen door.

"Zack might have left it here days ago," Beau suggested.

"Nope. It wasn't there yesterday." She looked around. "This pile of mail on the counter … I looked through it and stacked it neatly yesterday. Someone has looked through it."

She led them into the master bedroom where a large painting hung crookedly on the wall. Behind it was a wall safe, door closed.

"They didn't get into this," Jo said, "but someone knew the location."

"Or prowled around until they found it." Beau touched only the corner of the painting. "We'll dust for prints. With luck, something will match one of our suspects."

"You think this is related to Zack's death?"

"Someone came after you at your hotel last night. Maybe they came here first, couldn't get into the safe and decided to get you to come along and let them in."

"My god." Jo's face was the color of chalk.

"What's kept in the safe?"

"Everything of value. My jewelry, some cash, important papers and financial information."

Sam's mind raced. A thief after jewelry and cash would never have known where to find Jo at the hotel. But who would want their papers? No, it had to be something else, some other item Jo wasn't remembering.

Beau's thinking ran along the same lines. "The two incidents probably aren't related at all. Most likely, someone noticed the house has been empty for a few days and decided to see what might be easy to steal."

He retraced his steps through the other rooms and found a broken guestroom window. A single dark print, probably from a boot, showed clearly on the white carpet. Beau touched the print and sniffed the smudge on his finger. "He smashed his way in here, worked the latch and slid the window open. Wasn't your alarm set?"

"I—um—I thought it was. Oh, I don't know. Yesterday, I wasn't thinking very clearly." Jo trailed her finger through a layer of dust on the dresser.

"Careful not to touch anything. Maybe we'll get lucky and find identifying shoe prints outside," Beau cautioned. He handed her two pages from his notebook. "I need you to go room to room and make me a list of everything you see out of place or missing. Don't touch things, just make notes."

He pulled out his phone and got his forensics tech on the line.

"Lisa will be here in awhile to dust for fingerprints, photograph this footprint, and try to get molds of any others outside. Once she's dusted the surface of the safe, you should open it and make absolutely sure the intruder didn't get in. We can't assume anything, just because it's locked now."

Jo nodded and headed toward the kitchen.

"One of us should stay with her," Beau told Sam, "at least until Lisa gets here."

Sam saw her day slipping away. "I can stay a little while. Once Jo's made her list I can take her to her friend's house. That seems like a good plan now, don't you think?"

"As good as any, I suppose. Help me check the other windows and doors. An intruder will often come in through a window but find it a lot easier to exit through a door."

Sure enough, a slider leading to the back deck was unlocked. Within a few minutes Lisa's vehicle joined the others in the driveway. Beau took her to the areas he wanted dusted first: the mail and kitchen counter, the picture frame and front of safe, and everything surrounding the guestroom window.

"That boot print smells like grease," he said, pointing it out. "I want that tested."

Sam caught his sleeve when he walked out of the room. "Grease? Like automotive?"

He nodded. "Donny Vargas, the mechanic from the dealership, was one who threatened Zack."

"My thought exactly. But what would he come here for, especially now, days after Zack died?"

"If Ray Belatoni took the wrecked Lexus to that garage for repairs, maybe Vargas wanted to be sure no receipt or other paperwork could tie him to it. The intruder went through the mail."

Sam thought about his idea. She couldn't see how it would matter if the man repaired the car. On the other hand, some of the evidence certainly made Donny look like the one. The toolbox sitting in the kitchen puzzled her. Perhaps he'd taken it from the garage but forgot it as he was leaving the house. Or, more scary, maybe Jo's arrival awhile ago had interrupted him in the midst of his search. She voiced this thought to Beau.

"I'm going by the dealership right now. If he's not at work or looks flustered by my showing up … we may have our man."

At least for the break-in. Sam still didn't quite see how he could be tied to Zack Robinet's murder.

Beau was on the road when a sporty red convertible pulled into the driveway and Chandler Lane got out. He was dressed much more casually than Sam had seen before, this time in jeans, a sweatshirt and brown brogans, as if he'd just come from a long hike in the forest.

"What's going on?" he asked, eyeing the retreating law enforcement vehicle.

Jo's appearance at the front door caught his attention and he walked over and took her hand.

"I wanted to get by and express my condolences," he said. "Things got so crazy at the funeral and then when you didn't come by the office later … Well, I understand. Don't get me wrong. I just … well, I should have come by to see you a lot sooner than this."

"Thanks, Chan. I appreciate it. How are things going at the office?"

He waggled his hand in a noncommittal gesture. "A little rough. The gang doesn't quite know what to do. I mean, it's going okay. Just different, you know, without Zack."

"I know. Same for me."

He took her hand in both of his and pressed it. "I'm just so, so sorry. We were such a good team, all of us."

"The business will be fine," Jo said. "We have great products and the new game will take off like gangbusters. Really, Chan, don't worry."

Chandler gave Jo a quick peck on the cheek and released

her hand. "Let me know if you need anything. Anything at all."

He slid back into the sports car and it roared to life. Sam wished Jo would finish doing whatever she needed to so they could get on with the day. The morning was vanishing quickly and she'd not even begun their anniversary cake or made reservations for dinner.

Chapter 21

It's definitely motor oil," Lisa told Beau when she returned from gathering evidence at the Robinet house. "Unfortunately, I can't tell you where it came from. It seems to be a mix of several brands, which would indicate a garage where many cars are worked on. Maybe one of those oil change places."

"Thanks." Beau was pleased to see that his initial idea that the boot was worn by Donnie Vargas could be correct. It still didn't explain what he wanted inside the Robinet house or how this could possibly tie him to the murder.

"I'll see if I can come up with fingerprint matches from our databases. Maybe we'll get lucky on that," she said, leaving a copy of her handwritten preliminary report.

She was hardly out of his office before his phone rang. Kent Taylor, finally returning the call Beau had placed to him early this morning.

"I talked to the friends young Bentlee Robinet named as his latest alibi. Two prep school types who showed up with parents and lawyers in tow. Without admitting to any use of drugs whatsoever, both claimed to have spent the afternoon and evening of the murder with Bentlee. They were supposedly at a popular no-booze teen club here in town and I verified that with a waitress and the manager of the place. So, the son is out as a suspect."

"Okay, good. I didn't really think it would be him, but you know the drill. At least I can check him off my list."

"What about the guy from the country club?"

"The golfing buddy, Will Valmora? Still waiting on verification, but I'm just not feeling the right emotion from him, you know? He doesn't seem to be holding any anger toward our victim. However, on the chance that he's an Oscar-caliber actor, I'll let you know what I find out."

"Thanks. Gotta go." Taylor was obviously distracted by the other phones Beau could hear in the background.

"Hey, you," Sam said from the doorway. "This is a very quick stop to let you know I got Jo and her stuff delivered to her friend's house. She's arranging a rental car and will be helping me at the bakery this afternoon."

She didn't mention having stopped by their house where she succumbed to temptation and handled the wooden box. Given the fact that the night had consisted of almost no sleep and the day was already hours behind schedule, she would not let herself feel guilty about resorting to the extra boost.

"And … I wanted to wish you happy anniversary." She stepped into the office and closed the door. Leaning over his chair she took his face in her hands and gave a long and lingering kiss.

"Do we have any big plans for the occasion?" he asked, a little breathlessly.

"Hoping to. But so far I haven't made much progress putting it all together."

"You know what, darlin'? I don't mind. We could go home and fall right in bed, as far as I'm concerned."

She had the feeling he needed the extra sleep as much as she did. Then he wiggled his eyebrows. Okay, it wasn't *entirely* about sleep.

She noticed the report Lisa had just delivered.

"I tell you, I'm way more than puzzled about this case," he said. "Just talked to Kent Taylor and it doesn't sound like he's any closer to figuring it out than I am."

"What have you got? I might as well take a little more time away from the shop."

"The people who have motive to be rid of Zack seem to be clear of actually administering the fatal drug. From the surveillance video at the Kingston Arms, we can rule out Jo and their son. His alibi checks out, by the way, so he's completely off the list. Of the males caught on camera, it could be Will Valmora, but I sure as hell can't figure out his motive. Ray Belatoni could fit the size and description but Jo says he was in Taos and ran her off the road."

"Does the timeframe fit for that, though? Her accident happened in the early morning on Thursday. Zack probably died Wednesday night."

"According to Krystal, that would be true."

"She's another on your list, right?"

"She's the only one we can definitely place in the hotel room. She admits she was there and we've got her on camera."

"So she's the one."

"But what's her motive? She and Ray were trying to blackmail Jo. With Zack dead, they'd never get any money."

"Plus, if Krystal actually plunged the needle, the real killer is probably Jo. At least Krystal's lawyer will take that angle, a murder for hire by—" The intercom buzzed on his desk.

"Sheriff, there's a man named Chandler Lane here to see you."

"Bring him on back," Beau said.

"He stopped by Jo's house, just after you left this morning, offering condolences. He seems concerned about her."

Chandler had changed clothes in the past hour. Sam noticed he now wore khaki slacks and a polo shirt, his normal office attire.

"Sheriff, thanks for seeing me. I don't want to take up your valuable time. Just thought I would check in to see how the investigation is going. Are you close to finding out who killed Zack yet? Jo seems at a loss for how to carry on with her life and I'm very concerned for her. While that killer is out there, I'm worried for her safety too."

"We're doing everything we can, Mr. Lane. Our department is working closely with APD and we're narrowing it down."

"Well, I'd say that's good news. Really glad to hear it." His eyes cut to the folder on Beau's desk but the cover was now closed.

"Okay, then. I'll let you get to it. Be sure to let me know if there's any way we can help." He shook both their hands and left.

Beau waited until Chandler had been escorted to the front of the building. "Jo, at a loss for how to get on with her life? I was under the impression she was enormously relieved to be out from under the thumb of her abuser."

"That's how she tells it."

"Does that mean Chandler Lane knows our recent widow a lot better than either of them are admitting?"

Sam walked across the room and closed his door.

"Beau, I just got a weird feeling from him, when he shook my hand."

"Weird, how?"

"Okay, you know it's been months since I've handled the wooden box but I got it out of the safe yesterday."

"Uh-huh." He leaned back in his chair, waiting for the story.

"I handled it awhile ago. After I left Jo at her friend's condo, I stopped by home."

His eyes didn't waver.

"And, well, you know the effects it has on me sometimes." The time she saw fingerprints no one else could see, the time she spotted a murderer in a crowd because of the color of an aura around him, the unbounded energy she sometimes used to accomplish a lot of extra work. She'd never quite admitted that last part to him.

"And?"

"Chandler Lane was hiding something just now."

"I got the feeling he's already showing an interest in his partner's widow. She's a wealthy woman as soon as Zack's portion of the business passes to her. Lane marries Jo and suddenly as a couple they own the whole thing."

"Are you saying she might have planned it that way? Because I haven't caught any sign of interest on her part."

"Maybe it's one-sided. Maybe it's an idea that only occurred to him in recent days."

"Just keep an eye on her, Sam. She's coming back to work at the bakery, right? Pay attention. See if she gets unusual phone calls or if he—or any other man, for that matter—stops by to see her."

He was probably right. The scent of money could be a powerful aphrodisiac.

* * *

Sam went back to Sweet's Sweets, dismayed that so much of the day had slipped away. At least Jo would be there finishing the order of chocolates for Mr. Bookman, with a whole day to spare before their deadline. That little dream burst like a fragile soap bubble the moment Sam walked in the back door.

Her carefully selected decorative box sat in the midst of the worktable, small lumps of indefinable brown shapes sticking up in the bottom of it, gooey drips of chocolate oozing down the sides. Sam's eyes went wide. Jo and Becky stared up at her, looking like schoolgirls caught smoking in the bathroom.

"What—?" Sam couldn't take it in.

Becky backed away and Jo's lower lip began to tremble. Julio had apparently left for the day, while Jen stood aside, staring in horror.

"Don't even—" Sam said, advancing on the mess, trying to fathom what could have happened. "No tears!"

"It's my fault." Becky and Jo both said it at once.

"Mine," said Becky. "I had a big cake to set up so I picked up the box and moved it. I wasn't even thinking. It was on top of the oven."

Sabotage? Becky had not wanted Jo here from the

beginning. Sam's vision blurred and cleared. She'd taken the man's money. Not only would she have to refund it all, she would disappoint him and possibly tarnish the name of her business forever.

"This is an important customer," she said, working to hold her emotions in check. "How do you propose we fix this?"

"I'm supposed to pick up my boys from soccer but I'll call my husband to get them. I'll work all night." Becky's remorse was genuine, but a whole night of her time wouldn't bring the knowledge or talent needed to re-do the order.

"I can stay too," Jo said. She shook her head. "But I don't think the two of us can finish it in one day."

They couldn't. No way. It had already taken a week to get this far. Sam's head began to pound. She turned her back on the chocolate mess, went into the bathroom and splashed cold water on her face. There was only one solution.

Back in the kitchen, she picked up the ruined box and dumped it in the trash.

"Becky, get your kids and go on home. We'll talk about this tomorrow. For now, I have to concentrate on solutions. Jo, inventory our supplies and start tempering a fresh batch of chocolate. Call me on my cell and let me know what ingredients I can pick up at the supermarket. I'm heading to Millie's Attic, hoping the lady has another box like this one."

Becky moved in a daze. Sam patted her shoulder to offer a scrap of reassurance. She got in her van and covered the four blocks to the antique shop in a blur. The woman was locking the door when Sam double parked and ran up to her. Ten minutes later, she had another cat-patterned container under her arm. The fact that it was slightly smaller than the first actually came as a welcome relief.

One more thing to do. She forced herself to slow down and watch the afternoon traffic as she headed home. The carved box was going to provide her escape from the disarray her life had suddenly become.

On the coffee table sat the two dozen yellow roses Beau had brought home yesterday. Their anniversary. There was no choice now. The dinner plan would have to be scrapped. She called his cell as she climbed the stairs and made her way to the master bath. Bless him, he didn't question the decision, just wished her luck.

The lumpy wooden box waited, quiet and dark, in its place. She picked it up and sent up a little prayer that it not fail her now. By the time she locked the front door and got back into her van, the odd little artifact had already begun to glow and to warm her hands.

Back in the alley behind Sweet's Sweets, Sam puzzled over the appearance of a car she didn't recognize. Of course. Jo was driving a rental now. Next problem, how to convince Jo to leave? Although the help would be nice, there was no way an outsider could witness the power of the box.

She killed the van's engine, put the magic box into her backpack and sat there a minute, deciding what to do.

Jo looked up when she walked in. "Were you able to get the box?" she asked.

It took Sam a second to realize she meant the cardboard box for the chocolates. She held it up.

"Excellent! I've already ground the beans and set out all the ingredients. I'm ready to start cooking."

Sam eyed the array of items on the worktable—cream, butter, flavoring. Aside from the secret powders and her own touch, everything was ready.

"Hold off for a minute, Jo. We need to talk."

Jo's smile faded. "Oh, Sam, I'm so sorry for what happened. I should have been watching more carefully. I could have saved the pieces we had already made."

Sam waved off the apology. "It's fine. It's not that. Accidents happen."

She took another deep breath, debating as she had all the way here about what she would say.

"Jo, I'm going to do the chocolates myself."

"I understand your disappointment in me, really I do, Sam. But two of us can work twice as fast. And I really don't mind staying. There's nothing for me at home—"

"I don't mean to be insensitive, but I have to ask you to leave. I cannot explain how, but I will get the order done by myself. Please don't question me. And please don't say anything to anyone else about this because I promise I will deny whatever you tell them."

Jo studied her face for a long moment. "Okay then. I'm on my way."

Sam waited for the sound of the little sedan to fade away and checked the locks on the doors before pulling out the magic box. When its energy had thoroughly coursed through her body she set to work. It was something she had wondered in the past: when she worked under the influence of whatever powers this box transmitted to her, did she actually move about the room at the speed of light, or did it just feel that way?

Chapter 22

Sam braced herself against the stainless worktable and stared at the finished box of chocolates. They were as close to perfect as she could imagine, a collection of cats and kittens in dark, white and milk chocolate. Her personal favorite was the little calico on which she'd used essence of orange to create the rust-colored patches. Mr. Bookman's desire to present his wife with a gift of her two favorite things—chocolate and cats—had come to fruition. And Sam's blast of energy was completely gone. She set the lid on the candy box and walked to the sales room to brew the day's first pot of coffee. Julio would arrive soon to start the morning pastries, and Jen and Becky would come shortly after.

Gray predawn light filtered through the front windows. The parking lot was empty and no sounds came from the street. Sam pressed the button on the coffee maker and stared at the small view of Taos's adobe structures she could see from this limited vantage point. The coffee machine hissed and she felt an ache creep up her arms and into her shoulders. She would need to sleep off the binge, but at this moment the pains felt good. Accomplishment and prolonged creativity did that to her. The bittersweet part, the tradeoff, was that she and Beau had spent the evening of their first anniversary apart.

Disappointment crowded against exhaustion and physical ache. Why had she let business take priority over their time together?

Almost as if he'd read her thoughts, Beau's cruiser rolled to an almost silent stop at the front door. She unlocked it and beckoned him inside.

"I'm so sorry. I shouldn't have—"

He pulled her to his chest and rubbed her back.

"Nothing turned out right—the special cake I meant to bake for us, a nice dinner together, and our relaxing night at home …"

"It's okay. It's not as if my work hasn't interrupted our lives sometimes too." He held her at arm's length with a steady gaze. "The day started to get away from us early on. And I told you it would be fine to postpone the special dinner to another night. It's all good, darlin'."

The rumble of a Harley disrupted a kiss that could have lingered a long time. Sam heard the back door open and Julio's familiar movements as he began handling metal baking pans, starting his day's work.

Sam tilted her head in the direction of the kitchen and whispered to Beau. "At some point I want to talk to you about something. Now—coffee?"

He gave a puzzled look but accepted the cup she poured for him. Seated at one of the bistro tables with the warm mugs, Sam let herself relax and simply enjoy the fact that she was married to this wonderful guy. The cozy feeling lasted nearly five whole minutes before his shoulder mike squawked with an incoming radio call.

"Gotta go," he said, after answering with a bunch of coded cop-speak.

"I've got to get some sleep," she said. "If I get back here in time to make preparations, shall we plan on our special dinner tonight?"

"First things first. Get your rest and then we'll talk about it. I don't want you wearing yourself out." He was out the door as soon as he said it.

She took the used cups to the kitchen, happy to see Julio already pouring muffin batter into pans. Jo was next to arrive, wearing an anxious expression. She paused when she saw the box of chocolates on the table. A quizzical look toward Sam.

"Just remember what I said last night." Their own version of a don't-ask-don't-tell pact.

Jo nodded and Sam lifted the lid.

"Oh my gosh, they are fantastic!" Jo actually gasped. "How did—?" She clamped her mouth shut.

"Now for the taste test," Sam said, although she'd personally sampled a bit of each new flavor as she devised it.

She uncovered a plate filled with the inevitable goof-ups that were part of any decorative endeavor, the imperfectly formed pieces and those where her hand zigged when it should have zagged with the pastry bag. Jo took a sample of the cinnamon-nutmeg-molasses cream enrobed in dark chocolate and her eyelids closed in bliss as she rolled the flavors on her tongue.

"Will Mr. Bookman and his wife be impressed?"

Jo had already picked up a milk chocolate with raspberry and lemongrass. Another eye roll and she nodded vigorously. "They have to be."

Becky came in and tried a couple. "Oh, definitely. You guys have nailed this one."

Neither Sam nor Jo contradicted the impression they had both worked on the order.

"Okay, time to declare it done and let the customer know."

Sam cut a length of ribbon that coordinated with the box's cat design and tied it into a fluffy mass that topped the gift perfectly. She set the box on the shelf behind Jen's work area where it would be safe from harm. On the phone, Mr. Bookman seemed thrilled that the order was done a day early.

"You look tired, Sam," said Becky when she walked back into the kitchen.

"I'll admit it. I'm going home for a few hours' sleep— soon." She turned to Jo. "There was extra tempered chocolate after the Bookman order was finished, so I molded some basic squares and buttons. If you can decorate them today, we'll set them out with our other stock."

"Absolutely. Anything else?"

Until the holidays, they wouldn't need large quantities of chocolate and she really couldn't justify keeping Jo employed right now. Still, she had to admit the woman had a lot of talent. The unusual flavors and special molding techniques were things Sam wouldn't have known without working alongside her new helper.

"You probably could use some extra rest, too. How are things going? Personally, I mean."

"Well enough, I suppose. It's an adjustment. Staying with my friend is making it easier. I'd be going crazy alone in that big house. I started going through those papers I took home yesterday, but they just aren't making sense. I guess I have to get my head back into accounting and numbers and all that."

"Well, good luck with them. Okay, folks, I'm leaving for home and sleep. Unless the building's on fire, don't call me."

Since that had actually happened once, she amended the phrase. "Don't let the building catch fire." Then she was out the door.

Kelly was just getting out of her car when Sam hit the pavement.

"Hey, Mom. How's things? Did you and Beau have a great celebration for your anniversary?"

"Not exactly." Sam glossed over the way the day had gotten out of control and the fact she had worked all night.

"Mom? I have a question." Kelly shifted her purse to the other arm, gazed out past the building in a classic stalling technique.

Sam raised her eyebrows.

"How did you know Beau was the one? Your Mr. Right?"

Oh, wow. That was not the question Sam expected.

"Is this about your new guy, the one we haven't met yet?"

Again, Kelly shifted a little in her spot before nodding.

"Honey, you haven't known him very long."

"You only knew Beau a few months before he proposed. How did you know saying yes was the right thing?"

How indeed? "I suppose it was just a feeling. Some undefinable thing ... I'm not sure how to describe it."

Kelly smiled that cute, dimpled way which had melted Sam's heart from the time she was a toddler.

"Okay, Mom. Thanks." She stepped forward and gave Sam's hand a squeeze, then turned and disappeared through the back door at Puppy Chic.

Sam drove home in a daze, her mom-meter ringing like crazy. Could Kelly really be this serious about someone they'd never met? Or was it someone they knew well already? The more she thought about it, the more certain she felt. She patted the dogs on the head and trudged upstairs, swallowing a PM pill, peeling off her clothes and sliding under the comforter in her underwear. Her eyes closed but her mind would not shut down.

Kelly and Julio as a couple. Sam imagined the proposal, the wedding, the grandchildren to come. Whatever picture formed in her mind, the tattoos got in the way. *What is wrong with me that I can't see past the surface?* All this time, she should have gotten to know Julio better, to cultivate a bit of a friendship with him, rather than simply relying on his proven expertise as a baker. She liked the man, but well enough to welcome as a son-in-law? And how would he and Kelly mesh as a married couple—his quiet, almost taciturn disposition along with Kelly who exuded bubbles and giggles most of the time.

Sleep came, riddled with dreams. She rolled over. An hour had ticked by on the clock. Closed eyes again. Rolled over again. Fifteen more minutes.

Okay, this is ridiculous.

She sat up and called Beau. His cell went to voicemail immediately and she realized it wasn't fair to interrupt his work day because she couldn't rest. She would interrupt Zoë instead.

"Hey, what's up?" Zoë's breath was rushed, as if she'd run in from the back yard.

"Trying to sleep. Can't."

"Pull another all-nighter? Sam, I thought we'd talked about that."

"I know. And now I took a sleeping pill so I shouldn't drive. Otherwise, I would just go back to the shop and bake the cake I should have done yesterday."

"Oh, right. Your anniversary."

"It didn't happen. Beau's job, my job, no time."

"It's really bugging you. Want me to come over? I could rock you to sleep or something."

Sam chuckled over that image, slender little Zoë with her as the oversized baby.

"I'm coming by. Just a cup of tea and talking it out will help. And you can make me leave at any time by closing your eyes and getting yourself some real sleep. I'll be there in fifteen minutes."

The emotional bond between them tugged at Sam. How long had they been best friends? At least twenty years. She smiled. Meanwhile, she thought of a way to take one other concern off her mind. She dialed the bakery and asked to speak to Julio.

When his soft, slightly accented voice came on the line she paused. Mentioning Kelly would be out of line. It was up to her daughter to bring up that subject. Instead, she did the first thing that occurred to her, asked him to bake the layers for her anniversary cake. Beau's favorite cake for the lower tier and her own for the smaller top.

"No problem, Sam. Anything else?" he asked.

"No, Julio. That's fine."

"Sam? Are you okay? You sound really tired. We're a little worried about you."

We? He and Kelly?

"Jen says to get some sleep. Now. I mean, that's how *she* said it."

Of course he meant the bakery staff.

"Thanks, Julio. I will."

Outside, a car crunched through the gravel in the driveway and Sam peered out the upstairs window. Zoë here already. She put on a robe and went downstairs.

"I brought my favorite herbal tea," Zoë said. "It's got valerian root, chamomile and some other stuff. I'll put the kettle on and you go snuggle into your favorite corner of the sofa with this lavender-scented afghan. I swear, it's the best recipe for restful sleep I've ever used."

Sam took the knitted blanket and did as instructed. When Zoë delivered a gently steaming mug of the tea and settled into the overstuffed chair near the foot of the couch, Sam spilled the whole thing—all her concerns over Kelly and Julio and her own guilt over having put her first anniversary on hold because of an urgent bakery order.

"Was Beau upset over it?"

"Not at all. He's been so understanding … and those roses …"

"Then, you know what? I say don't stress over it. You guys are fine. Kelly's fine. So what if the boyfriend turns out to be Julio—you love the guy. She'll tell you what's going on when she's ready, and I know that girl. You cannot push her, and no man is going to push her."

Sam had to nod agreement over that statement.

"You've made your customer happy. You've got a great husband and a fantastic marriage. He'll wrap up his case, you'll get your work schedule on an even keel, and the two of you can take a weekend away. I'd offer a room at our place but I know you. You and Beau will both sneak out to check your respective work places. Go somewhere fun, sweetie. Maybe San Antonio or southern California. Take a quick flight and just hole up in a hotel somewhere."

Sam smiled as the effects of the warm tea lulled her.

"I'm setting your cup down now," Zoë said. "Put this pillow under your head and just close your eyes for a few minutes."

It felt good, hearing her best friend's solid, commonsense talk.

When Sam stirred, Zoë was gone. She pulled the cover over her shoulders and rolled to her side. She woke to find a lamp on in the room but it was dark outside. Her phone was on the coffee table and she saw that it was after seven o'clock. She'd missed a call from Beau.

Chapter 23

Beau bided his time in his office while Rico put Donny Vargas into the station's one detention cell. The grease on the boot print found at the Robinet home came back positive for motor oil mixed with dirt, a pretty certain sign it had come from a garage floor. Vargas could sit there awhile and sweat over what the lawmen knew or didn't know.

Meanwhile, Krystal Cordova was doing the same in an interrogation room. Beau had picked her up personally, before she'd had the chance to make up and fluff up for an evening of hanging around the men at The Scoreboard. Without the makeup and hair she looked younger and more innocent. Healthier, too. In a way, that made it more difficult for him to come down hard with his questions but he had to get to the bottom of this. The case was getting older and colder by the day.

He finished the sandwich someone had brought him hours ago for lunch, fortified himself with a cup of fresh coffee, and headed toward Krystal's room. She looked up, no more timid than the fiery little thing she'd been at four o'clock.

"What am I doing here, Sheriff?" she demanded. "Don't I get a lawyer?"

"Up to you. You haven't been charged with anything, so if you call one it's on your dime. I hear they're kind of pricey."

"So, what do you want?"

"Well, Krystal, I want to know just how far your plan went when you and Ray tried to blackmail Josephine Robinet."

"I have no idea what you're talking about."

"Now *that* is a lie. You admitted a couple days ago that you and Ray thought you could make more money than what Jo paid you to seduce her husband."

"I provided more services. I had the guy ready to take me away to the Virgin Islands. That's worth more money."

"Whose bright idea was it to kill Zack Robinet?"

The abrupt switch in topic startled her. She went back to the default answer: "I don't know what you're talking about."

"You don't know that Zack was murdered? Come on. Or you don't know who thought of it?"

"I, uh—"

"You think about that for a minute. Meanwhile, Donny Vargas broke into the Robinet home yesterday. What was he there for?" In fact, the intruder had worn gloves, so they only had the greasy footprint to go by. But it was worth the bluff to see what she knew. "I'm thinking some important little piece of evidence ties all three of you into this so deep you'll never get out. Donny was probably voted, or talked, into going there to look for it."

"Donny? What the hell does he have to do with anything? The guy's a douche."

"That's the best description you can think of? He's involved, Krystal. And I seriously doubt he's going to act so dumb about the details as you are. When we talk to him, I'll bet he's going to tell us every single thing you and Ray did, from the moment Jo Robinet hired you to the time of the murder, and probably including what all you've done to cover up your involvement. In court, it's going to sound like the stupid move of the century, you all trying to blackmail a woman but going ahead and killing the husband before you ever got any money from her."

Her eyes grew wide at the laundry list of problems Vargas could create for her.

"Look, Sheriff, I really don't know about any of this. I have no idea if Donny broke into that lady's house. I have no idea if he ever went to Albuquerque, much less to the hotel." Her voice cracked slightly.

He gave her a minute of silence, to let the implications fully soak in. "Krystal, I don't mean to be hard on you here. At this point I need to know who actually killed Zack Robinet. Who pushed that needle full of smack into his arm?"

He leaned in closer across the table. "Cause, quite frankly, Krystal, you are the only person positively identified as going in and out of that hotel room. The video cameras don't lie. We have the desk clerk and a maid who also remember you. They don't remember Ray. They don't remember Donny. But they remember you."

"Are you arresting me?" Her hands shook and she clasped them together to hide the fact.

"I'm building a case. Right now, according to the evidence, you're the one going down for this. If others were involved, I need to know it. If you can tell me how Ray or Donny got into the room and gave the shot, I'm listening. If you can give me something that shows it was their idea and they forced you to do it, I think a prosecutor and jury would be a lot kinder to you."

He shrugged as if he didn't have a care in the world. "That's all I'm saying."

A tear tracked its way slowly down her cheek.

"I swear, Sheriff, all I knew was the part about trying to get more money from the lady. Okay, that wasn't a nice thing to do. But life isn't nice, is it? She has a bunch of it, and I have hardly anything. I didn't see as how it hurt her to pay a little more. She got what she wanted out of the deal, right? She's rid of the man she claims treated her like dirt. I don't know nothing about the rest of it."

"Go through that whole day with me again," Beau said.

He brought out a yellow pad and pen, taking down her words which were basically a rehash of what she'd told them the first time. She was hired by Jo. She'd been seeing Zack Robinet for awhile. He promised to take her to Vegas for the weekend and maybe somewhere more exotic later on. They had sex in the hotel room in Albuquerque. She went out for pizza. He was dead when she came back. She got scared, gathered her things and ran away.

While it would have been helpful to have her add something to tie Belatoni or Vargas to the events of that day, Beau wasn't ready to give up on the men quite yet. A little time in the holding cell might improve Krystal's memory, although it bothered him a little that her version of the details had, so far, never varied. If only they could connect her to a known supplier for the heroin—who he believed to be Ray Belatoni—he could have her sent to Albuquerque and let Kent Taylor do the rest.

Having Albuquerque take over this mess would be fine with Beau. He sighed and stood up, telling Krystal he'd be right back. The clock on the wall caught his attention. Already approaching dinner time and he wasn't even close to being done. Last night, it had been Sam's work interfering with their anniversary celebration. Tonight it was his. He stepped into his office, dialed her cell and left a message apologizing all over himself for ruining whatever plan she'd made. He would make it up to her tomorrow night. Promise.

He rounded up two deputies who were lounging in the squad room, clearly uneager for work since both were only now recovering from that flu bug.

"Each of you take one of them. Handcuffs all the way. I want them to see each other but no chance for a clash or bodily harm, okay?"

Ramirez went to the holding cell and handcuffed Donny Vargas, who turned dutifully and put his wrists together. Waters followed Beau to the interrogation room where Beau explained to Krystal that she would be spending the evening here instead of at her usual haunts. She sobbed quietly as her wrists were cuffed.

The little entourage walked through the station until Beau opened the door leading to the separate holding cell area. Waters pulled Krystal aside as Ramirez led Donny Vargas out. Her eyes widened when she saw that Beau was not bluffing; Donny was indeed on his way to be interrogated. Vargas spotted Krystal and stared daggers at her. The warning was clear. As soon as the mechanic was safely out of the area, Beau instructed Waters to lock Krystal in the cell. His voice came out a little more gruff than normal. When he walked away he could hear her weeping quietly.

He let both suspects stew while he ate a sandwich at his desk, not exactly the nice dinner Sam had envisioned for them. When he entered the interrogation room twenty minutes later, Donny Vargas sat sprawled in a chair, tapping his fingers impatiently on the table.

"About time," he said.

"I'm sorry," Beau said, "I wasn't aware you were the one setting the schedule here." He took an extra couple of minutes to offer water, lay out his notepad and pen and pull out his chair. "Now, let's see. First off, there's the little matter of a break-in at the Robinet home yesterday morning."

"Don't know nothin' about that."

"Your footprint, with grease on it from the garage, was left on their white carpet."

"Not mine." Vargas had not flinched or straightened his posture. Cool as ice.

"We'll get back to that. You're friends with Ray Belatoni at The Scoreboard."

A tiny shrug. What of it?

"And Krystal Cordova."

Barely raised eyebrows.

"What's their relationship with the Robinets?"

"Relationship? You mean was Krystal screwing the guy's brains out?"

Beau tapped his pen against the notepad.

"Yeah, I suppose. I wasn't there at the time."

"Why do you suppose it's true?"

"The girl can't keep her mouth shut. She was all over the bar, bragging about how she was being paid by some lady to lure the husband. Krys has it all figured out that she can make the guy fall in love with her and the two of them will go away together. Says it's what the wife really wants, for him to leave town. Why not with her on some island or something?"

"That's a pretty unbelievable request from a wife."

Donny shrugged again. "Weird, yeah, but who can figure out people. They're all weird, especially the ones with money. The more they got, the weirder they are."

Beau couldn't necessarily disagree with that.

"You got into a big fight with Zack Robinet over something at the dealership where you work. Did the fight continue later, in some other place maybe?"

"No. I'm not that stupid. Geez, you think I'd kill a guy because he yelled at me at work? Half the customers in that place are unhappy about their bill. Friststone jacks up the prices of everything. That ain't my fault."

"Where were you last Wednesday?"

"Work. Went home after."

"No stop for a drink on the way?"

"Not that night. Just wasn't in the mood."

"Can someone verify that's where you were?"

"Check around. I live alone but my neighbors might have seen my car outside my apartment."

"I hear Ray Belatoni deals a little out at the bar. Ever see evidence that heroin passes through there?"

"Man, I know nothin' about any drug deals. My job requires tests and we aren't told when they'll happen."

It was the first time Beau sensed dishonesty in the man's statement. He probably had a way of finding out when his test would come around and he'd either lay off his recreational substances for awhile or he would manage to fake the results.

Nothing else about the man's posture or attitude showed signs of deceit. Beau made notes on the pad, thinking furiously, looking for a reason to hold Vargas longer, but he couldn't come up with anything solid.

* * *

Sam woke up wondering why she'd stayed all night on the sofa. Inertia, she supposed. She had listened to Beau's message on her phone, saying he was tied up questioning suspects and wouldn't get away in time for dinner, and after that she'd simply rolled over and fallen right back into a deep sleep.

Now, she saw that he'd been home. A handwritten note was propped against her phone on the table and she caught the scent of brewed coffee. She picked up the slip of paper.

I tried to be quiet—you needed your sleep. Call me when you wake up. xx Beau

She could tell he was distracted during the call, and a glance at the clock told her she had probably interrupted his morning briefing with the deputies. He promised to be available for dinner tonight and said he would call her a little later in the day.

Sweet's Sweets was already humming when Sam arrived. Three customers at the counter had Jen's attention, while two others sat at the bistro tables with their newspapers and coffee. Sam said hello to each as she surveyed the situation and saw all was running smoothly.

In the kitchen, Becky was going through a stack of order forms, prioritizing as Sam always did. Julio stepped from the walk-in fridge and told her he had put the layers for her anniversary cake in there. Jo stood at the stove, watching a copper pan full of bubbling chocolate. Sam stepped over to take a look.

"I'm glad you're here," Jo said. "We didn't really talk about exactly what you wanted done with this. I molded a pound or so of fairly plain shapes yesterday. Would you like creams, nuts or caramels today?"

"Sure. An assortment sounds good." She studied Jo's face. "Thanks for handling this while I rested. I hope you got some sleep last night, too."

"I did. It's still really weird, being at Brenda's. I should probably move back home. I managed to spend a little time last night going through those papers from the safe—Zack's will, the original partnership agreement between him and Chandler, the banking and investment accounts."

Something told Sam there was more. "Looks like the chocolate is ready for cooling. Want to chat a minute while it does?"

Jo turned off the flame and set the pan aside to cool, tilting her head toward the back door. Outside, she turned to Sam and the worry showed clearly on her face.

"Remember, I told you I had no money worries now? Well, something from the safe has me really concerned."

"Is it something I can help with?" Sam asked.

"No, not in the way you're thinking. I'm only bringing it up because there might be some connection with what happened to Zack."

Sam waited while Jo put her thoughts together.

"There's a significant amount of money missing. One of the investment accounts had over three million dollars in it. It's nearly empty now."

"A joint account?"

"No, business. We opened the account because there was no point in leaving large amounts of cash in the company checking account. It earns nothing there, so I suggested to Zack and Chandler that we put the money into some investments that would earn a better return."

"Maybe the investments themselves dropped in value?"

"No. These were cash withdrawals. Two fairly small ones, ten thousand apiece, over the last couple of months. I might not have noticed them, thinking one of the partners or Helen needed the money for operating expenses. But last month the balance of the account was virtually cleaned out. With everything going on this past week, I hadn't been online to look at it and the printed statements hadn't arrived yet. Of course, once the statements arrived I would have caught it immediately."

"Who was authorized to move money from that account?"

"Just the partners and myself. Helen had access but only through one of us. If she needed money for expenses she told us—usually either me or Zack—and we transferred the funds back to the checking account she uses for bills."

"You think Zack withdrew the money without telling you?"

"It looks that way."

"My first thought is that Krystal and Ray tried unsuccessfully to blackmail you. Maybe they tried the same with Zack and he gave it to them."

"They only asked me for fifty thousand. It's pretty bold

to up the ante by that much, don't you think?"

Sam wondered. Something must have changed. The blackmailers became bolder, they found out there was more money available and they might as well ask for it … It was only a guess at this point.

"Beau is questioning Krystal now. I think he needs this information."

"You're right. Call him. I can get the account number and pertinent data. The brokerage firm should have information about the circumstances of the withdrawal, who authorized it and such. Being that I only found this last night, I haven't taken the time yet to call them."

"Beau can tell you what he needs. Let's turn it over to him for now." Sam pulled out her phone and dialed his number, then handed the phone to Jo.

He took the relevant information, although Jo didn't have it all.

"I left all the paperwork at Brenda's. I guess I wasn't thinking too clearly this morning."

"That's okay," he said. "There are a few things I can check first. If you get the chance during the day, get the specifics. If we end up needing copies for evidence you'll have to contact the brokerage firm directly and authorize my access to the account."

She agreed to do it and they ended the call.

Back inside, Jo went back to her batch of chocolate, while Sam concentrated on the anniversary cake—at last. When Beau called back, close to noon, his news wasn't helpful at all.

"Krystal claims to know nothing about the money. I obtained warrants for Krystal's and Ray Belatoni's financial information. Neither of their accounts shows any large influx of cash, ever. In fact, The Scoreboard is basically hanging by a thread to stay in business. His drug deals must be very small-time. If Belatoni got hold of a lot of cash, surely it would have gone toward that."

Unless the pair planned to skip the country, in which case they could have opened an entirely new account, or they could literally be hiding a pile of cash.

Chapter 24

With Beau's news that Ray and Krystal did not appear to have the missing money, Jo left the bakery to gather the information he needed. Sam placed the final flounces on her anniversary cake. She would deliver it to the restaurant then go home and dress for the special occasion. She only hoped Beau wouldn't be running late.

She phoned Zoë and thanked her for yesterday's TLC.

"It was nothing any best friend wouldn't have done," Zoë said with a little laugh. "Come by later and I'll give you more of that tea. As relentlessly as you work, I have a feeling you could use a cup of it every evening."

Sam didn't care much about getting the tea but she really should take Zoë a little thank-you gift for taking the time to come and sit with her. She found a small foil-covered box and filled it with chocolates Jo had just finished.

She pictured Jo, stirring the new batch this morning and their conversation about the missing money. She'd mentioned each of the partners having access to the account. That would leave Zack and Chandler as the only suspects. If paying blackmail to Krystal and Ray wasn't the motive, why would either of them take it? Their games were so successful that each man's half-interest in the company had made him a multi-millionaire. Surely, either partner could request a draw of more money if he had a large purchase coming up. Helping himself to more didn't make sense. She would ask Jo about it later; maybe some provision in the partnership agreement would shed some light.

She closed the lid on the little box of candy. A bow and a card, and it was all set. If she left a little early, Sam could easily drop it off on her way home. She stowed the anniversary cake safely in the back of her van and placed Zoë's gift on the passenger seat. A quick stop at the restaurant where she was forced to park in a sunny spot. She set Zoë's gift on the floor where it was shady and a glimmer caught her eye.

The carved box. She picked it up. She'd taken it to work with her last night, knowing she would need every bit of extra energy she could get from it. Exhausted afterward, she'd obviously forgotten to take it in the house and put it back in a safe place. Once again, Isobel St. Clair's warnings came back.

There was nothing to do now but conceal the artifact until she got home. She pushed it completely out of sight under the car seat and double checked to be sure it wasn't visible. Already, her right hand felt a little warm and tingly from touching it. She hoped the box's glow would quickly fade and no one would notice it from outside the van.

Retrieving her cake from the back, she assured it was placed in a safe spot in the restaurant kitchen, her name and reservation time on it. Heaven forbid it accidentally got served to someone else. On to Zoë's house, a few blocks away.

The big territorial style adobe looked especially beautiful in the autumn with its glowing yellow cottonwood trees contrasting with the massive blue spruce on the east side. Out front, she spotted Zoë working in the garden, chopping spent hollyhock stalks and setting out colorful chrysanthemums in gold and purple. Zoë's green thumb was what kept the bed and breakfast one of the most picturesque and most desired in town.

Sam parked in the guest parking area, empty now, and picked up the gift.

"Hey there," greeted Zoë. "If I'd known you were coming this soon I would have quit this yard work and made us some tea already."

"Don't worry about it. I can only stay a minute." Sam showed the gift box. "A little thanks for yesterday. I can put it in the kitchen if you—"

A car pulling in very close beside her interrupted the thought as she stepped closer to her van to get out of its way.

The red convertible seemed familiar and she realized why when she saw Chandler Lane get out.

"I saw your van," he said. "I was just on my way to talk to the sheriff. I heard they arrested a couple of people for Zack's murder."

It took Sam a moment to switch gears and process what he was saying. She didn't recall Beau saying he'd formally charged Krystal or Ray or Donny. Only that he was questioning them all. She stepped closer to Chandler's car.

"I'm afraid I really don't know much about the progress on the case." Her eyes dropped to the interior of his car.

There on the light-colored floor mat was a dark spot, a footprint that made an ugly mark on the pristine carpet. Light carpet, dark footprint. The other one—at Jo's house—flashed through her mind. The print was the same, that distinctive patterned shape from a boot. Chandler had shown up as they were leaving the Robinet house and he wore boots then. She glanced at his feet but he now had on sneakers.

Suddenly, the break-in at Jo's house and the stalker at her hotel made sense. Sam swallowed hard and dared a glance at Chandler's face. He knew that she knew.

His right hand had remained in the pocket of his lightweight jacket. Now a firm, cylindrical shape distorted the fabric as he pointed the barrel of a gun at her.

"I had really hoped to get this thing solved without you figuring it out," he said.

Gone was the smile. The wide-eyed inquiries about progress in the case weren't so innocent at all. Chandler Lane wasn't asking out of concern for his dead friend or justice or anything like that. He wanted to know if the lawmen were on to him. A sick feeling settled into Sam's gut.

She glanced at Zoë, who stared open-mouthed without a clue about what was happening.

"Get into my car, Mrs. Cardwell. I need those papers Jo Robinet gave you and to persuade your husband to let me leave."

Sam was so accustomed to her business name that Cardwell didn't immediately click. And papers? What papers? He took her hesitation as a refusal.

"Okay then. I guess you aren't so worried about your friend." His voice became more menacing with every word.

Sam looked frantically up and down the short street. Not a soul in sight. The lack of traffic that appealed so much to Zoë's guests was not such a good thing now.

"I don't have the papers," she said, stalling. "I left them at the bakery."

"In the car then." He meant it.

Sam knew going along with him would be stupid. The man had killed once. Even as the thought occurred to her, she realized it had to be true. She still wasn't clear on the reason—maybe an argument over the stolen money, maybe something else—but the man in front of her was crazy and dangerous.

"Let's get the sheriff here and you can tell him your story," she said, reaching for the phone in her pocket.

The moment the phone appeared, he rushed closer and kicked it from her hand. It went flying toward the street and landed with the sound of smashed glass. When she looked at Chandler again he was laughing, a high maniacal sound.

"You're crazy. I'm not telling the sheriff my *story*. There is no *story*, as far as I'm concerned. Zack got mixed up in drugs and overdosed. It looks like he took a bunch of money from the company's funds too."

"Really?" No one knew about the missing money until Jo discovered it last night. Another fact that would nail Chandler's ass, if Sam could manage to survive the next few minutes. How could she get help or get control of the gun, she wondered. Two seconds later, she heard the sound of a vehicle making the turn onto the narrow lane where they stood.

Unfortunately, Chandler heard it too. He lowered the

hand with the gun. Sam calculated her odds of dashing out and getting the driver's attention before he could raise the gun again and shoot her. It didn't look good.

The car passed them, a tiny white-haired woman at the wheel. Good thing Sam hadn't rushed for help from that sector. When she looked at Chandler again, he was studying her face and the gun hand was back up.

Zoë had finally caught on and was edging her way toward her house. With a hedge and wide porch between herself and safety, that wasn't a good bet either. Sam started to warn her to stay put, but Zoë took it the wrong way and began to run.

Chandler Lane had no compunction about using his weapon. He whipped it free of the jacket fabric, raised it with a practiced eye and fired. The shot reverberated and echoed through the neighborhood of closely built houses. Sam froze, horrified, as Zoë stumbled sideways and went down.

Chapter 25

Heedless of any danger to herself, Sam raced to Zoë's side. Her best friend lay on the ground, writhing in pain. Blood covered the shreds of her left sleeve.

"Oh god, Zoë, can you hear me?"

Zoë groaned, rolling to her side and gripping the wounded arm with her other hand.

"Hold on. I'll get help." But when Sam looked toward the street, Chandler Lane blocked her view.

He was standing above the two women, holding the gun at Sam's head.

"This isn't one of your video games, Chandler," she said, fearing the waver in her voice. She had to stay strong for Zoë now. "You don't want to kill us. Your life would be over."

A tiny flicker of hesitation showed in his eyes.

Sam made a plan. "Drive away. Let me get medical help for her."

The flicker had not been compassion. His expression hardened. "Get her in the house. I don't want anyone to see us out here."

"That's right. Dozens of people heard that shot. We're only two blocks off the plaza. I'm sure they are rushing over here right now."

"You're not helping your case, Sam." He almost smiled as he said it. "Get her inside. Now."

Zoë's injury seemed confined to her left arm. Sam put both arms around her and managed to get her to her feet, although Zoë's face lost all color when she stood.

"Stick with me," Sam murmured. "We'll get you inside and I'll think of something. Hopefully, he'll let us go in and then leave us alone."

Obviously, Darryl wasn't home or he would have come running. Sam knew it was up to her to save her friend's life. She took most of Zoë's weight, guiding her wobbly legs along the driveway beside the house. By the time they reached the kitchen door, Zoë, surprisingly, seemed to have a little more strength. Sam half expected Chandler to get them out of sight of the road and shoot them both, but he let Sam open the door and guide her friend into the house.

The big kitchen with its commercial-grade appliances and Saltillo tile floors offered no comfortable spot for an injured person. Sam kept moving, going down the hall toward the room Zoë called the parlor, one with soft sofas and chairs where guests met in the evenings for wine and snacks. She eased Zoë onto one of the couches.

"I'm going for some gauze and alcohol," she told Chandler.

"No, you're not. Stay right there." To reinforce the order, he blocked the doorway and kept the pistol trained on Sam.

"Fine. You can get away now. I'll stay with her and call paramedics once your car is gone."

"And you'll call the sheriff who'll have an alert out for me. I won't get a mile away, will I?"

Well, that was sort of the plan, Sam thought. She saw his dilemma. Leaving them here gave him no way out. Staying with them didn't either. Sadly, she couldn't think of any chance this was going to end well.

Her best bet was to keep the status quo. If Chandler stayed here, providing he didn't go wild and start shooting, eventually Beau would either try to call her or go to meet her at the restaurant for dinner. When he learned she had left Sweet's Sweets hours earlier, he would begin looking. If Becky told him Sam had meant to deliver a gift to Zoë, it would send him this direction and he would see her van out front. Unfortunately, he would assume she and Zoë were in the house, talking endlessly until she'd forgotten the time. Unless he realized the car out front was Chandler's, that it didn't belong to one of Zoë's guests, he would walk right into a trap, never suspecting a thing. How could she warn him?

As long as Sam was defiant, Chandler's mood stayed hostile. He stood in the doorway with the gun aimed toward the sofa where Zoë lay and Sam knelt to attend to her injury. She could tell that the bullet had not entered the arm. A long, ragged gash had ripped the skin, but it went through muscle, not into bone or artery. The more frequently Sam touched the injured area, the better it looked. The box's power, even in the brief time she'd handled it earlier, still offered potent effects.

She watched Chandler surreptitiously while wiping Zoë's forehead. When Sam went quiet, thinking of what she could say to summon help—how to phrase it most effectively in the fewest words—their captor became restless, almost bored. He paced to the window and looked out through the lace curtain.

"Who else is likely to show up here?" he asked. "Do you have guests tonight?"

Zoë moaned without answering.

That agitated him. He was accustomed to control, to issuing orders. He didn't mind unknowns, up to a point. The nature of the gaming world had taught him that, Sam supposed. As long as you held the weapon it didn't matter what enemy sprang out at you. But he was used to being the mastermind behind the games. He knew how many potential enemies lurked, how many levels it took to reach the top. Now he didn't. She needed to figure out how to use that against him.

She murmured soft words to Zoë, initially asking how she felt, telling her to stay calm. When she sensed Chandler's distraction she added instructions. "Don't let on it's getting better." Zoë complied by screaming with Academy Award persuasion.

"You can't let her lie here in pain," Sam insisted. "At least find me something to clean the wound and some bandages. There are six bathrooms in this house, and I'd bet there's a first aid kit somewhere near the kitchen. Let me go get *something*."

He ignored the request until the next scream.

"Where's the closest bathroom?" he demanded.

"Go to the hall. The first door on the right," Sam said.

He looked around and spotted a telephone on one of

the end tables. Sending Sam a knowing look, he walked over to it and unplugged the cord, taking the phone with him.

Snag number one.

"Quick, Zoë, is there another phone I can get to?" Sam whispered close to her friend's ear.

Zoë took a ragged breath. "Darryl had a spare cell phone for a long time. In one of the desk drawers over there, across the room. If the battery isn't dead—"

Chandler came back, holding out a box of tissues. "It's the only thing I could find."

"This is useless," Sam told him. "Can't I just go look?"

He peered at Zoë's sleeve. "It's not bleeding anymore. It'll be fine."

He pulled an armchair to the doorway and sat on the edge of the seat, his legs bouncing with pent-up energy. The jumpiness finally registered. He was high on something. Any chance of getting to the desk or somehow shoving past him and running outdoors went away.

At the window, daylight was fading fast. It had to be only another hour or so until full darkness. She might be able to do something then. Zoë kept going with her litany of moans. Then she said something that chilled Sam.

"Darryl," she whispered.

"What?" Then it hit her—with the loss of daylight, Zoë's husband would soon come home from whatever construction job he was on. He would walk right in unless something alerted him not to. They couldn't afford to wait this out much longer.

"Beg for something," Sam whispered, "something in another room."

"Aahh, the pain," Zoë cried loudly. "I need something for the pain."

Sam stared accusingly at Chandler. "Come on. Some Tylenol or something. I think she keeps in it the kitchen. Let me get it."

She stood up as if to walk right past his chair.

"No way. I'll get it. Which cabinet?"

Darn. They couldn't even gain extra time by making him search.

"The one nearest the microwave," Zoë said, gasping the words.

The moment Chandler left the room, Sam raced to the desk and the drawer Zoë told her to look in. The cell phone was there. She flipped it open and pressed the power button. It lit up. She watched it search for a signal—ten seconds, twenty, thirty. Chandler was being none too quiet in the kitchen, thank goodness. By the time a few bars showed a signal on the cell phone she heard him in the hall again. She dropped the phone into her pocket.

"We have to think of something else to send him for," Sam whispered. "In a couple minutes. By then we should have a better signal."

Their captor stood in the doorway. Sam had a moment's awful feeling he might have overheard her last words. But he merely tossed a pill bottle her direction. She instinctively reached for it, grabbing it in midair.

"What about some water?" she said. "She can't swallow these without water."

Chandler's expression darkened.

Zoë cried out again, grabbing her wounded arm and rolling into a fetal ball on the sofa.

The heel of his hand smacked the back of the armchair he'd left in the doorway. His face contorted in anger and Sam had a brief flash of him going completely berserk, shooting them and trashing the house before leaving. Then, in an instant, his jerky movements settled and he turned back toward the kitchen after sending an impatient scowl her way. With these mood swings, hc was likely to go over the edge at the very next slight provocation. They most likely only had one chance to live through this ordeal.

She whipped out the cell phone and punched Beau's number with shaking hands.

She got out only a few words before Zoë shrieked her name. She could only hope they were the right words.

Chapter 26

Beau felt his cell phone vibrate as he got ready to get into the shower. He glanced at the readout, didn't recognize the number. Debated whether to answer. If he lost much time he would be late to meet Sam at the restaurant. She was probably running late, too. There was no sign she'd been home to change clothes and shower. After the third ring the call went to voicemail. He sighed. He would listen to the message but whatever it was would have to wait until morning. He would *not* ruin their anniversary plans again.

He tapped the button and turned up the speaker volume. What he heard froze him in place. "Beau, help! Zoë and I are held hostage at the B&B. Bring reinforcements." It was Sam's voice.

What the hell had happened? He straightened his clothes, his mind racing furiously. The danger had to be real—Sam would never say something like that if it weren't absolutely genuine. He ran downstairs, started his cruiser. Before he reached the end of his driveway he'd got dispatch on the radio and ordered all units to the end of Zoë's street.

Hostages. The worst of all scenarios. He couldn't let his men or vehicles be seen until they were certain of what they were dealing with. He didn't dare call that strange cell number back. It could make the whole situation explode. His small department didn't have SWAT teams or hostage negotiators. He had to solve this himself.

He visualized the layout in his mind. The bed and breakfast sat on a short lane. At the south end was Kit Carson Road, one of the busiest in the central part of town. The north end dead-ended near the park but didn't connect with it. So, basically, one way in and one way out. He immediately went to a secure frequency and began issuing orders: block the lane at the intersection; let no one in or out; send an officer in a plain car to cruise by and observe the location. He would be there himself in ten minutes. He hit his lights and siren and roared through traffic.

Kit Carson Road was already a mess by the time Beau arrived at the blockade. Two lanes were barely enough to accommodate the normal traffic but throwing in police vehicles and barriers caused every driver to slow to a crawl to see what was going on. He whipped into the oncoming lane and angled his cruiser next to the barrier, pleased to see how quickly his men had responded. He sent one of them to act as traffic control and keep things moving.

"She'll be fine," Rico said when he joined Beau beside the cruiser.

Somehow, the word that Sam was involved had leaked. He didn't recall he'd actually said her name.

"I drove a plain car to the end of the block and back. Sam's van is out front. There's also a red convertible." He gave the plate number. "It's registered to Chandler Lane. The building is dark except for a light in one of the front rooms."

"No other guest cars?"

"No, sir."

That was one less worry.

"Do you think you were spotted?"

"No sign of anyone near the window that's lit. It looks like one of those lacy curtains that you can see through. They might still be able to see the street, but once it gets dark outside he may decide they're too visible. He could order them to shut off the indoor light or close some heavier drapes."

"What about other residences on the street? We need to decide whether it's necessary to evacuate them."

Rico nodded. "There are only about a dozen. We could have Dixie use the reverse directory and phone each house, warning them to stay indoors. People are just now getting off work, so there might not be anyone home in some of them anyway."

"Good thinking. Get right on that."

Headlights lit his cruiser as a vehicle pulled out of traffic. Beau started to order the driver to move on, then he recognized the white pickup with lumber rack as Darryl Chartrain's. He walked over to inform Zoë's husband that he couldn't go home. Although he didn't want to say why, he felt bound to let the man know the overall situation.

"How can I help?" Darryl said.

A man of action rather than hysterics. Beau appreciated that. Unfortunately, he couldn't let Darryl anywhere near the house.

"Take my keys," Darryl said. "If you have the chance to approach, at least you can get in."

Beau weighed the circumstances. In a big city, factoring in the hyper-dramatics presented in movies and relentless coverage by media, any number of things could happen: the entire building rigged with explosives, the perpetrator cunning enough to have some sort of infrared way of seeing everything and desperate enough to shoot every human who crossed his path.

But Beau had to assess this realistically. This was Taos and he was dealing with a businessman who had somehow gotten into a bad situation. Granted, a *very* bad situation, but still. Chandler Lane, from all they knew of him, was not a criminal mastermind. He had entangled himself in some type of financial fiasco. Perhaps Zack had caught him embezzling funds from the investment accounts. Things had spiraled downward and Zack was dead. How low had Chandler Lane sunk? Beau had to be careful that Sam and Zoë didn't meet the same fate as Zack before Beau and his team could capture the killer.

Chapter 27

Sam pulled Zoë's bloody, ripped sleeve over the wound, which her own touch had nearly healed. It was vital that Chandler continue to believe Zoë was helpless.

"We need some light in here," she told their captor. "From the street it's going to look suspicious that there are cars out front and no lights inside. This place is always lit up." Plus, I need to be able to watch your hand on that gun.

He had been pacing the room for the past ten minutes, making Sam believe more than ever that he'd taken another snort of whatever he was high on when he went to the kitchen for the glass of water. The pistol worried her. In his agitated state, he could easily pull the trigger when he didn't intend to. She wanted to watch his face, to hope that she could read his expressions well enough to have a bit of warning before he aimed at her.

He peered around the edge of the lace curtain, toward the street . Apparently it was quiet enough for his liking.

"One lamp," he said.

Sam reached for the floor lamp beside the sofa before he could make the choice. She twisted the little plastic switch several clicks, causing the light to go on and off twice.

"Sorry. I thought maybe it was a three-way bulb." *Or that I could get a signal out to someone.*

His eyes became hard.

"Sorry." Sam kept the gun in sight. He'd stopped holding it up, aimed at the women all the time, but it had never once left his hand.

She spread a knitted afghan over Zoë, who by now had toned down the moans and was watching everything through half-closed eyes. Sam sat in one of the chairs near Zoë's feet. She tried to give the impression of being calm and non-threatening, but her mind was racing. Beau would have been home by now, getting ready for their dinner out. She prayed with everything she had that he'd received her message and made sense of it. Meanwhile, she had to go on the assumption that she and Zoë were on their own here. They needed to overpower Chandler or distract him long enough so they could get away. Unfortunately, she didn't see any way for that to happen.

He paced the length of the room twice more and finally went back to the armchair at the doorway. Again, the jittery leg. What was his goal in holding them? How long before he became bored and shot them both?

* * *

Beau directed Deputy Waters to park next to Darryl

Chartrain's pickup truck. The back of Waters' cruiser was full of weapons and teargas canisters. Overkill, most likely, but he wanted to be sure they could take Mr. Lane with a minimum of resistance. Leaving two officers in charge of traffic and onlooker-control, the rest suited up with Kevlar vests and high-power rifles. Beau led the way. In under ten minutes they had disabled both the red convertible and Sam's van as getaway vehicles and established a perimeter around the nearly dark bed and breakfast.

Beau moved stealthily to the back door, gently twisted the knob and found it locked. He pulled Darryl's key from his pocket and prayed the construction man kept the lock and door hardware well oiled and noise free. It worked. He and Rico slipped in and moved, weapons drawn, toward the light that showed faintly into the kitchen from the hall.

Voices. He made out Sam's. She sounded tired. A male voice responded to something she said.

"... not that hard to override an electronic hotel key," the man said.

"Were you just trying to scare Jo? Why?"

A chair scraped. Beau wished he could see into that room. He stood with his back to the wall, weapon aimed upward, and signaled to Rico to be ready. On his signal— one finger, two, three—they filled the doorway. Chandler Lane spun around, shock registering on his face.

"Drop the gun!" Beau ordered. "Facedown on the floor!"

Lane looked for a fraction of a second as if he might defy them. Then he dropped to his knees.

"Down!"

Lane went face down and released the pistol. Beau kicked it toward Rico and held his rifle over their suspect while Rico secured his weapon and cuffed their man.

"Sam, you ladies all right?" He took his eyes off Chandler long enough to see Sam standing at the end of a sofa, Zoë sitting up with a cover over her lap, blood on her blouse.

Beau called down the men on the perimeter and told them to come inside to take their suspect into custody. With Chandler Lane on his way to jail, Beau turned to the women. Sam gave a quick recap of what had happened. Zoë's wound looked superficial. Beau allowed Darryl into the house and recommended he take his wife for medical care, even though Zoë protested that a little herbal cream would heal it just fine.

Outside, Rico awaited instructions. Beau told him to lock Chandler in their detention cell and call Kent Taylor in Albuquerque. As for himself, he planned to take his wife out for their anniversary.

Chapter 28

Sam protested, saying Beau had far more important things to do at the moment, but once he'd pointed out that it would take Kent Taylor nearly three hours to drive up from Albuquerque and that their own plans had been on hold far too long already, she acquiesced.

"We aren't exactly dressed for fancy," she said, looking down at her disheveled clothing as they walked to their vehicles.

He reattached her distributor cap and looked at his watch. "We have thirty minutes before they'll give away our reservation. Do what you can with it."

It's amazing what a four-minute shower and change of shirt will do, she discovered. They walked into the restaurant at one minute after seven and were given the choicest table in the house. Beau chose a good wine and by the time they'd decided to order the chateaubriand for two Sam finally began to relax.

"At the risk of making this sound like the work day never ends," he said, "I have to say I'm still having a hard time putting today's events together."

She smiled. "We can talk about it. I don't mind."

"What did he admit to you, while he had you and Zoë trapped there?"

Where to begin? "Chandler's got some heavy-duty drug problems, Beau. Being around him, especially when he's stressed out, I really saw it for the first time. I think that's at the bottom of all this. Plus, he rambled a lot while we were in there—things about his Manhattan apartment that cost ten million, how he's bought a castle in Europe, and how he was buying a private jet. That takes a crazy amount of money to support those things. I think he started looking for ways to take Zack's share of the business. He broke into the Robinet home to steal papers from their safe. At first I thought he was after the financial records, in order to cover up the fact he'd cleaned out a rather large investment account, the one Jo just now discovered."

Beau nodded as he dipped a hunk of bread into the olive oil and garlic mixture their waiter had brought.

"But he said something at one point this afternoon that made me realize what he was *really* after was Zack's copy of their original partnership agreement. Chandler was very hyper, talked a lot, muttered on about how 'it wasn't like that.' I asked him what he was talking about. Their agreement, he said—if one partner died, the other was to take over ownership of the whole business."

"Giving Chandler access to all the millions in company assets."

"Yes. But then he said it wasn't like that, and I wondered what *that* was. It turns out each partner's share becomes part of his estate, so upon Zack's death Jo inherits his half. Chandler didn't gain a thing by killing Zack. Now he had to get Jo as well."

"So he tried to get into her room at the El Monte Hotel because no one knew she was there and no one would come checking on her."

"He came right out and told me how easy it was to create a little device that circumvented the key card. But I think it started even earlier. I'll bet if you investigate very carefully, you'll find that it was Chandler who ran Jo off the road last Thursday morning. Maybe she spotted Ray Belatoni at the gas station, but I don't think he's the one who chased her down. She doesn't remember the actual crash. My guess is another vehicle came along and Chandler had to drive away before he could be sure she was dead."

"His car wasn't damaged," he said.

She gave him a knowing stare. "The rich have their resources. If Jo's car miraculously got repaired in just a day or two, doesn't it make sense his could have, as well? Or, maybe he has more than one vehicle. Have you ever met a rich, single guy who didn't?"

The waiter brought their dinner and went through the ritual of carving and serving. Sam could tell Beau's wheels were turning until the server left.

"So he went to the Kingston Arms in Albuquerque and killed Zack. Once Krystal left the room, it wouldn't be difficult to get Zack to open the door to his own business partner. Quickly, he shot the heroin into a vein, left the room, drove back to Taos. I want to review the video tapes from the hotel. Two or three businessmen were seen walking along that hall. I suspect Chandler was one of them, being careful not to let his face be seen on camera."

Again, Sam saw his mind working, making a mental note to get back to that aspect of the investigation, as she took her first few bites of the incredibly tender beef.

Beau continued, thinking aloud. "Then Chandler came back here and tried to get rid of Jo. Killing her wouldn't have solved his problem, though, because half the company—in Zack's estate—would have simply passed to their son, Bentlee."

"I imagine when he realized it, that was when he decided he needed to get his hands on the partnership agreement. He could destroy the old copies and replace them with a new version. As long as Jo had amnesia he had no worries that she could mess things up. Even later, he could always point out her knock to the head as a reason she wouldn't remember the document accurately. Except once her memory came back, she was very clear on everything. The chance of the whole problem being forgotten was now gone."

Beau smiled at her. "You know, for a lady who just went through a traumatic ordeal you have a remarkably analytical take on all this."

Perhaps she did. Sam felt herself blushing a little at the compliment. Or maybe it was just the wine. She gazed out the window and a moment later, movement caught her attention. A familiar tangle of brown curls, the slender figure in a perky floral dress. Her daughter.

At first Sam didn't see the man but then he walked into view and Kelly reached for his hand, laughing at something he'd said. He wore dark slacks and a tweed sport coat.

A rush of emotion flooded through Sam. She caught it, thought about the reaction.

"Sam?" Beau's eyes followed hers.

"It isn't Julio," she said. "I'm ashamed to say it, I'm relieved that Kelly's new guy is someone else."

"Julio? Your baker? Why would that bother you?"

Why indeed? Despite the fact she'd had this argument with herself over the past two weeks, despite the fact that she knew and liked Julio and really respected him, something told her he wasn't the right one for her daughter.

"I wish Julio all the best in finding the perfect woman in his life. I just—I don't know how to say it. A guy with a record and a bike and all those tattoos … I'm not sure I could have welcomed him into the family."

"Darlin', I really don't believe that. I've never seen a scrap of prejudice in you and I think if you saw Kelly happy with someone you knew to be a decent and hard worker, you'd accept him."

Sam realized he was right. Whatever was best for Kelly would make her happy.

By this time Kelly and the man had entered the restaurant and were speaking to the maître d'. When Kelly glanced toward their table, Sam gave a little wave. She couldn't tell whether the reaction was exactly joyful, but at least Kelly put on a smile and did the right thing. She linked her arm through her date's and brought him to their table. Beau stood and shook hands with the man who, Sam guessed, was about forty. He had longish, wavy brown hair, wire-rimmed glasses and a tentative smile. This was probably not exactly how he'd envisioned meeting the parents, walking in with no preparation whatsoever.

"Mom, Beau, this is Scott Porter."

Scott's expression relaxed when Sam and Beau both greeted him warmly.

"Scott is a history professor at the UNM campus here."

How on earth had Kelly met a professor? Sam could foresee a girl's lunch out where she would ferret out all the answers.

"Join us," Beau offered. "I'm sure we can arrange a couple more chairs and place settings."

"Oh, no, we don't want to interrupt," Scott said. "You're partway through your meal. Plus, I understand it's your anniversary. Congratulations."

"We'll catch up later, Mom."

The maître d' was standing discreetly to one side, menus in hand. He led them to the only empty table in the place, on the other side of the room.

"Well, imagine my surprise," Sam said.

"Yes. I am." Beau gave a smile and a wink.

Sam's mind whirled as she finished her meal—too many new revelations in a very short time. When their cake came to the table, everyone in the place applauded.

"There's plenty of cake here," Sam told the server after he'd cut and served slices to them. "Offer it to everyone, and be sure that young couple over there gets some."

By the time they arrived home Sam wasn't sure she would ever fall asleep. Wired with the stress of the day and the excitement of the evening she declined coffee, opting for a small raspberry liqueur when Beau offered. Bundled against the chilly September air, they sipped their drinks outside on the back deck. Ranger and Nellie settled nearby, happy to have the pack together again.

Beau had called the station on the way home, hoping he wouldn't be needed for another late-night interrogation session. Kent Taylor was there, assuring Beau things were moving as well as could be expected. They would hold

Chandler Lane in a cell until morning. He'd called upon his high-power attorney and would not say another word. Transport to Albuquerque and arraignment would take place tomorrow.

"Something just hit me," Sam said, turning to Beau, watching his face in the moonlight. "Kent Taylor awhile ago mentioned a slip of paper in your case file, one with numbers on it. It was the note Jo found in her pocket the day after she wandered into my shop. She was onto the embezzlement even before her accident."

Beau's forehead wrinkled.

"Think about it. The numerals 3679854. We thought it was a phone number at first. But instead of a dash, insert commas. The figure represents over three-point-six million, the amount taken from the investment account. Even though she told me she assumed Zack had moved the money, Chandler must have known she was looking into it and thought she knew what he was doing. It explains why he came after her."

Beau smiled at her. "You are one smart cookie, you know."

She sighed, happy that the last piece of the puzzle now finally fit. The moon cast a silver streak across their pasture land and a chill autumn breeze riffled her hair. Beau noticed her shiver and suggested they go inside.

Despite her earlier alertness, Sam felt her eyes drooping. She trailed behind Beau up the stairs and fell asleep within minutes, her last sensation the feel of Beau's kiss on her forehead as he tucked the covers around her shoulders.

She woke to daylight and discovered he'd left early, with a note explaining it would be a busy day for him. When Sam arrived at her shop, Jo showed up at her van door before she had set a foot on the ground. Judging by her lack of makeup and flustered appearance, she'd heard the news.

"Sam, I don't know what to say. I'm completely shocked about Chandler. I never saw that coming."

"No one did, Jo. It certainly wasn't your fault."

"I talked to Bentlee last night," Jo said. "I felt that I should break it to him personally. He's very relieved. We talked a long time and I think things will be good between us."

"I'm happy for you, Jo. Really glad."

"I also called my uncle back east. I won't say he was happy to learn of Zack's death, but the two of them clashed right from the start. Zack was a big part of my estrangement from my own family. Anyway, Uncle Peter offered me a job in the family candy company. I'm going to take it. There are great schools there, and it will do Bentlee a lot of good to get away from everything he's been facing here in New Mexico."

"What about ChanZack Innovations? It's all yours now."

"I'll do some deep thinking about that. I could make a huge amount of money with it, but it's not where my heart is. I'll probably look for a buyer. Luckily, it's the kind of business that can operate from anywhere—I mean, who would guess a venture of that type originated in this little town? With the recent introduction of the new game, the timing seems right to look at some offers."

"Well, I wish you luck in everything. Who would have guessed that the scared woman who walked in here with no memory would turn out to have such a fascinating life?" Sam hugged her and they headed inside.

Word had spread of yesterday's action and Chandler Lane's arrest, Sam learned, when Jen plopped the morning newspaper on the worktable in front of her.

"When did you plan to mention this?"

Becky, Julio and Jo crowded around, catching the headline: Two Local Women Held Hostage. Beau had never mentioned the presence of media people. She felt half-irritated and half-grateful. At least he hadn't spoiled their anniversary celebration with this additional stressor.

With no other choice, Sam gave a very quick summation, leaving out the way Zoë's wound had healed so quickly and making light of the fact that they'd been at gunpoint during the whole ordeal.

"We are fine now, and Mr. Lane is facing a trial in Albuquerque," she said. "Now, it's time for us all to get back to work."

"There's one more piece of news," Jen said, standing taller and ceremoniously clearing her throat. "I checked our website this morning for new orders and there was a very nice email from Mr. Stan Bookman."

Sam felt puzzled. He was supposed to be in Paris, wowing his wife with her birthday trip and gift.

Jen held up a sheet of paper and started to read.

Dear Ms. Sweet and the entire Sweet's Sweets crew,

I write this informal note to express my sincerest thanks for the excellent job in designing and presenting your fantastic box of chocolates. My wife declares it the best birthday gift she has ever received. I must say, I agree.

The chocolates have been so popular with our guests that I have come to an important decision. I want every traveler who books through my agency to experience the exquisite flavors and classic presentation (minus our personal cat theme, of course!) with which you have delighted us. Attached please find a contract for Sweet's Sweets to be the official provider of chocolate gift boxes for Book It Travel.

Hoping you will find the terms agreeable,

Yours sincerely,

Stanley Bookman

"I printed the attachment. Sam, this is huge. We're talking thousands of travelers, a lot of celebrities and important people," Jen said.

"What? My gosh." Sam took the pages and speed-read through it. This would mean hundreds of thousands in extra revenue. "I—I think I'm speechless."

Jen chuckled. "Maybe for the first time!" she said, which started all of them laughing.

"Okay, back to work everyone," said Becky. "There's going to be a lot of chocolate flowing around this place very soon."

Sam picked up her baker's jacket and slipped it on. She thought of her daughter and the way Kelly and Scott placed their full attention on each other last night at their restaurant table. Would they have a future together; if so, where would that future take them? Jo, whose forgotten memories had threatened her very sanity a week ago, would soon be off to a new adventure in her own life. She looked around the busy kitchen, her gaze landing on Bookman's contract— Sweet's Sweets might look like an entirely different business a year from now. Nothing felt certain anymore.

You never know where fate will take you, she mused, but if you're open to the possibilities, exciting things really can happen.

Thank you for taking the time to read *Sweets Forgotten*. If you enjoyed it, please consider telling your friends or posting a short review. Word of mouth is an author's best friend and much appreciated.

Thank you,
Connie Shelton

Learn about the histsory of Samantha's magic
box in Connie Shelton's historical novel,
The Woodcarver's Secret.

For the latest news on Connie's books,
announcements of new releases, and a chance to
win great prizes, subscribe to her monthly email
newsletter. All this and more at
connieshelton.com

Connie Shelton is the USA Today bestselling author of
two mystery series, as well as several award-winning essays.
She taught writing courses for Long Ridge Writer's Group
and was a contributor to *Chicken Soup For the Writer's Soul*.
She and her husband live in New Mexico.

Made in the USA
San Bernardino, CA
14 March 2019